Free
Pass

ALSO BY ELIZABETH SCOTT

Naughty Housewives
Spin the Bottle

Free Pass

ELIZABETH SCOTT

HEAT

HEAT
Published by New American Library, a division of
Penguin Group (USA) Inc., 375 Hudson Street,
New York, New York 10014, USA
Penguin Group (Canada), 90 Eglinton Avenue East, Suite 700,
Toronto, Ontario M4P 2Y3, Canada (a division of Pearson Penguin Canada Inc.)
Penguin Books Ltd., 80 Strand, London WC2R 0RL, England
Penguin Ireland, 25 St. Stephen's Green, Dublin 2,
Ireland (a division of Penguin Books Ltd.)
Penguin Group (Australia), 250 Camberwell Road, Camberwell,
Victoria 3124, Australia (a division of Pearson Australia Group Pty. Ltd.)
Penguin Books India Pvt. Ltd., 11 Community Centre,
Panchsheel Park, New Delhi - 110 017, India
Penguin Group (NZ), 67 Apollo Drive, Rosedale, North Shore 0632,
New Zealand (a division of Pearson New Zealand Ltd.)
Penguin Books (South Africa) (Pty.) Ltd., 24 Sturdee Avenue,
Rosebank, Johannesburg 2196, South Africa

Penguin Books Ltd., Registered Offices:
80 Strand, London WC2R 0RL, England

First published by Heat, an imprint of New American Library,
a division of Penguin Group (USA) Inc.

First Printing, December 2008
10 9 8 7 6 5 4 3 2 1

LIBRARY OF CONGRESS CATALOGING-IN-PUBLICATION DATA:

Scott, Elizabeth, 1955–
    Free pass/Elizabeth Scott.
        p. cm.
    ISBN 978-0-451-22503-0
    I. Couples—Fiction. I. Title.
    PS3613 .A958F74   2008
    813' .6—dc22   2008016238

Set in Centaur MT
Designed by Ginger Legato

Printed in the United States of America

To the ladies of Hermit Week #1, 2007. . .the setting was idyllic, the weather delightful, and the company beyond compare. May all of you enjoy sunny days ahead as you walk life's shore, and may the books you publish, like the stars, be too many to count.

Free Pass

Prologue

Cherisse wiped a bead of sweat from the tip of her nose, shoved a damp hank of her wavy brown hair behind her ear, and sighed. Her two good friends, pedaling furiously on either side of her, loved working out at the House of Fit. For Cherisse, it was nothing short of torture. But she endured it for the sake of wearing her favorite bikini and to ward off the scary reality of her gene pool.

She was only thirty-two, but the heavy-waisted women on her mother's side of the family had a lot to answer for. They had a history of "bulking up" during their childbearing years, and never losing the weight. The fact that Cherisse was short and full-breasted only made matters worse.

Add to the mix her mostly sedentary job as a bank teller, and regular exercise became a must . . . especially since she and her husband, Wesley, were contemplating getting pregnant in the next year or so. Staying as thin as possible had become her focus.

Dark-headed Melanie, who owned the facility along with her husband, was a poster child for the healthy athlete. She looked far younger than her thirty-eight years, and her smoothly muscled arms and legs were a great advertisement for the benefits of gym membership. Her endless energy made Cherisse feel like a slug.

Mel ran on superspeed and, despite her undeniable business sense, often went off on crazy tangents in her personal life. She got a kick out of trying every unusual thing that came down the pike, whether it be organic vitamins from Tibet, New Age crystals for mood enhancement, or even an unlikely commitment to trying every recipe in a hot-off-the-press heart-healthy cookbook. Not that Melanie didn't enjoy culinary challenges on occasion, but her attention span was abbreviated at best.

Debra, the baby of the trio at twenty-nine, still had the dewy skin of youth and could eat anything she wanted with impunity. Her silky blond ponytail drew male attention almost as much as her long tanned legs.

Debra was a sweet, gentle woman . . . a bit shy on first acquaintance, but lots of fun to be around. She and her cute husband, Gordon, both worked in real estate.

On the surface, the three women had very little in common, but they had met when the gym first opened and had since become fast friends. They enjoyed one another's company, and it was probably their differences that made the friendship so rewarding.

Cherisse had zoned out for a minute, but Debra's gasp of shock dragged her back to the present.

"You can't be serious, Melanie. You're actually going to encourage Thomas to have an affair?" The last word trailed off into a screech.

Melanie smirked. "No. Don't be ridiculous. Not an affair. But I believe in being proactive. The seven-year itch is more than a classic Marilyn Monroe movie. It's a psychological and sociological phenomenon. And I have no intention of being a divorcée before I'm forty."

Cherisse caught the gist of the conversation and frowned. "But Thomas adores you. He wants to take you on a cruise for your anniversary. His face lights up when he talks about it." The trio of couples socialized occasionally, and Thomas often dropped by the gym to see his wife or to do his own workout. He clearly doted on his wife.

Melanie puffed out her cheeks as she exhaled. "And that's the way I want to keep it. So tonight I'm going to suggest to him that we each get a one-time-only free pass for a fling with a stranger."

Debra's ponytail bounced to the beat of her rapidly moving legs. "A stranger?"

Melanie nodded. "Can't be someone we know . . . too messy. And afterward, we have to spill the beans to each other about all the details."

Cherisse slowed to a crawl, hoping her friends were too wrapped up in the discussion to notice her lackluster performance. "But what if he refuses?"

Melanie chuckled breathlessly. "What man in his right mind would say no to consequence-free infidelity? Although, technically speaking, it wouldn't really be infidelity if we both agreed to it in advance." She paused to check the screen on her machine. "If you two are smart, you'll do this, too. We all have the same anniversary coming up. Let's nip this itch in the bud."

Cherisse felt an odd burn in the pit of her stomach that had nothing to do with endorphins. It was either trepidation or uneasy excitement. "I don't know, Mel. It might be asking for trouble."

Debra nodded solemnly in agreement. "I'm not sure I like the thought of Gordie hooking up with another woman. It scares me."

Melanie's grin was smug. "Give the idea a chance," she panted breathlessly. "Think about it. . . . *You* get to take a walk on the wild side, too."

Cherisse gulped. "That might be the most terrifying part of this," she muttered. "I'm not sure I'm ready for a stranger to see my naked thighs."

In the flurry of laughter that followed, the conversation moved to other subjects, but the seed had been planted. . . .

Chapter One

Cherisse winced as Wesley cursed under his breath and tried to cross five lanes of vehicles to the exit they had just missed for a second time. The Miami traffic was like a psychotic video game. She'd read stories of foreign tourists getting carjacked in rental vehicles down here. As far as she could tell, she and Wesley, being from northern Minnesota, qualified.

Thank God they had flown into the Ft. Lauderdale airport instead of Miami International. She wasn't sure they would have escaped unscathed otherwise.

Wesley swung the wheel and, if she wasn't mistaken, closed his eyes as he darted between a silver Lexus and a big rig to reach the next exit. He was sweating despite the car's efficient air-conditioning. And his neck was red, a sure sign his blood pressure was up. His dark hair was rumpled where he'd raked a hand through it.

Guilt pinched Cherisse hard. This whole trip was her idea, and Wesley had been reluctant from the beginning. He was the kind of man who was content mowing the grass and then relaxing with a cold beer and a baseball game.

His dad had been active military for thirty years, and the family had moved at least a dozen times before their only son was out of college. Perhaps it wasn't a surprise that Wesley had no particular wanderlust and was happy to spend vacations at his grandparents' cabin on the lake.

But a year ago, Cherisse had cajoled him into planning a trip to Miami for their upcoming seventh anniversary. She'd convinced him that they needed to shake up their complacent lives . . . to get out of their rut. On the Internet they'd found a condo that rented for a song compared to the big-name hotels. They'd paid a deposit, and month by month, they had chipped away at the balance.

They'd reassured themselves that they weren't buying a pig in a poke, because the lovely pictures on the Web documented the property's stylish furnishings and spectacular view of South Beach. For the next fourteen days, Cherisse and Wesley would be living the high life.

Another fierce, frustrated oath from her dear college professor husband called her blithe enthusiasm into question. Wesley's domineering father had drilled into his son the mantra that men didn't show emotion. Consequently, it was like pulling teeth to get Wesley to open up about his feelings. He was quiet and reserved as a rule, but he had a formidable temper, and when it blew, things got ugly. To his credit, he'd learned to control it . . . most of the time. At least when his wife wasn't driving him bonkers.

She laid a hand on his arm. "Breathe, Wesley. We're almost there. The letter says to take a left turn at the light, and in a tenth of a mile, we'll see the parking garage on the right."

The tall, rather ugly building was exactly where it was supposed to be. Not precisely in the middle of the action, but close enough to satisfy Cherisse.

By the time they had parked, unloaded the suitcases and carry-ons, and ridden the smelly, small elevator up to the thirty-fifth-floor breezeway, Cherisse was panting and slightly less optimistic.

But once they went through the double doors into the lushly carpeted hallway of the condo proper, things improved. They found number 3517 and tried the key that had been FedExed to them a week ago. The lock turned smoothly. Wesley followed Cherisse into their home away from home.

Cherisse couldn't wait. She dropped her bags in the narrow entryway and hurried through the hall into a large, beautifully decorated living room. Rattan ceiling fans circled lazily overhead. The cream leather furniture grouping was accented with bright tropical print pillows.

A high-tech entertainment center took up most of one wall, and large native plants in terra-cotta pots added an exotic flavor. All in all, it was about as far from their Minnesota home as it was possible to get.

Cherisse grinned. "Thank God. It's perfect."

Wesley nodded and stretched the kinks out of his back. "I'll have to admit that I had my doubts, but you picked a winner. Let's see the rest of it." They began exploring, and all went well until they reached the bedroom. At first glance it was amazing—sexy, luxurious, extremely tasteful. Even the telescope at the window, as promised.

But when Cherisse drew back the drapes, she groaned. "Wesley, come look. I don't believe this."

Sometime during the past twelve months, the spectacular view of South Beach had been obscured by a brand-new high rise. A strip of ocean was still visible to the left, but it certainly wasn't the blissful photograph they had printed out and hung on the refrigerator—the vista that had warmed Cherisse all during the long, cold winter months.

She expected Wesley to go ballistic, but he surprised her. He put his arms around her from behind. "It's not the end of the world, baby. We'll have plenty of opportunities to see the ocean up close and personal. Besides, I'm planning to keep you too busy in this room for you to worry about any damn view."

He kissed the side of her neck. She shivered. Seven years of marriage, and he still made her melt when he touched her like that. Her still-waters-run-deep husband was a tiger between the sheets, and she was giddy at the thought of having him all to herself for the next two weeks.

He scooped her up, threw back the covers on the bed, and deposited her gently in the middle of the big mattress. She tried to protest, but he had already kicked off his shoes and come down beside her to pluck at the buttons of her blouse. She batted his hands away. "Shouldn't we at least unpack?" She wasn't serious, but it didn't hurt to put up a bit of a protest . . . especially when Wesley was so darn good at persuasion.

He found bare skin and nibbled at the curve of her breast.

"We're christening our new abode," he muttered, nuzzling the damp lace covering her nipple.

She groaned, surprised to feel a raw edge to her arousal. Was it the new surroundings, or was it the conversation she had shared with Wesley the night before? The free-pass discussion. He had been surprisingly noncommittal on the subject, and she'd been unable to read him.

Now he ripped her top and slacks away, along with her pretty new sandals. Clad only in her panties and bra, she watched, breathless, as he stripped to the skin. His black hair was mussed, his hot blue eyes sleepy with passion. He was lean, with muscles that were sleek and firm. His penis was a marvel of genetic engineering, and her mouth (and other parts) watered just from looking at it.

He grinned smugly at the glazed look on her face. "See anything you like?"

He was kneeling at her hip, and it was all she could do not to drag him down on top of her right then. But they had all afternoon and evening to play around, and she was determined to get this vacation off to a good start.

She slid off the bed and put her thumbs beneath her bra straps. "I'm *so* hot," she said in a pouty little voice. "Let me just get comfortable."

She released the back closure and wiggled her arms free one at a time, until the bra hung, barely secure, from her breasts. She held it in place with one hand and touched herself with the other hand.

Wesley's prick bobbed eagerly.

She smiled innocently as she straddled one leg of the telescope. The slender piece of wood nestled between her thighs, and she pressed closer. A tiny gasp of breath escaped her parted lips as her clitoris made contact with the unyielding pole.

She bent her knees slightly and moved up and down. She'd initiated the naughty game for Wesley's benefit, but the auto-massage was turning her on, almost enough to come, especially with Wesley watching her. His narrow gaze promised retribution.

As though by accident, she allowed the bra to drop as she leaned forward. Now the smooth metal barrel of the telescope nestled between her breasts. She moved her hips slowly, keeping the telescope leg pressed firmly against the center of her sex. She closed her eyes, breathing heavily.

It was a shock when Wesley grasped her waist and jerked her away from her toy. "You're having *way* too much fun without me," he muttered, pressing her down to the carpet. He entered her from behind with one forceful motion, making her cry out. His hands clenched her hips, anchoring his vigorous thrusts. They both came quickly, and then collapsed in a heap.

After long, heavy seconds filled with rough breathing, Cherisse turned her head. "Let's try out the shower."

Wesley adjusted the water temperature and stepped into the large, glass enclosure with his wife. As he soaped her shoulders and back, he couldn't resist sliding the slippery bar down her spine to the slope of her ass. She had a lush, curvy body that had knocked him for a loop the first time he saw her and ever since.

Cherisse was always trying to lose weight, but hell, as far

as he was concerned, she was perfect. He reached around her and began moving the bar of soap over and between her full breasts. She made a small sound and backed up against his rapidly rising boner.

He licked a drop of water from her earlobe. "We need to talk." Last night's little discussion had left him unsettled and furious, if the truth were told.

She laughed softly, rubbing her butt against his crotch. "Isn't that my line?"

He dropped the soap and pinched her nipples gently. "I'm serious."

Her head fell forward as he bit the back of her neck. "Now?" The word was a moan.

He lost the urge for conversation. "I guess not." He supported her with an arm as she rose on her tiptoes. Then he aligned their bodies and entered her slowly. The warm water hitting his back should have been soothing, but his unsettled mood was propelling the encounter.

The position was hard to maintain against the slick floor of the shower. He reached around and fingered her, putting pressure where he knew she wanted it. She stiffened and quivered in his arms, then braced her hands on the wall as she groaned and came. He was barely aware of her climax as his own release consumed him.

When he could stand straight, he reached behind them and turned off the water. In the resultant silence, his anger and unease returned like a freight train. Cherisse chattered happily as they toweled off and retrieved their suitcases to change clothes.

While she dried her wavy brown hair, she spoke loudly

enough for him to hear over the hair dryer. "Where do you want to go for dinner? I have that Fodor's travel guide in my carry-on."

He buttoned his shirt slowly and stared at her in the mirror. "Cherisse, we were up at five this morning to catch the plane. I'm beat. How 'bout we stay in this evening and order carryout?"

Her face fell, and he felt like a heel. It was their first night in Miami. But he wasn't lying. He was exhausted, and ticked off, and the time for a showdown was coming, vacation or not.

He held his tongue until they had devoured a large pizza and an order of bread sticks. They drank water, because neither of them had wanted to go to the trouble of finding a grocery store. Cherisse seemed to have picked up on his mood, because she had quit talking, allowing the television to fill any awkward silences.

When the pizza box was empty, he hit the POWER button on the remote and slouched in one of the comfy chairs, his leg slung over an arm. "We need to talk."

She curled up on one end of the sofa, her expression troubled. "You've already said that."

"Yeah, well . . ." He scraped a hand through his hair, feeling the anger bubble up again. He had to get this out in the open, but if he did, there was a good chance that their vacation would be ruined.

He swallowed hard, feeling his pulse throb in his temple. "What you said last night pissed me off."

She paled. "I don't understand."

He got to his feet, unable to sit still. "That free-pass shit. What were you thinking, Cherisse? Am I not enough for you anymore? I know I'm not the most exciting guy in the world. But I thought we were in a good place in our marriage. And I definitely thought things were good in the bedroom. Shows what dumb asses men can be. Clueless, I guess. But you didn't have to make up some elaborate charade to get what you want. You could have just told me."

Cherisse was staring at him with big brown eyes and a trembling chin. "You've totally twisted this around, Wesley. The free-pass idea was for *you*."

He snorted. "Yeah, right. Have I given you any indication that I want to be screwing strange women? Hell, I don't even look at other females when we're out together. So I think it's pretty clear which one of us is unhappy." He squared his shoulders, acid burning in his stomach. "Go ahead. Tell me the truth."

A single tear rolled down her cheek, and she twisted her hands in her lap. "Wesley, I swear you've got it backward. Melanie said—"

He cut her off. "Melanie? That woman's a loose cannon. Please tell me you haven't been taking relationship advice from her."

Cherisse frowned. "She's a very smart businesswoman."

"Maybe so, but isn't she the one who made her husband go to a couples' retreat at a nudist colony?"

"That was a joke she played on Thomas. They really went on a Napa Valley wine tour."

"Still . . ." He shrugged his shoulders. "What on earth did she say to make you come up with such an off-the-wall idea?"

Cherisse wrapped her arms around her waist in a defensive

posture, and curled as tight as a porcupine into the corner of the sofa. She scowled. "She merely reminded Debra and me about the seven-year itch."

It was his turn to frown. "The movie?"

"No. Of course not. We all have seventh anniversaries coming up, and that's the time in a marriage when men often get restless and cheat. So Melanie suggested that we give you guys a free pass for a hookup with a stranger."

He shook his head in disbelief. "That's insane. Whose idea was it that the women be included, as well?" His suspicions still rankled.

His wife thrust out her chin, glowering at him. "That seemed only fair." She cocked her head. "And admit it. All guys think about having sex with other women."

He winced. She had him there. "Okay. I'll cop to that. But we're talking fantasy, not reality." He refused to acknowledge that this conversation was arousing him in any way.

Cherisse put on her earnest, pleading face—the one he was never able to resist. "I want our marriage to last, Wesley. Let's face it. We're dull. And once I get pregnant next year, or whenever it happens, we'll be permanently tied to a conventional life in suburbia. I wasn't keen on the free-pass idea when Melanie brought it up, but the more I thought about it, the more I decided we need to step outside the box while we have the chance. I don't want to wake up one day and find out you've run off with a coed from the university. I want you to be happy and satisfied, and if that means injecting a bit of unconventional sex into the mix, I'm all for it."

"Is that what this vacation is all about?"

"Of course not. We've been planning this for months.

But when Melanie brought up the free-pass idea, it did occur to me that these two weeks would be our best opportunity. We're far away from home. No one knows us here."

"What happens in Miami stays in Miami?"

Finally, she smiled. "Exactly." She held out her hand. "Come sit with me."

He got up and went over to the sofa, allowing her to pull him down into the dual embrace of soft leather and softer woman. He stretched out with his head in her lap. The knot in his stomach had eased, enough for him to appreciate the unique view of her breasts. He could smother happily in those curves.

She stroked the hair from his forehead. "Doesn't the idea turn you on just a little bit?"

He adjusted the crotch of his pants. The answer was there in plain sight. "Of course it does. But I guess I'm not as enlightened a male as I thought I was. I'm having a hard time envisioning you and some strange guy. Already I want to punch his lights out."

Now she was playing with his ears. She knew what that did to him, the little minx. "I have the same feelings about you, Wesley."

He closed his eyes, feeling the soothing caress of her cool fingers along his jaw, his neck. "Then why the hell are we even contemplating this?" He had a gut feeling, but he wanted her to be honest.

The silence was fraught with tension. Finally Cherisse answered him. "Don't you want to know if you're still attractive to the opposite sex?"

Bingo. Lightbulb moment. Suddenly everything made

sense. Cherisse had some serious self-image issues. Was this her way of testing her desirability? He spoke slowly, weighing his words. "I think you're sexy as hell, sweetheart. But if it would make you feel good to know that another man sees you that way, too, I guess I shouldn't stand in your way."

She didn't deny it. That told him a lot. Her evasion was as good as a confession.

She continued stroking his face. "We don't want to become complacent, Wesley. If our marriage is as strong as you say it is, and I agree with you by the way, then we can enjoy all the perks of this little experiment without suffering any damage to our relationship. This will be purely physical."

"I thought women couldn't separate the physical from the emotional."

"Not with someone we love. But this will be totally different."

"How can you be so sure? What's to say you won't fall for this guy?" He knew his insecurities were showing, but he couldn't help it. He was scared, damn it. Scared for their marriage and scared that some other guy would rock her world. Fear and jealousy. Yep, that was the perfect way to start a vacation.

She massaged his shoulders. "I have the same reservations, Wesley. I keep seeing you with a naked woman, and it makes me crazy."

"Good crazy or bad crazy?" He managed to joke, but he didn't feel at all amused.

She pinched his nipple through his shirt. "I'm serious, Wesley. Do you think it thrills me to imagine you screwing someone else?"

"I guess not. So why do this at all?"

"Because we can. Because we're happy. Because we don't want to get in a rut."

Because you're too damn insecure to realize how beautiful you are? He choked back the words. "So that's our assignment for the next two weeks? Find someone and get laid?"

He sat up abruptly and stared at her. At his blunt words, her face changed. Now she definitely looked uneasy.

He wrapped his arms around his chest, barely keeping his hot, unsettled emotions in check. "Not so simple to think about when you put it like that, is it? And what about your safety, Cherisse? Have you considered the possibilities of harm?"

She thrust out that chin again. "I'm not stupid. I'll take precautions."

"I'm not just talking about condoms. I'm thinking about your physical safety."

She wrinkled her nose. "I guess I could bring him back here."

Wesley's semiquiescent erection quivered and flexed. "Well, that would be one solution." He had a sudden vision of him peeking through the doorway as a strange man fucked Cherisse on this very sofa. His throat tightened and his tongue felt thick in his mouth.

She lifted her arms and ran her hands through her hair, looking thoughtful. "I guess the logistics might be problematic. But we can deal with that as we go. I'm not sure it's possible to plan for every eventuality. Sex is spontaneous. At least I'm imagining it will be under these circumstances."

"So that's it?" he asked, his body numb with apprehension. "We each troll for an easy lay?"

"Don't make it sound cheap."

"What would you call it? It's not exactly taking the moral high ground."

She frowned. "I never knew you had such scruples. If this bothers you that much, forget it."

He drew in a breath, wanting to take the out she was offering. But on the slim chance that Cherisse needed this experiment to prove something to herself, he held his tongue. "We'll do it," he said roughly. "But I hope to God you know what you're getting us into. There's no way to stuff the genie back in the bottle once it's out."

She nodded slowly. "I know. And it's scary. I won't deny it. But I think it will be fun. For both of us. We'll scratch an itch and then we'll compare notes."

"You make it sound so romantic."

"But that's just it, Wesley. This isn't about romance at all. It's about having sex with a stranger."

Chapter Two

Melanie opened the door to her office and winced. No magic fairy had come in while she was gone. The stacks of paper on her desk were still as high, the phone-message light blinking as furiously as ever.

She plunked her toned ass into the chair with a disgruntled sigh, and stared at the mess. It wasn't fair. Cherisse had been in Florida for a while now, and Debra had left for Greece yesterday. Melanie, on the other hand, was chained to the gym for eternity.

Well, that was a bit of an exaggeration. Her assistant would be back from maternity leave in eight weeks. But eight weeks could be a hell of a long stretch.

She winced, remembering her husband's face when she had told him she couldn't get away for an anniversary trip anytime soon. Thomas had been disappointed but resigned. He'd long since grown accustomed to her workaholic ways.

But it wasn't fair to him, not at all. Melanie had had every intention of hiring a temp to cover the maternity leave. But interviewing required time, and time was in short supply at the moment. The strain of running a large business was beginning to get to her.

The gym had done well from the beginning. She and Thomas had been meticulous in their planning, down to the last basket for dirty towels. They'd wanted to open a top-notch workout facility, and they had.

But Thomas had a job already, and once things were up and running at the new gym, he'd had to get back in the swing of things at his own assignment. He ran the sporting-goods store that had been his and Melanie's first business venture. Thomas was much better at delegating than Melanie was, and not only that, he knew how to keep his personal life separate from work, a skill Melanie had never mastered.

Now the gym was more than doing well. It was hugely successful. They'd opened a new wing six months ago, and memberships were up twenty-five percent. More members meant more headaches, and Melanie was stretched to the max. It wasn't unusual for her to stay an hour or two every night after the gym shut down at nine to catch up on paperwork and anything else that required her attention.

Sometimes she did her own workout then, but she much preferred carving out forty-five minutes in the middle of the day to exercise with Cherisse and Debra. It was a nice little break, even though she was still available for employees' questions. She did, however, draw the line at phone calls. There was no emergency so great that it couldn't wait until she had finished her routine.

It was probably her own guilt that had prompted the genesis of the free-pass idea. She heard stories every day of unsuspecting wives who were blindsided when their husbands ran off with other women. It had happened to Melanie's own mother. And Melanie had sworn never to make the same mistakes.

So last night, she had broached the free-pass plan with Thomas. She'd assumed he would jump at the idea. He had a phenomenal sex drive, and he was always ready to fuck her, no matter what the circumstances.

But Thomas had surprised her.

"Is this another one of your jokes, Melanie?" His lack of immediate enthusiasm had caught her off guard.

She shook her head. "I'm dead serious. I thought you deserved a chance to be a free agent for one night. Let's face it. Several of your friends run around on their wives. I'm merely suggesting we be up front about it."

His expression reflected his discomfort, almost as if he couldn't bring himself to even think about such a thing. "I made a commitment to you, Melanie. Why would I want to cheat?"

"But that's just it," she said earnestly. "It wouldn't be cheating. Consider it my gift to you." Even as she tried convincing him what a great idea it was, she shared some of the same reservations voiced by her two friends. Would Thomas find a woman who was not only good in bed but also attentive to his other needs, as well?—a woman who might actually cook, or pick up his dry cleaning, or run a load of laundry?

He stared at her, his eyes dark and troubled. "I think

you're fooling yourself, Melanie. I don't believe this is about my potential infidelity at all. You still have issues with your dad. But don't project those onto me."

He stalked out of the room, leaving her to wonder if he knew her better than she knew herself.

Melanie had no illusions about her own appeal. She was fit and attractive, but she was getting dangerously close to the big 4-0. There would always be younger, prettier, sexier—and perhaps more nurturing—women.

She and Thomas had decided a long time ago not to have children. Sometimes she regretted their choice, but she probably would have made a lousy mother. She was impatient and had been diagnosed with ADD in high school. She ran the gym well, but it helped that it was an active, ever-changing environment. She was easily bored and needed that stimulation.

It occurred to her that Thomas might eventually get tired of her incessant energy. All the more reason to let him get any discontent out of his system with a free pass. As long as the plan didn't backfire, she'd be in business.

But his comments the night before had stung. Was she really still reacting to her father's desertion—something that had happened almost twenty-six years ago? And was there an even darker question? Was she too much like her father? Did her short attention span mean she was destined to follow in his footsteps sexually? That fear was one she'd rarely allowed herself to face. But if she were honest, was it the big, ugly thought that lay behind the free-pass idea?

Her stomach churned, but she deliberately avoided any

further self-analysis. There was nothing she could do about it now. The cat was out of the bag. She glanced at her narrow-banded sports watch. Ashanti would be expelling the stragglers and locking up in another seven minutes. Time for Melanie to dig in.

The quiet rap on her partially open door made her grit her teeth, but she schooled her face into a pleasant expression. "Come in."

The man who entered almost had to duck to clear the door to her small office. He was easily six feet five inches, and his shoulders were broad. He was a big guy, but not fat, not in the least. The sleeves of his tan suit jacket were maybe a half inch too short, and his curly chestnut hair needed a trim. When he smiled, her tummy did a funny little flip and curl.

He leaned against the doorframe, one hand in the pocket of his slacks, the other raking his hair from his forehead, only to have it fall back again. "Are you Melanie?" His voice rumbled out in a slow, melodic Southern drawl that said he was far from home.

She nodded and rearranged a jar of paper clips, feeling unreasonably nervous. His presence seemed to suck the air out of the room. "I am. Can I help you?"

His smile was as slow as his speech, but the wattage made up for it. "Sure hope so. I'm in town for a week or ten days, and I need a place to work out. I was hoping you could help me."

She wrinkled her nose. "We don't do short-term memberships. I'm sorry."

He focused his eyes on her, the irises so dark they almost

appeared to be black. "I'd really appreciate it if you could make an exception. Sitting in a hotel room at night can pack on the pounds." He rubbed a hand over his flat stomach, giving lie to the notion that there was an ounce of spare flesh anywhere on his large, solid body.

She swallowed. "Well . . ." For a man so soft-spoken, his will was an iron force. "I'd have to bill you for a single month, and that's the most expensive way to join."

He shrugged. "If you have to."

She nibbled her lower lip. "But I would feel terrible charging you that much for only a week." She motioned to a poster on the wall. "What if you write a check for the charity we're supporting, and we'll call it even? I'll give you some temp passes."

His slow, lazy smile dawned a second time. "That's mighty nice of you, Melanie."

The way he said her name sent a caress of heat down her spine. Feeling unaccountably flustered, she rummaged in her drawer for a pen and the blank cards.

Without waiting for an invitation, he settled into the chair against the wall and pulled a checkbook from his inside coat pocket. He scribbled quietly, tore out the check, and handed it to her.

She took it, glanced at the amount, and her eyebrows shot up. "A thousand dollars? Good grief, you could have joined for a year and a half for that amount."

He shrugged, now only a whimsical grin tilting the corners of his sensual mouth. "It's not the same thing at all. I don't believe in wasting money."

She was totally flummoxed. His careless generosity

stunned her, even as she reacted helplessly to his strong, masculine vibe. "Well, thank you."

He inclined his head. "You're welcome, Melanie. Are those mine?"

He reached across the desk and took the passes from her nerveless fingers. "I appreciate your flexibility. I'll be seeing you soon."

When Melanie climbed in bed beside her husband later that evening, Thomas was almost asleep. She crawled on top of him and sighed with pleasure. They always slept nude, and the feel of his warm frame pressed against every inch of hers was both a stimulant and narcotic.

He ran his hands over her ass. "I missed you, love." His voice was drowsy.

There was no criticism in his quiet words, but she felt guilty, nevertheless. "I'll try to interview some people this week for the assistant spot. If I can find anyone good, we'll take that cruise, I promise."

He flipped her and settled between her legs. The slow entry of his erect penis made her catch her breath. "It's too late for that," he mumbled, kissing her neck. "They're all booked. But we could go *somewhere*—anywhere I can have you to myself."

Her body stretched inexorably to accommodate his girth. He pumped lazily, letting the gentle, rolling pleasure deepen. Her breath caught in her throat as shards of sensation raked her pelvis. "Thomas..." His name fell from her lips in a long, aching sigh. He knew her so well. Knew just how to probe, just how to hit the hot spots.

He picked up the rhythm, letting her feel his power, his

hunger. She tried to hold back her climax, wanting to extend this lovely, spiraling joy. But unbidden, images of her visitor at the gym slid into her brain, ratcheting up her arousal. Remembering that brief encounter made her shiver with inexplicable sexual tension. His eyes had mesmerized her, almost as if he had been offering something—something illicit and wonderful. Guilt and excitement filled her as Thomas rode her hard to his own completion.

Just as her husband shouted and filled her with his warm bursts of come, she cried out as well, her orgasm sharp and fierce. And in that moment, when everything inside her crystallized in drugged pleasure and then shattered, it was a pair of warm, dark eyes that sent her flying.

Thomas was awake then, and inclined to talk. He flicked on the bedside lamp, its illumination so gentle it barely moved the shadows in the bedroom. His reddish brown hair stood on end. He kept it short, and without gel it was inclined to sprout in a hundred directions. He was a health nut like she was, and his abs, even though he was in spitting distance of forty, were firm and sculpted. He was average in height, and his frame was sturdy.

He leaned on his side and propped his head on his hand. "Tell me something, Melanie. Why did you get it in your head that I might want sex with other women? Be honest. Is this really about your dad?"

She flinched. "Maybe. No. I'm not sure."

His hazel eyes were sober. "I'm not ever going to leave you."

He said it simply, not dressing it up. His conviction was comforting, but in her gut, her own insecurities remained. "I know," she muttered. "But don't you think you'd get a kick out of having sex with someone else just this one time to see what it's like?"

"Is this a test?" His piercing gaze made her wish they weren't having this discussion naked.

"Of course not," she huffed. But was she being entirely truthful with him ... with herself? She dragged the sheet over her hips. "Debra and Cherisse are going to do it, too." *God, was that her whiny voice sounding like an adolescent in full-fledged self-justification mode?*

He narrowed his eyes. "But who came up with the whole seven-year-itch, free-pass thing?"

She couldn't quite meet his eyes. "Me."

"Ah."

She could feel his disapproval like a weight on her narrow shoulders. His steady regard stripped away all of her defenses and saw through to the woman who was never quite confident in her femininity. The girl who didn't get breasts until she was almost in college. The young female who alienated most guys with her assertive ways. The woman who was afraid she couldn't hold on to her own husband.

She twisted the sheet between her fingers. "I do trust you, Thomas. I do. But what could it hurt to be a little crazy?"

He sighed. "I'll think about it," he said. "But you forget that I had a fair amount of experience before we got together. Any wild-oat sowing is long behind me. I'm fine with you going for it. I'm not the jealous type. And as for me ... well, we'll see."

He reached for the sheet and lowered it, once again revealing his wife's slender, angular body. It was lovely to him, healthy and strong. The shiny black of her boyish haircut might have a little help from the hairdresser, but he never asked. Women's private vanities were their own business, and since Melanie kept her pussy completely shaved, there would be no gray hairs there to tell the tale.

Her blue, blue eyes met his warily. Although she was a strong, take-charge gal, it didn't take much to scratch through to the uncertain girl beneath. Her father had abandoned the family when Melanie was at a particularly vulnerable age, and her scars ran deep. Thomas did everything he could to reassure her, but in the long run, only time would win that battle. He wasn't going anywhere.

He glanced at the clock. It was almost one a.m. He'd dozed before she climbed into bed, and now he was wide-awake. He took her wrist and pulled her closer. "Could I interest you in round two?" he asked softly.

She came willingly, allowing him to draw her across the mattress and into his embrace. He knew the docility was temporary. She was as likely as he was to take control of their lovemaking. And no matter who ended up on top, metaphorically speaking, the sex was always explosive and deeply satisfying.

Which was why he didn't understand her insistence on the free-pass idea. Even if sex with another woman might be fun, it wouldn't be what he had with his wife.

She touched his cock, and he lost any interest in thoughtful pursuits. Hot, carnal, and immediate—those were his urgent needs.

He tugged her out of bed.

Her face reflected surprise and confusion. "What are you doing?"

He stood her with her back against the wall. "Stay there."

She closed her eyes, and he saw her posture relax. For the moment, she would obey. Rapidly, he strode to the spare bedroom and rummaged in the closet for a pair of solid, twenty-pound wrist weights.

Back in the bedroom, he led her to the sturdy oak quilt rack and made her bend at the waist. Then he fastened the bands to her wrists. With the heavy weights pulling her down, she would be unable to stand up without his help.

The position displayed her nice ass to perfection. He got hard just looking at her. He spread her legs carefully and secured each ankle to the rack with ties.

Through it all, his Melanie remained silent. He crouched beside her and ruffled her hair. "I should punish you, you know . . . for wanting to screw other men."

Her face was flushed, and when he slipped a hand beneath her to play with her tits, she squirmed. "I never said I wanted to be with anyone but you."

He pinched the nearest nipple. "The free-pass idea was yours, right?"

"For you," she gasped.

He stood and went behind her, thrusting a couple of fingers between her legs to play with her pussy. She was wet, really wet. He massaged her ass. "Methinks the lady doth protest too much. You're horny as hell just thinking about it."

He went to the bedside table and opened the bottom drawer. Over the seven years of their marriage, he and Melanie had collected an eclectic assortment of vibrators and sex toys. After several moments of consideration, he selected a long, thick, rubbery penis. Melanie loved the way this one stretched her.

She was still silent, which for his wife must be some kind of record. Perhaps she was in an unusually compliant mood tonight. He found the lubricant and smeared it over half of the fake cock. Then he approached his quarry, feeling his blood rush south as his anticipation mounted.

First, he caressed her bottom with his free hand. Melanie squirmed and pressed against his palm. Then, with the same hand, he trespassed between her legs, stroking her labia and probing her swollen flesh. She was hot to the touch, and he clenched his jaw at the jolt of heat that tightened his groin. He separated the folds of her sex and put the head of the toy at her entrance.

He rubbed the small of her back. "How badly do you want this, my sweet?"

Her answer was an inarticulate groan. Gently, he pressed deeper. Her whole body trembled in a sharp shudder. He stopped a few inches in to let her adjust. Then he continued invading her pussy with the foreign, unyielding length. Even though his prick wanted in on the action, he was getting off on this scenario.

"Is this what you want?" he asked in a deliberately bland conversational tone. "Something besides my cock for your entertainment? Or do you just want to get fucked hard, period?"

He moved more quickly now, firm, steady strokes that made her moan and cry out. When he thought she was poised on the brink of her orgasm, he withdrew the toy abruptly.

Melanie struggled wildly. She was strong, and she managed to lift her arms a few inches, but the awkward position defeated her. "Let me up," she hissed, temper born of thwarted satisfaction evident in her voice. *"Now."*

He bent and untied her quickly, stripping off the weights and then backing up to see what would happen. Her utter unpredictability was one of the things he loved best about his volatile wife.

She launched herself at him like a wildcat, climbing his torso and wrapping her legs around his waist. He staggered backward until he hit the wall. With something to brace against, she was able to join their bodies with a sharp, downward motion.

He had to grit his teeth and summon every last bit of control he could muster not to come instantly. His chest was tight, and his arms trembled, not from supporting her negligible weight, but from the effort of controlling his raging hunger.

She did that to him on a regular basis, no matter how many times they'd had sex. She triggered a caveman response in him that made him feel like a randy teenager.

He sucked in a lungful of air, his hands full of sweet ass, and his erection throbbing painfully. "Easy, babe. I'd like to enjoy this for more than thirty seconds."

She squeezed him with her inner muscles, and his eyes crossed. "Damn it, Mel. Stop that. Give me a second to get control."

She bit his nipple hard enough to send a sharp pain from the tight bud to his cock. "I like you wild," she said, the four syllables lush with sexual promise. "Now quit holding back and give it to me."

Some things were beyond a man's capacity to endure. He flipped their positions so that now *her* back was against the smooth surface. His vision grew hazy. His throat went dry. He pounded into her desperately, hearing the slap of her butt banging the wall.

Her arms around his neck nearly strangled him, her legs around his waist a vise. Her back arched, and she screamed a split second before his own climax smashed into him and dragged him over the edge.

Long moments later, Melanie tried to lift her head from his shoulder. Her neck and limbs felt like spaghetti. It was a wonder Thomas was able to stand. His chest still heaved with his fractured breathing.

She relaxed her legs and slid to the floor, aware that the room was spinning in a groggy circle. She wet her lips, leaning into him for support. "That was a little intense." Her words sounded croaky to her ears.

He had his hands on her shoulders, almost as if he was using her to hold himself upright. "Yeah."

His lack of vocabulary didn't particularly bother her. Thomas was a man of few words in normal situations, and after an encounter like that, even she was barely able to speak coherently.

They stumbled into the bathroom to clean up and then collapsed into bed. Her heart still pounded, despite her regular aerobic activity. She curled into her husband's embrace, physically content, but no closer to resolving her feelings about the free-pass idea.

Should she forget about it? Accept the fact that her husband was unlikely to leave her? Concentrate on finding ways to extricate herself from work and spend more time with her spouse?

Unbidden, she thought once more of the out-of-town businessman. She turned her back to Thomas's chest and spooned him. His heavy arm slung across her waist was comforting and familiar.

Before he fell asleep, she felt the need to confess, though why, she wasn't sure. "I met a man at the gym tonight."

"Oh?" His voice was three parts drowsy and one part interested.

"He's from out of town. Said he might be here for a week or ten days, and he wanted a place to work out."

"Did you tell him we don't do that?"

"Yeah."

"And?"

"He was persistent."

She felt him tense. "How persistent?"

She patted his leg. "Not like that. He wasn't rude, and he didn't cross any lines, but he was . . ." She paused, not sure how to explain. "I wanted to give him what he asked for. So we made a deal. He wrote a check for charity, and I gave him a handful of free passes."

Thomas made a sound beneath his breath, and she realized what she had said. "For the gym—you know, the ones we give trial members."

She rolled onto her back, trying to see his face in the gloom. "What are you thinking?"

He touched her breast. "I hear something in your voice, love. You were attracted to him, weren't you?"

His perceptive comment made her flinch. "He was a nice-looking man, that's all." The way Thomas toyed with her nipple made her restless. "Nothing happened."

His voice was mild. "I'm not accusing you of anything, Melanie." He moved to the other breast, stroking her almost as if he was unaware of his actions. "But I'm interested in hearing more. He could be your free pass, don't you think? He meets the requirements. He's a stranger. He'll be going home in a week or so. Sounds perfect."

She closed her eyes to absorb the feel of his gentle touch on her sensitive skin. "The free-pass idea was for you." She said it by rote now, no longer sure of her original motives.

She felt him move over her, and then his mouth covered hers in a rough kiss. "I think you should do this, Melanie . . . if you want to. Remind yourself what it's like to be intimate with someone who's discovering your beautiful, sexy body for the first time. And I'll promise to think about doing the same."

"You swear?" She felt really guilty now. Instead of her husband getting a freebie to break up any potential tedium from marital sex and ward off the seven-year itch, suddenly *she* was contemplating seducing a handsome stranger. How had that happened?

She stirred restlessly, pulling his mouth back down to hers. She kissed him anxiously, afraid he wasn't really as sanguine about her confession as he appeared. "I'll never love anyone but you, Thomas." She prayed it was the truth. Genetics weren't everything, and she was a strong, principled woman.

"I know." He tugged her into a warm embrace and kissed her forehead. "Go to sleep. We'll deal with it tomorrow."

Chapter Three

Debra stood on the steps of their sun-washed villa and gazed across the hilltop village of Oia. It was like something out of a dream. She and Gordon had been on Santorini less than twenty-four hours, and already she had fallen in love.

Sparkling white buildings, blue-domed churches, and sunshine, always sunshine. Many things in life were disappointing at second glance. But not Greece. It was every bit as lovely as the calendars and movies portrayed, probably even more so.

The sun-warmed stone beneath her bare feet was surprisingly sensual. But then again, the entire island struck her as erotic and unabashedly hedonistic. She yawned and stretched, suddenly eager to explore. Gordon was still sleeping, but she had no qualms about waking him up. After almost an entire day of travel, they had arrived at their ultimate destination absolutely exhausted. They'd fallen into bed and slept for hours.

She had no idea what time it was locally, but her stomach was growling loudly. She wandered back inside and opened the short, old-fashioned refrigerator. They had been promised some minimal provisions to get them started, and there they were: milk, fresh squeezed orange juice, and some sort of honey-and-almond-laced pastry.

Suddenly, she laughed out loud. This place was amazing. And they had an entire week to wallow in the sights and sounds of the fabulous island. As recently as yesterday morning, a part of her wished they had gone somewhere Stateside like Cherisse and Wesley had so they could have afforded to vacation for a full two weeks. But now that she was here, she couldn't regret the choice. This was paradise.

Suddenly, she had to talk to somebody. She felt ready to burst. She peeked in on Gordon and then left him to slumber undisturbed. Instead, she rummaged in her purse for her cell. Gordie had splurged on an international phone, and although they had agreed to use it judiciously, she couldn't wait to tell her friends about Greece.

It would be rude to disturb Cherisse on her anniversary trip, but Melanie wouldn't mind being woken up. After punching all sorts of numbers, Debra waited impatiently. At last, someone picked up, and Mel's sleepy voice came over the line, surprisingly clear.

"Hello."

"Mel, it's me . . . Debra. I'm in Santorini, and it's fabulous. I'm sorry to call at whatever hour this is, but I wanted to talk to you."

"So it's really awesome?" Mel sounded more awake by the second.

"It's incredible, and so romantic. Not that we were able to take advantage of it last night. We were zombies by the time we got here."

"Too bad. I was expecting to hear about wild monkey sex."

Melanie's teasing words made Debra grin. "Give us time. And by the way, how did Thomas react to the free-pass idea? I haven't had the courage to bring it up with Gordie yet. Although this week would probably be a good opportunity. We're not likely to know anyone here."

After a split second of silence, Mel replied, "He was surprised mostly. And not all that excited about it, frankly. Although he urged *me* to go for it, if I wanted to. That seemed more interesting to him. Go figure."

Debra leaned against the low stone wall. "Well, that's no surprise. Thomas has never been the jealous type, and he would do anything for you, including, I imagine, letting you do the nasty with a stranger."

"Very funny." Then Mel's voice changed. "Listen, Debra. That free-pass proposal was kind of a crazy idea. Don't do it just because I brought it up. You know your own marriage better than anyone. Seven years is a number, that's all. I'm sure you have nothing to worry about."

Debra sighed, shielding her eyes to look out at the Aegean. "Well, I haven't told him yet, but I'm thinking I will. We'll see what happens." She glanced at her watch and moaned. "Oh, heck. I've got to go. Who knows what this is costing us? Love ya, Mel. Tell Cherisse I said hello if you talk to her."

She hung up and turned back toward the house to find that Gordon had finally surfaced. He was standing just outside the door in his favorite pair of boxers. As he yawned and scratched his chest, he gazed at her with suspicious eyes. "Tell me what?"

She tucked the phone into her shirt pocket. "It will keep. Let's eat. I'm starving."

Thankfully, he allowed her to change the subject. If she decided to introduce the idea, she wanted to do it very carefully. And it would definitely not be a good idea to drop this particular bomb on an empty stomach . . . his *or* hers.

With Gordon's help, she gathered the simple breakfast items onto a tray and carried it outside. She had a notion that they might be eating most of their meals alfresco in the coming week. The spectacular view alone was sustenance enough.

The morning sun was hot, but not unbearable. Although she and Gordon were both fair-headed, their olive skin enabled them to tan rather than burn. A light breeze ruffled the blossoming shrubs along the patio wall and kept the heat at bay.

The villa they had had rented sat at the top of a hill, and unless someone actually climbed over the wall, it was doubtful their privacy would be disturbed. They ate companionably in silence, soaking in the atmosphere. Sunlight glittered on the ocean, and in the distance, the island of Thirassia beckoned.

Neither of them was a morning person, so this slow start to the day was a delicious luxury. Gordon sighed and leaned back in his rough wooden chair. "I might just sit here for the entire week."

She smiled faintly. "I know what you mean. I'm trying to summon up the energy to think about a plan for the day. I feel like we have such a short time, and I don't want to miss anything."

Gordon put his arms over his head and stretched. "But I thought you wanted to relax."

She propped her feet on the wall. "Well, that, too. But shouldn't we at least do some of the touristy things?"

"Translation—shopping?"

She flicked a crumb of pastry at him. "Don't be so sexist. I can live without shopping for a week."

He rolled his eyes. "Right. No handpainted Greek pottery, no embroidered tablecloths, no sandals, no gold jewelry? If you say so . . ." His voice trailed off in a skeptical sigh.

She chuckled. "Well, if the right bargain comes along. But seriously, sweetheart, this is your vacation, too. I want us both to have fun. So you'll have to speak up and tell me what you want to do."

He looked over his shoulder. Tucked under an eave of the house was a striped canvas hammock. It hung in a pocket of shade at this hour. Gordon turned to look at her. "How about sex in a hammock?"

"Really?" She was cautious but intrigued. Exhibitionism had never been high on her list of fantasies, but then again, their little balcony was very private.

Gordon reached for her hand, squeezing it and then tugging until she stood as he did. "No time like the present."

Gordon didn't have much clothing to take off. His boxers were gone in a flash, leaving him buck naked in the brash sunlight. She scooted back closer to the house and stripped off her panties and sleep shirt. The breeze on her sun-warmed flesh brushed over nerve endings and made her feel like Eve in the garden. Her Adam moved closer.

Here on this ancient island, she and Gordon might well be channeling carnal pursuits from aeons ago. A lot of those Greek gods and goddesses had been lusty in their sexual habits. She felt oddly bashful. Gordon wasn't saying anything. But his green eyes were watchful. They looked almost aquamarine today, perhaps reflecting the blue of the sea and the sky.

His penis might have been the model for one on a classical statue, except that his was fully erect and bore no resemblance to cold marble. She sensed the life pulsing in him, felt drawn to his hunger as though only she could satisfy him.

He slipped his hands beneath her sleep-tousled hair and cupped her head, drawing her closer for a kiss. She tasted the honey on his tongue, felt the slight rasp of his whiskers on her lips and chin. His body was hard and warm against hers.

She slid her arms around his neck, exploring the muscles in his shoulders. He was built like a rock—solid, tough, someone to cling to in a storm. His cock nudged her belly. She trembled. They hadn't made love outdoors since a camping trip four years ago. Now she felt naughty and excited all at the same time.

She loved the feel of his hair-roughened chest against her breasts. "How do we do this?" she whispered.

He cupped her butt and squeezed. "I imagine I'll have to be on my back." He released her with obvious reluctance and settled himself on the wide, sturdy fabric. It looked like it might have been made from the same sort of cloth used to fashion fishermen's pants or triangular sails.

Watching Gordon sprawl unself-consciously in the hammock made her knees weak. She glanced over her shoulder, but only the birds gliding high above them on the thermal currents were watching. Gingerly, she put a knee on the hammock and tried to climb on.

Gordon chuckled as she lost her balance and fell against him. "Careful," he groaned. "Don't hurt my boys."

After a couple of minutes of decidedly unromantic grunting and squirming, and with her husband's help, Debra finally sat astride Gordon's thighs.

He put his hands on her hips. "Come here, woman." He lifted her enough to align his cock with her pussy and then lowered her gently. They both murmured in pleasure as the connection engaged.

It was an odd feeling. The hammock bobbed and swayed each time she tried to lift up and come down. And with no hard surface beneath them, the angle of penetration was more shallow than she was accustomed to.

Arousal built in slow, trembling waves.

Gordon's eyes were closed. His jaw was tight and the

cords in his neck stood out in relief. Sweat dampened his forehead. She leaned forward to kiss him. He groaned and thrust his tongue in her mouth. She bit down and at the same time rotated her hips.

In the distance, music played faintly, a lyrical counterpoint to their breathless, awkward passion. Gordon hissed suddenly and lunged upward, holding her tight until they were almost in a sitting position. Now her clit got the full effect of his thrusting erection.

She cried out. Gordon clamped one hand over her mouth, and they both shuddered and groaned as they climaxed almost in tandem.

Gordon fell back, taking her with him. Beneath her cheek, she could feel the rapid beat of his heart. The sun had shifted enough that she felt hot rays on the backs of her legs. She was enervated, lost to any consideration of time or rational thought.

They dozed.

When she finally became aware of their surroundings once more, she was intertwined in an embrace that was both comfortable and embarrassing. Had anyone been watching? As they slept nude as the day they were born, had a careless observer made note of their exhausted passion?

Gingerly, she tried to extricate herself, but it was a two-person job.

Gordon reacted when she tried it on her own a second time. "Easy, Deb, my love. Those elbows of yours are sharp." He supported her as she rearranged her legs and finally managed to stand without tumbling either of them to the hard surface below.

She was sweating, and her heart was beating rapidly. Guiltily, she slipped into her panties and shirt. "What time is it?"

He had tucked his hands behind his head and seemed in no hurry to get up. "How should I know? Isn't there a digital clock on the phone?"

She slipped the tiny phone from her pocket and peered at it. Her eyes were watering from the unforgiving sun. Her sunglasses were somewhere in the house. "It's almost noon. I'm going to take a shower and get dressed."

Gordon looked like the lazy male he was. "I'll just rest a bit more while you're in the bathroom."

She picked up his boxers and dropped them over his lap. "Well, let's not press our luck. I don't know what the decency laws are around here, but I have no desire to spend a night in a Greek jail."

"Prude," he said with affection in his voice.

"Show-off." As she entered the house, she thought about the fact that her husband had *plenty* to show off. If she brought up the free-pass idea, Gordon would have no problem finding a young Greek woman to satisfy his onetime tryst. But Debra didn't have his self-confidence. She was shy and not inclined to dress for attention.

So maybe she would just follow Melanie's original plan. She would offer Gordon the chance to play, and be happy knowing she had made the sacrifice for the sake of their marital longevity.

But as she showered and washed her hair, an inescapable feeling of dissatisfaction plagued her. Why should Gordon have all the fun? He was secure enough in his masculinity to let her flirt with another man. Would he be able to tolerate the turnabout-is-fair-play side of the free-pass idea?

She finally coaxed him inside to dress and clean up, and they headed out for a stroll to locate groceries and have lunch. She was glad they had chosen to stay in Oia, because it was much quieter than Fira, which they had seen briefly yesterday on their way from the airport.

Gordon dragged her around exploring until the heat forced them to seek out a taverna and escape from the sun. Over traditional glasses of ouzo, they squabbled about the menu. Gordon wasn't an adventurous eater, so he chose the Greek salad topped with grilled prawns. Debra ordered tomato-keftedes, which turned out to be tomato and fresh spearmint dough balls laid on crispy vine leaves with a sun-dried tomato and feta cheese pesto.

The portions were huge. Debra had to beg Gordon to help her finish after she convinced him it was an innocuous dish. She waited until he chewed with his mouth full, and then leaned closer. "What would you think about having sex with another woman?"

He choked on a grape leaf and had to swallow down his glass of water and hers before he could speak. His face was red, and his eyes continued to water as he croaked out a response. "Is that one of those trick questions females like to use on a man? If so, I plead the Fifth."

She rarely drank, and the ouzo had given her a pleasant buzz. She leaned back in her chair, feeling magnanimous. "I suppose you've heard of the seven-year itch?" She didn't wait for him to answer. "It's a documented phenomenon that causes men to cheat on their wives when they feel trapped in a marriage."

He wiped his mouth with a heavy cloth napkin. "You think I feel trapped?"

She shrugged. "Well, no. But this is more of a preemptive strike."

His eyes narrowed. "Don't tell me. I'm guessing such a wild idea has Melanie written all over it."

His perspicacity surprised her, but perhaps he was remembering the last time she had done something kind of freaky. Melanie had convinced Debra to sign up with her for an online dating service so they could research the possibility of opening an *in-person* dating business in conjunction with the gym.

One of the men Melanie had hooked up with in an e-mail conversation tracked her down, and the police ended up getting involved. Gordon had been furious with Melanie for involving his wife.

Debra spoke calmly, though her heart was thumping in her chest. "Melanie might have been the first one to mention it, but it makes a lot of sense. Men stray. It's a fact, and apparently after seven years, things can happen."

He shook his head in apparent confusion. "I'm a guy. Of course I think about screwing other women from time to time. It's a mental exercise, though. It doesn't mean I don't love you."

She knew that. But they had both been virgins when they'd married, and surely he had wondered what it would be like to have sex with someone else. They occasionally shared fantasies in bed about being with other people, but up until now it had been nothing more than a game.

She put her elbows on the table and leaned forward. "So wouldn't it be fun to have a once-in-a-lifetime, purely sexual hookup with a stranger . . . here in Greece . . . where we don't know anyone?"

Now she had his attention. "We?" His eyes narrowed and he folded his arms across his chest.

"I assumed the offer would be reciprocal."

He drummed his fork on the table. "I thought the point of this anniversary trip was for us to be romantic and lovey-dovey."

It was her turn to scowl. "You make it sound so appealing. Be fair. Haven't you ever wondered? Since we've been married, I mean."

"Well, at the risk of getting my nuts chopped off, sure. Everybody wonders. But that's as far as it went." His eyes didn't quite meet hers. She saw him try to unobtrusively adjust himself beneath the table, and she was pretty sure he was getting excited about her offer.

"Don't you see, Gordie? If we each give the other permission, i.e., a free pass, we can experience all the wicked excitement without any of the guilt. And then, when it's over, we can remember."

His expression was one part caution and two parts arousal. She could tell he was trying to be cool about the conversation. "Since when did you develop such a liberal attitude about sex?"

She hadn't, but she was trying to expand her horizons. "We're hopelessly inexperienced, Gordie. Most people our age have been with at least a half dozen partners at this point in their lives. We tied ourselves down when we were very young. I don't want you to regret that. Just think about it," she urged. "That's all I ask."

She saw him swallow, and his face flushed crimson. "You don't have to sell me. I like the idea, honey ... in the abstract. But let's give it some time to make sure this is a solid idea. I don't want us to do something you'll regret later. But if you're sure ... *when* you're sure ... Well, hell—I'm your man."

Gordon followed his wife inside their cool, pleasant villa and wondered how amenable she would be to an afternoon nap. Not that sleeping was really what he had in mind. Her latest bombshell had him hard and aching, but if he told her how horny he was, she would assume he was ready to score with another female on the spot. And while the idea had definite fantasy appeal, he had a feeling that the fallout from such a thing might be damaging.

When Debra bent over to put something in the small refrigerator, he bumped up against her. "You're just doing that to taunt me, aren't you?"

She straightened up and grinned. "Whatever works." She glanced at the clock. "You up for some sunbathing?"

He considered it. She would be mostly naked. He was in. "Sure. I'll get the sunscreen."

They changed into their swimsuits, and he got his first look at Debra's new leopard-print bikini. He'd bet his last dollar that she'd never have the guts to wear it at home. The bottom barely covered the seam of her butt, and the two flimsy triangles of fabric over her nipples were no more than four inches across.

By European standards it was probably not all that unusual, but it sure as hell made his heart race. As he stood in the bedroom smearing suntan lotion all over her back, he reminded himself that it would be rude to throw her down on the bed and fuck her.

He sighed inwardly. A polite husband would at least wait for an invitation, considering that they had already screwed their brains out once today. He followed her like a lapdog out onto the patio, salivating over the fabulous rear view. Debra spread out her towel and then perched cross-legged on the stone wall.

He tossed his towel beside hers and went to stand behind her, nibbling her shoulder. "What are you doing?"

She sighed, her expression dreamy. "Just looking. The volcanoes, the islands, the water. I wish I could paint."

"We brought a camera."

She gave him that look that women use when they think their spouses are being particularly thickheaded. "There's no way a photograph could capture this—the light, the brilliant colors, the sense that we're walking on ground that people have walked on for thousands of years."

Wesley chuckled. She was so cute when she waxed poetic. He leaned his chin on her shoulder, his arms linked loosely around her waist. It was romantic. He had to admit. This was probably the most beautiful place he and Debra had ever visited. They had only been twenty-two when they got married, and even now money was still an issue, though they both had decent jobs.

But it had only been recently that they had finally paid off their student loans. The resulting positive swing in their budget had made it possible for them to plan this anniversary trip.

A lot of people had cautioned him about getting married so young . . . warned him it wouldn't last. But he and Debra were levelheaded people, and aside from the fact that they were still head over heels in love with each other, they both came from stable families and parents who were working on thirty-five-year marriages.

He was just about ready to suggest that they stretch out and enjoy the late-afternoon sun when Debra gasped and nearly tumbled off the wall. He grabbed her, even though the drop was only a few feet. "What is it, angel?"

She scrambled off the wall and crouched beside it, her cute nose peeking over the top. "Get down."

The urgency in her voice convinced him, but damn if he could figure out what was wrong. "Debra—"

She shushed him. "Look," she whispered hoarsely. "Right there." She pointed a finger and then quickly drew it back as though it might get bitten off at any moment.

Totally perplexed, he scanned the expanse of villas that covered the hillside. Finally he saw what she saw. About twenty-five yards below them and to the left . . . on a lovely, flower-decked stone patio, much like the one where Debra and Gordon were now hiding out, a couple was having sex.

They weren't flaunting it, but they sure as hell weren't being discreet. At least a half dozen other houses besides Debra and Gordon's must have had a similar view of the action.

Both of the naked lovers were dark headed, though it was

difficult to make out much else from this distance. A white blanket spread beneath the writhing bodies cushioned them from the hard stone floor.

There was nothing titillating about the sexual position. The guy was on top. The woman had her legs wrapped around his waist. He was fucking her vigorously, and she appeared to be enjoying it.

Gordon couldn't tear his eyes away, even though Debra was only allowing him to peek up to eye level. His dick got hard, and he swallowed, wishing they had brought water bottles outside.

No sound carried this far, but the tableau was erotic, nevertheless. Suddenly, the couple swapped places. The woman got on her hands and knees. Gordie winced in sympathy. Man, that must have been killing her shins.

Debra's eyes were open wide, her mouth a little "O" of shock. But she never let her gaze waver from the two strangers going at it like rabbits.

Gordon slid her bikini bottom to her knees. She barely noticed. He inserted two fingers into her plump, wet pussy and frigged her slowly.

Her breath caught audibly, and when her fingers clenched the edge of the wall, her knuckles turned white. He upped the tempo. Debra's breathing was ragged now, her hips moving against his hand feverishly. He bit gently on her ass cheeks, one at a time, and she came with an almost soundless cry. Below them, the strange woman did the same.

Gordon lowered Debra into his arms, holding her tightly as she recovered. He glanced one last time over the wall and saw that the couple was standing. They were a nice-looking pair. Just before they disappeared inside their villa, Gordon saw them kiss tenderly.

Debra wriggled in his grasp. He released her and watched as she gathered up their towels.

He cocked his head, his boner throbbing like a toothache. "I thought we were going to get some sun."

Debra took his hand, her smile coy. "Not at the moment. I suddenly have the urge to screw my husband, and I must be a prude, because I want to do it in our bedroom on our soft mattress."

He hustled her along. "Get moving, then. I think that's the best idea you've had all day."

Chapter Four

Cherisse rolled over in bed and peered at the clock. She couldn't believe that a week of their vacation had already passed. They'd done a little of everything. Monday they drove over to the Everglades and saw more sleepy alligators in one afternoon than on all the Discovery Channel shows combined.

They'd tried a dolphin cruise. Gone parasailing. Visited art galleries. Another day they took a walking tour of the fascinating Art Deco district.

Most afternoons, Wesley sat patiently on a bench and watched the world go by as Cherisse shopped to her heart's content. He got a kick out of following the Rollerbladers, though Cherisse pleaded with him not to try it. She could tell that he was tempted to overlook her protests, but the thought of actually breaking one of his limbs must have deterred him. Thank God.

She got out of bed and went into the living room, yawning and stretching. Last night they had called for a cab and gone to a snazzy club on Twenty-first Street. They both wanted to be able to drink, and after a few killer cocktails, she'd even persuaded Wesley to dance. It was crazy and fun, and by the time they had finally tumbled into bed, they'd only had the energy for a quickie.

Now she sat on the sofa and flipped to the Weather Channel to study the forecast for the upcoming week. Nothing but day after day of incredible sunshine and blue skies. She felt a bit guilty. She had talked to Melanie twice, and apparently, it was raining buckets back home.

Cherisse hit the MUTE button and stretched out with her hands behind her head, staring absently at the lazily rotating fan overhead. During the past week, neither she nor Wesley had spoken aloud about the free-pass idea, but she had a feeling it had been on his mind as much as it had been on hers. But time was slipping away, and neither of them had done anything concrete to pursue the idea.

Maybe that was all it was—a fun idea. Perhaps neither of them had the guts to go through with it. Which confused her. If it was such an arousing idea, why had nothing happened? Were they such an old married couple already that they were afraid to take risks? Were they never again going to do even one sexually crazy thing?

She sighed and lifted a leg in the air to admire the pedicure she had gotten before she'd left home. With the exception of a tiny chip on her left pinky toe, the polish still looked perfect. She lifted the other leg and studied the pair of limbs side by side. All her life she had yearned for long, slender calves and thighs. Instead, she had to live with short and a bit too shapely. But strong . . . and nicely sun warmed thanks to the tanning bed she had used before coming to Miami.

Would a strange man find her sexually attractive? Her stomach quivered. The thought of intentionally seeking out a sexual partner made her nervous as hell. Was it possible to have sex fully clothed? She couldn't imagine getting naked in front of a stranger, especially one who might be more critical than Wesley of all her jiggly parts. Was she really going to do it?

She jumped up and headed to the kitchen for a bagel. Maybe the odd sensation in the pit of her belly was hunger, not lust.

Now that she and Wesley had hit the highlights of all the major tourist stuff, they'd decided to let this week be more laid back. And they had also agreed to go their separate ways for a bit. Wesley needed to work on syllabi he was preparing for two new economics courses he would teach in the fall. Cherisse wanted to spend as much time as possible exploring the glitzy stores on Ocean Drive, and also wandering through more of the antiques places in the Lincoln Road area.

By the time she had finished her breakfast and returned to the bedroom, Wesley was beginning to stir. The faint frown creasing his forehead might signify a hangover.

She scooted under the covers and curled against him. "Do you care if I head out to the beach this morning?"

He mumbled something and groped her breasts. She rolled to her back, shimmied out of her undies, and urged him on top. Morning fucks were lovely and slow, especially on vacation. Wesley moved between her thighs and entered her with a steady push.

She bit her lip and arched her back, moving in sync with his rhythm. Her orgasm built languidly, almost as if it would never peak. Wesley's skin was hot. He screwed her slowly. Her brain latched on to familiar fantasies, and then suddenly... her breath caught as a vision of herself and a strange man scrolled like a sexy movie behind her closed eyelids.

Just as the mystery man kissed her, Wesley pumped one last time, shouted, and came, leaving her hanging on the precipice of hot, achy, frustrated arousal.

He rolled off her and brushed the hair from his face, still breathing heavily. "Sorry, sweetheart. I didn't mean to come so fast. Blame it on yourself. I love how your body feels in the morning."

She was ready to beg, but Wesley was no dummy. She was practically quivering with unspent hunger. He gave himself a moment or two to recover, and then he trapped her wrists over her head with one strong hand.

The position poured fuel on the fire. She squirmed, her arousal deepening. Carefully, he put his other hand between her legs and stroked her, avoiding her clitoris. Sometimes she relished the care he took with her body. Now she just wanted relief.

He played with her teasingly, roving around and up and over the bull's-eye, but never making contact. She begged. She pleaded. He kept up his gentle torture until her climax sneaked past him, even without any direct stimulation, and sent her over the edge.

Wesley held her, stroking her hair until her tremors subsided. She felt like her bones were made of mush. For two cents, she would go back to sleep. But the thought of how quickly the days were passing spurred her at last to a sitting position. "I think I'll go to the beach."

He dropped her off so she wouldn't have to struggle with parking. With a large straw tote in her hand, and a beach towel slung over her shoulder, she leaned one arm on the car door to look at him through the open window. "Sure you don't want to come with me?"

He blew her a kiss. "Enjoy your day, Cherisse. And don't worry about me. I'll be perfectly content back at the condo."

She smiled wryly. "I know. You probably won't even miss me."

As he drove off, she made her way over to a small kiosk and paid for an umbrella and chair. She had arrived early by Miami standards, and the beachgoers were sparse. After spreading her orange-and-yellow towel on the canvas lounger, she rummaged in her bag for the sunscreen.

She had fair skin that burned easily, so she wasn't taking any chances. She'd had Wesley do her back before she put her suit on. She was kind of proud of her new bikini. It was fire-engine red, a color she seldom wore, but it made her feel sexy, and the fact that it had cost an astronomical amount was irrelevant.

The legs were cut high, but the rest of the bottom half was fairly modest . . . if you discounted the two gold rings that held the sides together. The top was halter-style, and the deep V in front flattered her generous cleavage. She tugged the chair into the sunlight. She would enjoy the blinding rays now, before it got too hot, and then move back into the shade later.

She started on her back, closing her eyes and savoring the sounds and scents. The heat of the sun seemed to bake down into her bones. The roar of the waves crashing on the beach mingled with laughter and the fainter noise of traffic in the distance.

The scent of coconut-based sunscreen lingered in the air. She might have dozed except for the fact that she and Wesley had slept in so long this morning. After ten minutes, she turned her head to the side and opened her eyes, shielding them with her hand.

Not far away, a lifeguard kept watch from his perch. She squinted and studied him. He was blond and tanned, and his features, what she could see of them, were pleasing. He held himself with careless grace, and she felt a lick of arousal in that vulnerable spot between her thighs.

She closed her eyes again and wished she dared touch herself. Her mind took over, painting pictures of the young man and her, their limbs entwined on a broad bed in a dimly lit room. She felt his lips on her throat, her breasts, her belly.

She squirmed on her chaise as the dream man moved lower, parting her thighs with gentle hands. He buried his face at her core. His tongue flicked a tiny spot that made Cherisse moan with fever.

Her hands clenched in fists at her sides. She sat up abruptly and reached for the bottle of water she had brought along. Feeling ridiculously self-conscious, she turned to look at the handsome lifeguard.

Her heart fluttered and sank. He was greeting his replacement. And the new man didn't do it for Cherisse at all.

Her disappointment was all out of proportion. She couldn't even see her dream lover's eyes beneath the wraparound sunglasses he wore. He might have been unexceptional up close. Though from this distance, his firm jaw looked masculine and his tousled hair appealing.

She turned to her stomach and buried her face in her hands. This was stupid. She had come to the beach to sunbathe and relax. Unfulfilled fantasies were frustrating and unproductive. Maybe she should have brought a book to keep her mind occupied.

After another half hour, she was getting too hot to keep still any longer. The Miami sun was brutal. She had expected to find much warmer temperatures than in Minnesota. But June back home was a lovely month. Here, practically in the tropics, it was suffocatingly hot, much more so than she could have imagined.

She slipped her credit card beneath the edge of her bikini bottom for safekeeping and left the rest of her things behind as she wandered to the water's edge. The sand burned the bottoms of her feet until she got them wet. She'd put on her sunglasses, but even so, the glare was blinding. The water slapping over the tops of her feet actually felt cool against her hot skin.

For a moment, she wished Wesley had come with her, and then she shook her head in self-disgust. Surely she could entertain herself for one day without feeling lost. They didn't have to be joined at the hip 24-7.

She went back and moved into the shade, spending the next hour people watching. It was endlessly entertaining. She actually saw a seventyish old man in a thong bikini, his once-white skin the color of rich mahogany. Decades in the Miami sun had turned his body to teak.

The women were even more fascinating. Beautiful females were a dime a dozen down here, she had discovered. She'd read somewhere that more than fifteen hundred models made their homes in Miami because of the many opportunities for location shoots, not to mention movies and television shows. It was enough to make an ordinary woman self-conscious.

At noon, she was ready to go. In the midst of a Minnesota winter, the idea of sunbathing in Miami had been appealing, but for her, the reality was less so. She folded her towel neatly and stuffed it in her tote. After a quick call to Wesley to let him know what she was doing, she reached for the simple cover-up that would serve her well the rest of the afternoon. She'd actually found it in a boutique the first time she had shopped on Ocean Drive.

It was made out of a lightweight ecru fabric that resembled linen, but without the wrinkles. Once she tugged it over her head and smoothed the skirt, she was good to go. Bands of embroidery in two shades of brown accented the deeply scooped neckline and short hem that showed off her legs. A narrow gold chain accented the waistline. With her brown leather sandals, it made an entirely acceptable ensemble for a summer outing.

She decided to have lunch in the luxurious hotel just behind her. It offered at least four full-service restaurants. La Perla was a pricey tearoom that boasted an eclectic menu along with a nice ocean view.

The hostess didn't blink an eye at Cherisse's casual attire. The woman led her to a cloth-draped table by the window and handed her a leather-bound menu. "Danny will be your server today. The specials are listed on the left panel. Enjoy your meal."

It didn't take Cherisee long to decide on a mandarin and almond salad with baby shrimp. She might even have room for dessert.

The waiter approached from behind her right shoulder. "Good afternoon, ma'am. My name is Danny. I'll be taking care of you today. What can I get you to drink?"

She turned to look at him and dropped her menu. It was the lifeguard. Her face must have registered her mix of emotions, because he gazed at her in concern. "Is something wrong?"

Her face flamed. "Um, no. I was just surprised. Weren't you lifeguarding at the beach this morning? Or am I totally confused?"

His smile was cheerful. "Nope. You're not confused. You got me. I work several part-time jobs so I have the flexibility to go for auditions when they crop up."

"You're an actor?"

Now his grin was sheepish. "Aspiring only. Also model, dog walker, and occasional bartender."

"A man of many talents." She gulped as she realized how flirtatious her words sounded.

They didn't faze him. "I like to think so." Now that same flash of white teeth was definitely cocky.

She cleared her throat. "Well, good luck with that." She straightened her silverware and fussed with her menu. "I think I'm ready to order."

He plucked a pad from his pocket. "Let's hear it." He seemed to approve of her choices and promised to be right back with her water. She'd had more than enough alcohol last night, and she wasn't big on colas.

When he disappeared toward the kitchen, she took out her compact and examined her face. She had stopped by the restroom in the hotel lobby as she came in from the beach, so at least she had touched up her minimal makeup. Her cheeks were flushed, and her eyes stared back at her with what was almost certainly guilt in their depths. Had she found her free-pass man?

When he came back with the goblet of ice water and a silver mesh basket full of warm bread, his arm brushed hers as he set them on the table. She shivered inwardly and tried not to look like an idiot. His scent was light and masculine, tangy with lime.

They chatted a bit more. On a Monday afternoon, the restaurant was almost deserted. She commented on the view. He pointed out a few landmarks. His hands brushed hers when he reached for her water glass to refill it. She'd been drinking thirstily, ostensibly because of the hot day, but in reality because his simple, friendly sex appeal made her edgy and uncertain.

Other customers finally drifted in, and Danny was called away. But he stopped by a few minutes later to drop off her salad and give her another cheeky grin.

As she ate her meal in solitude, she gazed blindly through the window. Huge clumps of bougainvillea splashed color over the manicured lawn that ran between the hotel and the beach. Beyond that, the ocean basked in the sun like a momentarily serene lady. But Cherisse knew the peacefulness was deceiving. That huge expanse of water could be dangerous on occasion.

Her hands were perfectly steady when she finally laid down her fork and dabbed her lips with a napkin. Danny reappeared to offer dessert. It seemed the perfect metaphor for the moment.

She wet her lips and looked up at him. "What time do you get off today?"

His quick blink was the only sign of his shock. "Two," he said quietly, studying her embarrassed face and then her breasts.

She swallowed and clenched her hands in her lap beneath the tablecloth . . . where he couldn't see them. "Would you like to join me later for some ice cream?"

His eyes narrowed, locking on her tremulous gaze with masculine assessment. "Ice cream?"

She nodded jerkily. "For starters. I usually order vanilla, but I was thinking of branching out . . . maybe trying one of the local specialties."

Now he looked at her lips, his intensity almost tactile. "Sounds like an appealing idea. I love ice cream."

She tucked her credit card in the folio he had set on the table with her bill.

He started to speak and then shook his head. "I'll be back with this in a moment."

She slumped in her seat and lifted a hand to her lips. Holy cow. Was she actually going to go through with it? Her heart thudded like she had run a marathon.

He was gone longer this time. The party across the room

demanded his attention. Finally, he headed her way. He placed her receipts on the table with a pen. "Were you serious? About the ice cream?"

She nodded slowly. "Yes. I'll be in the lobby at two. If that's okay."

He picked up her hand and lifted it to his lips. "I'll look forward to it."

For the next hour and fifteen minutes, she wandered blindly, first in the hotel's air-conditioned shops and then out on the street, her feet leading her in aimless directions. When the unforgiving midday heat drove her back inside, she found a chair in the marble-floored lobby and sat quietly, her feet side by side, her hands clenching the arms of the plush armchair.

At a quarter till two she called Wesley. She asked about his day. She mentioned her tasty lunch. She didn't talk about Danny. The free-pass agreement included full disclosure. But after the fact, not now. Not when she was so nervous she could barely breathe.

When she closed the cell phone and dropped it in the tote, she happened to look up and catch the eye of the concierge. He smiled pleasantly. She wanted to crawl under the chair. Good Lord, what was she doing?

Danny was prompt. At ten after, he came striding into the lobby from the direction of the restaurant. She thought his expression was a bit tense . . . until he saw her. Then his face broke into a big smile. "It dawned on me that I didn't know your first name," he said as he joined her. "It's not on your credit card."

Her face grew hotter. "Cherisse," she mumbled, hoping no one at the front desk was paying them any attention. "And I guess I should ask your *last* name."

He put an arm around her shoulders and steered her toward the street. "Does it matter? Let's leave it at Danny," he said smoothly. "For the moment."

His answer troubled her. Was he accustomed to doing things like this? Did he think she would hang around? Try as she might, she couldn't think of a reason for him not to tell her his last name. Unless he'd had some bad experience in the past. Maybe a psycho woman who had slept with him and then become his stalker.

She snickered under her breath and struggled to keep up with his long legs. He had taken the tote bag from her and slung it over his shoulder. Some men might have felt awkward about carrying a bag trimmed in pink floral ribbon, but Danny seemed unconcerned.

The ice-cream place was two blocks away. It was popular, so they had to stand in line. Danny insisted on paying, which struck her as sweet. Then she wanted to smack herself. This wasn't a date.

She panicked once when she thought that her husband might call in the midst of this. Maybe she should have clued him in. Danny handed her a homemade waffle cone stuffed with an enormous scoop of Pop Her Cherry. Only in Miami. Back home in Minnesota, the morality police would have jumped all over that. And even worse, Danny selected Fuckin' Fudge. She wondered if he was really a chocolate lover, or if he had chosen the suggestively named flavor deliberately.

Outside they found a table with a modicum of shade. For

several moments they licked their rapidly melting ice cream in silence. He sat close to her on the bench, his bare leg, covered with golden hair, touching her thigh now and then. His khaki shorts and pristine white shirt were required hotel garb.

She finished off her cone and licked her fingers. It came as a complete shock when Danny snagged her hand and finished the job. He pulled her index finger into his mouth and sucked on it. Cherisse felt the tug in her womb. She couldn't see his expression. His eyes were hidden by his dark glasses.

He gave each finger the same attention. At the end he bit down gently on the pad of her thumb. It was all she could do not to moan.

She tugged her hand away. "I'm not sticky anymore." The words came out prim and stilted.

"Too bad." Deliberately, he took the last of his dripping cone and smeared it on his left hand. "I am." He wiggled his fingers in front of her mouth, and the challenge had to be met. She held his wrist in both hands and bent her head.

She started with his middle finger. His skin wasn't smooth. She felt calluses beneath her tongue. He cursed under his breath when she took his ring finger between her teeth and scraped it deliberately.

She sucked at his pinky and then his forefinger before licking delicately at his thumb.

Through it all, he watched her. She couldn't see his eyes, but she knew he watched her.

When his long, narrow fingers were completely clean, she leaned back. He put his palms on his knees, bent his head, and seemed to be having trouble breathing.

When he finally sat up, he reached beneath her hair and pulled her closer. "I need another taste of you," he muttered.

Her hand on his chest slowed his progress. She removed his sunglasses and set them carefully behind her. "I want to see your eyes." The green had darkened to emerald. He looked less like a boy and more like a man. "How old are you?" she asked.

He nuzzled her nose with his. "Twenty-six."

She was thirty-two. Not cradle robbing, but still. She pulled back a fraction more. "Am I the first woman to proposition you?"

He brushed his lips over hers, tasting, feeling, exploring. His mouth felt different from Wesley's. The contrast rattled her. "Danny?"

"Does it matter?"

"Is that your answer for everything?"

Without bothering to respond, he covered her lips in a lazy kiss. He was a good kisser. World-class. His tongue, still tasting of chocolate, thrust past her teeth and explored her mouth. His hand on the back of her neck kept her captive, not that she was trying to evade him. If anything, she wanted to crawl into his lap.

Arousal that had been simmering all day burst into full-blown hunger. Her fingers clenched on his shoulders. He was hard where she was soft. He smelled good, and his hands on her neck were firm but gentle.

If they could have stretched out right there on the bench and had sex, she would have done it.

But it was a long way from ice cream on the sand to

screwing in some unknown location. Her head was too fuzzy to follow through. She broke the kiss, struggling for a sane thought. "Do you like walking on the beach?"

He touched her cheek, his eyes surprisingly vulnerable. "Too hot right now," he murmured. "We should do it at dawn. The ocean is amazing at that hour. And not many people are out yet."

She knew in that moment she wasn't quite ready for intimacy with a stranger. She kissed him softly. "Will you walk with me . . . in the morning?" They both knew she was asking for more.

He kissed her again—long, drugging kisses that made her so hungry she almost changed her mind. "Yes," he muttered hoarsely. "I'll walk with you. Just say where and when."

Chapter Five

The next day at the gym, Melanie was busy as usual.
It was depressing to know that her friends wouldn't
be dropping by. She'd heard from Cherisse, and
Debra had even called from Greece. Both of them sounded
as if they were having wonderful vacations.

Sadly, Melanie was worrying about a broken-down washing machine and two hundred dirty towels, a clogged hot
tub drain, and a leak in the roof.

It was her own damn fault.

Before lunch she had called an agency in town that dealt
with managerial-level temps, and set up a handful of appointments. It might not be too late to salvage an anniversary trip after all. She owed it to herself and to Thomas to
try at least. And if they had to wait until her assistant came
back, surely it wasn't the end of the world. Thomas wasn't

angry with her. He might be disappointed, but no one ever had died from that. She would make it up to him.

All day she kept half an eye open for the mysterious businessman. She thought she might see him around noon. Lots of people worked out on their lunch hours.

But he never showed. And she refused to admit she was in any way concerned. She'd given him the passes. It was up to him whether he used them.

She'd promised herself she would leave at closing time tonight. Thomas wouldn't benefit, because he and his crew were doing inventory at his store, and he wouldn't be home until after midnight. But it seemed the healthy thing for her to do on her own behalf.

It would give her a chance to take a bubble bath, do a pedicure, read a book—all the things she told herself she enjoyed and yet never seemed to make time for.

Around dinnertime she slipped away for an hour to pick up some takeout and steal a quick moment with her hubby. He was pleased to see her. They sat in his office eating chicken pitas, and she told him about setting up the interviews for a temp assistant.

The flash of pleasure on his face made her glad she had pushed herself to do it. He took a swig of his diet soda. "We can save the cruise for another year. Where would you like to go? Somewhere easy to plan, I think—a place that won't be booked up months in advance."

She shrugged. "I don't know. Maine? We could hike in Acadia."

He nodded slowly. "That's not a bad idea." He reached for his calendar and flipped it open. "If you can get someone in place at the gym, we could do it three weeks from now. But later will work, too. I don't want to stress you out. That's not the point of the vacation."

She dropped her garbage in the trash, went to him, and curled up in his lap. "Why do you put up with me?" she murmured, resting her forehead against his.

He kissed her and tightened his arms around her waist. "Somebody has to," he teased.

She felt his erection flex beneath her butt. "Are you always ready?" She wiggled and straddled his lap. "Don't you ever stop thinking about sex?"

He groaned and trembled. "Yes and no. In that order." He ground his teeth. "Leave, my love. I can't do this now, and it's killing me."

She slid obediently from his lap and went to the door. "Have fun with inventory."

He shot her a dirty look. "Yeah. It's a blast. Be glad you don't have to count golf tees."

She chuckled as she walked away. "Believe me . . . I know how lucky I am."

Richard pulled up in front of the gym and shut off the engine. It was almost eight fifteen. He was bone-tired, and the thought of working out was not really appealing. Not to mention the fact that doing it this late might make it hard to sleep. Exercise tended to jazz him up for several hours.

But then again, he needed the stress relief. He'd been working twelve-hour days for several months, and often Saturdays as well. At first, the promotion and the travel had been exciting. He had no family to tie him down, and he was ambitious.

The money was good, really good. He was socking it away hand over fist in hopes of retiring in his late forties and enjoying life. But if he missed all of his life in the meantime, what would he have left to enjoy? God, he hated being a cliché.

He gazed through the windshield at the gym. Someone had gone to a lot of trouble to make the facade warm and welcoming. The woman he'd met last night might have been responsible. She struck him, even in their short acquaintance, as someone who could do just about anything she set her mind to.

Energy practically radiated off her. Her hands were quick and decisive in their motions; her sharp gaze reflected intelligence and drive. He'd been struck almost from the first second by the notion that she'd be hell on wheels in bed.

He adjusted his shorts and muttered a profanity under his breath. Nobody had told him that living on the road included celibacy. Before the promotion . . . back when he'd had a good desk job and plenty of free time, women frequently came and went in his life. He liked women. And they liked him. So his sex life had not been a problem.

But now . . . well, in the first place, it took a bit of time and effort to pick someone up for a one-night stand. And frankly, he'd been raised to think such behavior was less than admirable. But he certainly wasn't in a position to develop any kind of relationship.

Which left him horny and cranky.

He glanced at his watch one last time and knew if he didn't go inside in the next two minutes, he wouldn't be able to finish his usual workout. As he stepped out of the car, a steady drizzle dampened his hair and made him shiver. He'd stopped by the motel to change into his gym clothes and pick up one of the passes. As he was tossing clean clothes in the trunk of the car right before he'd headed out again, he decided he might to go out for a drink afterward.

A pleasant young man at the desk welcomed him as he entered the lobby. Richard surrendered the pass and made his way into the workout area. He took a moment to orient himself and then settled in for a punishing forty minutes. The machines were slightly different from the ones he was used to, but not that hard to figure out.

Maybe if he upped his weight enough, he could exhaust himself to the point where he could sleep without having sex dreams.

Melanie looked at the clock and then at her desk. For once, she was doing pretty well. She was going to leave at nine on the dot.

She shut down her computer and decided to walk a few laps before she headed out. As soon as she stepped onto the track that circled the workout area, she saw him. He was lifting weights, the muscles in his powerful arms and torso flexing and rippling.

She actually stumbled and had to catch herself on the railing. Deep inside her, something quivered and sprang to life. She walked slowly, trying not to look his way. His back was to her, but the weight area faced a mirror, so he could see her if he was paying attention.

She studied him surreptitiously. Last night in his suit, he had looked like a rumpled, slightly geeky businessman. Now, wearing thigh-hugging shorts and a tank shirt, he was a powerful sexual being.

The sheen of perspiration on his skin merely added to his appeal. It was easy to spot a newbie in a gym. They were the ones with pristine exercise togs that looked as if they had come straight from the department store.

Not this man's. He was entirely comfortable in his attire, and it was clear his clothing was well-washed and -worn. She watched him. She couldn't help it. But what would he do when she circled in front of him?

He stopped dead. That was what he did. And he smiled. That incredible, knee-weakening smile. "Well, hey there, Melanie. Good to see you."

Something about his accent made her think of sex even when he was speaking prosaically.

She slowed to a halt and cleared her throat. "Hello, Richard." She'd read his name off the check the night before. "Has everything been to your liking? We try to keep our customers happy." Was it her imagination, or did her words come out sounding like flirtation?

His even smile didn't change, so perhaps she was being oversensitive.

He put the equipment back on the rack and picked up a towel to wipe his face. "It's a top-notch facility. I'm impressed."

His praise warmed her. She folded her arms around her waist. "Well, good, then . . ." Feeling awkward, she turned to keep walking, but he stopped her.

He shrugged, looking surprisingly vulnerable for such a powerful man. "Do you have a minute? Just to talk? I'm getting to hate that motel room."

Her mouth opened, but she couldn't quite think of a response. "Well . . ."

He twisted the towel in his hands. "I know it's closing time. But could we maybe get a protein shake at the bar? Sit and chat in your office? I won't keep you long, I promise. I know you want to get home."

She thought of Thomas and his inventory. She visualized her quiet, lonely house. "Okay. Sure," she said abruptly. "But do you want to shower first? Not that you need to," she said hastily. "I wasn't implying that—"

He cut her off, grinning hugely now. "I get it. And sure. I'd love a shower if you don't mind waiting."

She knew her face was red. "I'll fix the shakes while you're changing."

He strolled past her, all hot and sweaty and utterly male. "Sounds great."

By the time she'd made sure the gym was empty, locked the front doors, and mixed up the drinks, Richard had reappeared. He carried a gym bag, and now he was wearing a casual white knit shirt and faded blue jeans. His hair was slicked back from his forehead, and he smelled faintly of cologne.

Without speaking, they walked through the outer room, where her assistant normally worked, and into Melanie's office. It had never struck her as particularly small, but with Richard sitting in the chair opposite her desk, the space seemed cramped. He was just so damn big.

Over their shakes, they made chitchat. She thought she was picking up on a sexual vibe, but maybe it was just the stupid free-pass idea that was making her jumpy.

She set her shake on the desk and managed to look at him without blushing. "So tell me, Richard. What business are you in?"

He sprawled in the chair like a lazy tiger, his chestnut hair springing to life as it dried. His long legs were stretched out in front of him. He chucked his empty drink container into the trash. "Pharmaceuticals," he said with a crooked grin. "Not all that romantic. My company has come out with a new med that drastically reduces the effects of the common cold. We're marketing it aggressively right now in the upper Midwest and the Northeast, hoping to have it in place for the fall cold and flu season."

"Does it work?"

He frowned. "Of course it works. I wouldn't be selling it if it didn't."

"Some people would," she said mildly.

His annoyance faded away. "Well, not me. I believe in honesty. In every situation." His eyes narrowed, and he stared at her until she wondered if she might be unbuttoned or unzipped. The intensity of his regard made her feel almost naked.

He leaned forward. "Which is why I have to tell you that you are one of the most striking women I've ever met." His voice was low and husky. "I'm deeply attracted to you, Melanie."

She clutched the edge of her desk. Was this a line he used from town to town? Was he the proverbial traveling salesman with an available woman in every little community on his route?

It occurred to her that she might have inadvertently given

him the wrong impression. She didn't wear her wedding ring at work. "I'm married," she said bluntly.

He cocked his head. "Ah. Still," he said softly. "There's something about you...."

"You're very handsome." The three words popped out of nowhere.

His big frame stilled, his eyes watchful. "What are you saying, married Melanie?"

She couldn't quite meet his gaze. "Well, my husband and I are happily married, but lately we've discussed the possibility of having a fling with someone else. You know ... to spice things up."

His gaze was hot now, his full lips set in a sensual line. "I'd be happy to put in an application," he said drolly.

Her spurt of laughter momentarily defused the tension. "Well, you fit the profile." At his raised eyebrow and inquiring glance, she elaborated. "Temporary."

"Ah. True. I am that." He rested his elbows on the arms of his chair and steepled his fingers under his chin, staring at her with unblinking eyes. "I don't believe I've ever met a husband as complacent as yours."

"So you've been with a lot of married women?"

"None."

She didn't know whether to be relieved or worried. Did this mean she was out of luck?

He continued studying her face, although she was pretty sure he had surveyed her breasts as well. She was wearing lime green—and-black spandex. Without conceit, she knew she looked good. But most men liked breasts, and hers were almost invisible.

She wrinkled her nose. "I've never cheated on my husband."

"Is it cheating when he agrees to let you play?"

"I'm not sure. We were still working that out. And then you showed up."

Now he folded his hands across his flat stomach. *She* was nervous as hell. He seemed relaxed, comfortable. Everything about his posture suggested easy confidence. But then, why shouldn't it? He was a man in his prime. He radiated strength and self-possession.

He let the silence drag after her last statement before he finally spoke. "I'm not in a relationship. I've been doing this new job for four months. I haven't been with a woman in two. I'm horny and lonely, married Melanie. And if you need or want temporary, I'm your guy."

"Why do it?"

That confused him. "Excuse me?"

She leaned forward. "Why travel so much if you don't like it? Don't you miss having a home?"

He shook his head. "I didn't ever have a home, not of my own anyway. I had an apartment and some stuff. I had female companionship when I wanted it. This job offer came along, and I decided it sounded appealing. Lots of money that I could put in the bank for a rainy day."

She frowned. "But what about in the meantime? It can't be very much fun to be horny and lonely. Is it really worth the sacrifices you're making?"

He sighed and ran a hand through his hair. "You caught me on a bad week. I'm not always so maudlin."

She snorted. "Yeah, right. I wouldn't call you maudlin . . .

self-reflective maybe. But not maudlin. I have to tell you something, though."

His eyes perked up, though he didn't appear to move a muscle. "What's that?"

"My husband and I discussed this in terms of a onetime fling only. No do overs. No extended run."

Now his smile was faint and wry. "Is that supposed to dissuade me?"

She heard the underlying message loud and clear. This man wanted to have sex with her. She knew her nipples were standing up. He was gentleman enough to pretend not to notice. An ache in her sex reminded her that she was treading on dangerous ground. She'd been attracted to men before. But she had never deliberately tested the bounds of that temptation.

She loved her husband. He satisfied her sexually in every way. Their marriage was solid.

But she couldn't lie to herself. She was immensely flattered that this interesting, virile, sexy man wanted her. Her ego loved being stroked . . . and if nothing more than a simple conversation was having this effect on her, Lord knew how she would react if he ever touched her with one of those big, warm hands.

Now there was a lump in her throat. Was it apprehension or anticipation?

She wet her lips. "I can't just jump into this."

"Even though the time and place seem to be optimum at the moment?"

Shit. He wanted to do it right now. If she'd been standing, her knees wouldn't have supported her. She must have blanched, because he laughed softly.

When he smiled, he looked younger, sexier. "Don't panic. I'm not rushing you. But if you need help making up your mind . . ."

His naughty teasing made her restless. Should she just do it and get it over with? But in an instant of startled revelation, she realized that she wanted to discuss this outrageous turn of events with her husband. Before she committed to a course she might later regret.

She tried to be as carelessly confident as he was. "You're definitely on the short list, Richard. Right near the top."

He pretended to scowl. "Short? I think not."

In spite of herself, she blushed. Thinking about this man's penis was a seriously bad idea. She tried to regroup. "How long will you be in town?"

He looked up at the ceiling, visibly calculating. Then he turned his gaze to hers. "At least six more nights. Maybe longer."

"So we have plenty of time."

He winced and rubbed a hand over the unmistakable bulge below his belt. "You may," he said, his tone disgruntled. "I, however, am somewhat pressed at the moment."

"There are remedies for that," she said. "Cold showers. Autoeroticism."

He laughed out loud. "If you can't even say the word 'masturbation,' then I may be out of luck."

She was insulted. "I am not a prude."

He stood up, and her heart lurched. "Where are you going?"

His face was tight, his jaw rigid. "Listen, married Melanie . . . a man can take only so much provocation. You've said this isn't happening tonight. So I'd like to go back to my hotel and search for . . . remedies."

She stood up as well, the desk between them. "Have you thought about kissing?"

His mouth gaped for a split second before his jaw snapped shut, and he shook his head. "No way. Not now. Not in my condition."

"I can't screw a man I've never even kissed."

He put a hand to his forehead, muttering under his breath, "Fine. One kiss."

She quit hiding behind the furniture and came around to stand in front of him. Wow, now she really did feel dainty and small, even more so if she kicked off her shoes, which she didn't do. It might give him ideas.

She was trembling all over, much like the time she'd tried to do four miles on the treadmill without eating breakfast. Her blood sugar had dropped, and she had almost passed out. A candy bar wouldn't help her now.

She put a hand on his chest. "Don't look so scared. I won't bite."

He touched her cheek. "Even if I beg?"

She shook her head slowly, almost dazed by what was happening. She'd had her share of fantasies. What woman hadn't? But they had all stayed in her head. None of them had sprung to life and stood before her in the flesh, just begging to be seduced.

Melanie stepped closer, until Richard and she were breathing the same air. She had to tip back her head to study his face. Maybe she should stand on a chair. "I haven't kissed anyone but my husband in over seven years."

He smirked. "It's like a riding a bike. You never forget."

She appreciated his attempt to inject levity into the overheated moment, but the look in his dark eyes was far more serious than he was letting on.

She stroked her palm from his shoulder down to his chest. It seemed prudent to stop short of the belt buckle. Even through his shirt, he was hot. Really hot.

She searched his face. "I can't reach your mouth," she said softly.

He groaned and closed his eyes. "That's the only thing keeping me sane at the moment."

She spotted one of the stools from step class in the corner. Without stopping to think if her idea was absurd, she dragged it over between them and climbed up. He was still taller, but at least the playing field was more even now. At last, his grin was genuine.

He ruffled her hair. "You're a cute thing."

"You're not going to fall in love with me, are you?" she quipped. "I'm already taken."

He assumed a hangdog expression. "I know. Don't rub it in."

She put her arms around his neck. "I thought the man in these situations was supposed to take the lead."

"I wouldn't know. No married women—remember?" He held her waist. "We really don't have to do this tonight."

She lifted her chin. "It's just a kiss, Richard. Is it okay if I call you that?"

He chuckled. "Sure. After all, I'm at the top of your list."

They were both dancing around the issue of whether they were actually going to kiss. She had a feeling she was way more scared than he was. What if this was a huge, disastrous mistake? What if the kiss was awful? What if there was no chemistry? What if she decided she wasn't going to sleep with him, and he was offended?

He put an end to her dithering. His mouth moved over hers gently but forcefully. Her lips were open. She'd been about to say something profound. Instead, she found herself lost in a surprisingly erotic kiss. A bit awkward on her part, but erotic nevertheless.

His hands had moved to the small of her back and were kneading her spine. Between them, his erection reminded her how unfair this was to him.

Then he nipped her bottom lip. That little maneuver took things to a whole other level and derailed any chance she had of making a coherent judgment. She whimpered. He groaned. It should have bothered her that his taste and his touch were so unfamiliar. Instead, she found it deeply arousing. She kissed him back, letting her tongue explore the contours of his mouth while her fingers tangled in the silky hair at the nape of his neck.

Chemistry wasn't going to be a problem.

Slowly, regretfully, she pulled back. "Richard?" Her voice was husky.

He froze, and then a mighty shudder shook his frame. He kissed the top of her head and lifted her to the floor. Then he looked around him for his gym bag, picked it up, and started for the door.

"Richard?" This time there was alarm in her voice.

He turned to face her, his eyes hooded and his cheeks flushed. A muscle in his jaw flexed. "I'm leaving while I still can, married Melanie. Good night."

She stared at him, troubled. She hadn't meant for things to get so out of hand. "I'm sorry, Richard. This is a first for me."

He exhaled a sharp breath. "Yeah . . . me, too."

Chapter Six

Debra and Gordon fell into the habit of watching the other patio. The couple below them spent many hours outside ... eating, sunbathing, screwing. They screwed a lot. And every time it happened, Debra and Gordon reaped the benefits of voyeurism.

It was better than a second honeymoon. It was an extravagant, sensual love fest.

At the end of forty-eight hours, Debra was exhausted. She nudged her husband off her and glanced at the clock. "I know we're on vacation, but I've got to get out of this villa."

Gordon sat up and rotated his neck. "I guess you're right. At the rate we're going, we might fuck ourselves to death."

She scrambled out of bed, sleepy-eyed. "But what a way to go."

They showered and dressed, suddenly eager to get out

and see more of the village. Fabulous restaurants abounded, and they had only scratched the surface.

On this outing, Gordon was sated enough with sex to be in an expansive mood, more inclined than usual to tolerate being dragged around the shops. Soon, Debra had an armful of small, colorful bags. In one store she purchased a daring top. Short sleeved and scoop necked, it was made out of gold thread, tied with little pearls in a swirly pattern. The weave was loose. Her nipples were plain to see if anyone bothered to look.

Gordon had urged her to try it on, and it was now Gordon who insisted she buy it.

She looked at herself in the mirror. "I could never wear this back home."

He rubbed her arm below the sleeve, his eyes focused on her reflection. "You can enjoy it here. And besides, you could always layer something under it later. You look smokin' hot, Deb. Please buy it."

So she allowed herself to be persuaded. And what was more, he talked her into wearing it out of the store. She felt daring and Continental. And even nicer, she enjoyed the confidence of knowing she was a sexually appealing woman. She believed her husband found her attractive, and today, because she was wearing a deliberately provocative item of clothing, it wasn't beyond the realm of possibility that other men might as well.

The feel of the coarse thread against her nipples caused them to swell and harden. The warmth of the sun on her partially exposed breasts and the male appreciation in Gordie's eyes kept her in a state of simmering arousal. It was a good feeling.

They were on their way down through town when Gordie

grabbed her elbow and pulled her into the shadow of a small alleyway. "Look," he whispered. "Over there."

She froze, leaning into her husband's chest. "It's our neighbors, isn't it?" The couple from the house below theirs was wandering just ahead of them on the street.

Gordie urged her on, his gaze determined. "Let's go introduce ourselves."

She stared at him. "Are you crazy? I'd never be able to look them in the face."

He tugged her with him. "Come on. Aren't you curious about who they are? Where they're from?"

She followed a half step behind him, feeling like a stalker. "They'll know we've been spying on them."

"How could they know?"

The street was fairly crowded, and it was easy to close the distance. When they were abreast of the other couple, Gordie slowed his steps and pretended to look in a shop window at a display of scrimshaw.

The dark-headed duo paused as well, just to the left. Gordie looked at the other man. "Wish I could afford one of those big urns. Hard to imagine how many hours went into to producing that design."

The man's wife was on the far side. Debra stood nervously on Gordie's right.

The stranger looked up and smiled. "Indeed. I saw exhibit of this medium once at museum in British Columbia. It was quite impressive."

As soon as the man opened his mouth, Debra realized he was neither Greek nor American. Her guess would be that he was from somewhere in the old Soviet Republic.

The woman peeked around at Debra. "I love your blouse. Do you get it here?"

Debra felt her face heat and tried not to hunch her shoulders. "Yes. Just up the road."

The man held out his hand to Gordie. "I am Yuri. From Russia. This is my lovely wife, Katya. We are happy to make your acquaintance."

Gordie shook hands, stepped back, and brought Debra beside him. "I'm Gordon. This is Debra."

The woman cocked her head like a little bird. "You on honeymoon?" She was petite and her dark eyes flashed with interest and charm. She wore rings on every finger. Her features were angular but attractive.

Gordie shook his head. "Nope. We're celebrating our seventh anniversary."

Yuri made a small bow. "You are lucky man. She is beautiful." He stared at Debra. With no remorse. With blatant masculine assessment. With a keen appreciation for her scantily clad breasts.

Katya put a hand on Gordie's arm. "You are handsome couple. Come with us to dinner . . . yes?"

Debra saw Gordie blink and turn red. She'd tried to tell him, and now they were in a pickle. Unless they could make a polite refusal, they were going to be stuck eating a meal with this couple, all the while imagining them naked.

Gordie cleared his throat. "Well, we hadn't decided where we want to go yet. . . ."

Katya's hand closed over his. "No more thinking. We know best place on island. You like spanakopita?"

Gordie winced, his face priceless. "I'm not much for strange foods."

Katya threw back her head and laughed, her loose raven curls dancing in the breeze. "I show you what you been missing."

Yuri appeared unfazed by his wife's behavior. He smiled warmly at Debra. "We go now. Time to eat."

Gordon adjusted himself beneath the table and took another reckless sip of the local wine. Yuri and Katya sat on either side of him, with Debra across the small square tiled table. His stomach was queasy. Katya and Yuri had plied him with all manner of local delicacies.

Gordon had stopped asking for identification. He was having a hard enough time ignoring Katya's blatant flirtation. Every moment she handed him another bite of something revolting, her fingers brushed his lips.

Debra was faring no better, although she seemed genuinely appreciative of the Greek cuisine. His wife was adventuresome in her culinary tastes, though usually quite shy when it came to mingling in social settings.

Perhaps the alcohol helped. She was laughing and teasing Yuri and enjoying the meal in a way Gordon never could. He'd been raised on meat and potatoes. Beyond that, he was on unfamiliar ground.

The repast lasted two hours. Finally, Yuri motioned for the checks. He took both of them. "Our pleasure," he said formally. "We like to make American friends."

The four of them tumbled out onto the street, laughing and a tad unsteady on their feet.

Yuri took both of Debra's hands in his. "You come to our house now. Watch sunset from patio."

Katya was even bolder. She went up on her tiptoes and planted a sloppy kiss on Gordon's chin. "We sit and talk. Drink wine."

Gordon chuckled roughly. "We've had a lot of wine already, don't you think?"

The Russian woman waved a careless hand. "Never too much wine. We give you Russian wine at house."

The walk back up the hill cleared Gordon's head enough for him to wonder what the hell he and Debra were doing. She was walking along beside him, seemingly content, with a dreamy smile on her face.

Once, as she stumbled, Yuri caught her elbow and supported her before Gordon had the chance. The man held her strictly longer than necessary, his teasing laugh making Debra blush.

Gordon ground his teeth against a wave of jealousy and then had to laugh inwardly at himself. Katya was all over him. So he couldn't exactly complain, especially since he was enjoying the other woman's deliberately sexual banter and playful touches.

The Russians' villa, below Debra and Gordon's, was gloomy in the shadow of the hillside. Yuri led the way through the gate and began lighting candles on the patio. They were everywhere, large ones, small ones, fat ones, tapers. Gordon sat on the wall and stared out to sea, his heart pumping in his chest.

Surely he was imagining things. Surely this odd foreign couple was only being friendly in their own unique way. Just because the Russians enjoyed a healthy sex life didn't mean they wanted to have Debra and Gordon join them.

The women had gone inside. Debra was eager to take a look at the house and see if it was similar to theirs. Gordon watched Yuri move about the patio, fluffing cushions, brushing insects away, lighting more candles. It would be a miracle if they could even *see* the sunset at this rate with all the fire surrounding them.

When the females reappeared, Gordon watched his wife. Debra seemed fidgety, and her cheeks were red. He moved closer to her . . . casually. When the other two were occupied, he whispered in Debra's ear, "What happened in there? Your face is all funny."

She rubbed a hand across the back of her neck, not looking at him. Her voice was barely audible. "She touched my breast."

"She what?" His voice came out louder than he intended. Yuri and Katya glanced up from what they were doing. Katya had brought out bottles and glasses, and she and Yuri were squabbling about which wine to open first.

Gordon eased Debra a few steps farther away. "What do you mean, she touched your breast?"

"She acted like she wanted to see what my top was made out of, and then she very deliberately stroked my breast and my nipple."

"Sweet Jesus." Gordon was stunned. Stuff like this didn't happen in Minnesota, at least not in the circles in which he and Deb moved. "What did you do?"

She shrugged. "Nothing. I just stood there and let her feel me up."

His dick thickened along with his voice. "Did you like it?" The visual of the women filled his brain.

Debra rolled her eyes. "Men. What is it about two chicks that turns you on?"

"Don't know," he muttered. "Next time, please make sure I'm in the same room when you play doctor with the pretty Russian."

"You think she's pretty?" Deb's voice held a hint of vulnerability.

He took her hand. "She's pretty. You're a knockout. Don't confuse the two."

"And is this going to be your free pass?"

He tensed. He'd forgotten the stupid free-pass idea. Now his dick hardened even more. "It could be *ours*," he said slowly, monitoring her reaction.

He saw Debra look at Yuri. Her lips trembled. Her eyes were open wide. "Maybe so."

They had been murmuring in order not to be overheard by their hosts, but now Katya and Yuri came over and insisted on handing them glasses of wine and napkins full of cheese and olives. When no one was looking, Gordon surreptitiously pitched his olives over the wall.

The Russian couple had pulled four wooden chairs into a tight semicircle near the wall. The women ended up in the middle, but not beside their own spouses. Gordon wasn't sure how that had happened.

He and Yuri stretched out their legs and propped them on the stone balustrade. Debra and Katya had their heads together, discussing shopping or something. Gordon rested his neck against the back of the chair and closed his eyes. He'd rarely been as sloshed as he was at the moment.

His head was spinning, and his dick was still hard. Fortunately, he was wearing loose khaki shorts that disguised his condition . . . he hoped.

His mind wandered, imagining what Katya might look like naked. From there it was only a step to seeing his nude wife and the Russian woman embracing. He groaned and sat up suddenly, almost overbalancing his chair.

Katya turned to him and smiled, her warm, soft palm suddenly on his forearm. "You tired, young Gordon? Too many late nights?" He moved uneasily, wanting to remove her hand, but unwilling to be rude. Being touched by a strange woman with such a strong sexual vibe in the air made him itchy and restless.

He stood. The others ignored him as he wandered to the other end of the patio and stared out at an enormous tanker ship. Even from this distance, it looked huge.

Katya joined him, handing him an expensive pair of binoculars. "Take a look."

Gordon's eyes met Debra's across the small distance separating them. Her lips lifted in a faint smile, and he knew beyond a shadow of a doubt what she was thinking. If they'd had binoculars these past two days . . .

Katya continued speaking, something about shipping channels and such. . . . He stared through the binoculars blindly, not so much seeing the vast sea painted by the lowering sun as the two frolicking lovers, totally without modesty, fucking in the hot Greek light of day.

By now, the sun was a fat crimson orb barely touching the line where the purple-shadowed sky met the indigo sea. From below them in the village proper, there was a muted cheer as the flaming ball disappeared below the water.

Katya sighed dramatically, her hand over her heart. "This is why we come to Greece. Good food. New friends. And God's hand on the sea."

Gordon tried to give the binoculars back to her, but she shook her head. "You keep. You and Debra. Look at the ocean. The sky. The birds."

Your neighbors. Was that her unspoken addendum to the list? Or was he being paranoid?

Gordon and Debra made their excuses soon after. He sensed he and his wife were both on the same page. The idea of intimacy with the Russians was appealing. But not so fast. Not so lightly. It was a prospect that required at least some reflection. Some assessment.

They left as they had come, by way of the patio. Katya and Yuri were not bashful about goodbyes. Yuri took Debra in his arms and kissed her soundly. Katya did the same for Gordon. Then the couple stood side by side, offering waves and smiles as Gordon and Debra walked away. At the last moment, Katya called out to them in her lilting, heavily accented voice, "Which villa is yours?"

Gordon pointed vaguely toward the top of the hill. "Up there," he said. "See you later."

Even with the steep climb, it took them only fifteen minutes or so to get home. Gordon went immediately to the patio, working on a hunch. It was still twilight . . . a faint purplish haze cloaked the mountain with the promise of nightfall.

He lifted the heavy binoculars to his eyes and adjusted the focus. "Damn." He whispered it softly, leery of sounds that might carry on the night air.

Debra joined him. "What is it?"

He handed over the glasses. "See for yourself."

Debra had to fiddle with the knobs for a moment, and suddenly, the sea and Thirassia popped into crisp view. Slowly, she lowered the lenses until she was looking down and to the right. Yuri and Katya's house seemed so close, it shocked her. And then she gasped.

Gordie chuckled. "Interesting, huh . . . ?"

The Russians were screwing in a chair. Katya's curls tumbled to her shoulders, her head thrown back, Yuri's dark hands on her pale breasts.

They might have been on the same patio as Debra and Gordon, so clear was the image.

Debra lowered the binoculars, her hands trembling. "Do you think they know we're watching?"

He stood behind her and folded her in his arms. "I'd lay good money on it." He kissed the side of her neck. "Don't you want to see more?"

She did, but it felt wicked. Still . . . she lifted the lenses a second time. Shock ripped through her as she focused on Yuri's bent head. He was sucking Katya's breasts . . . most enthusiastically . . . taking turns. The ecstasy on his wife's face left no doubt about her response.

Debra jerked as Gordie's hands went under her simple cotton skirt. She still wore the woven top. Her nipples had been gently abraded for hours. He slid her panties down her legs and helped her step out of them.

In silence, as she continued to watch the tableau below, Gordie grabbed a cushion from a chair and placed it at the base of the wall. He pushed lightly on her shoulders until she knelt at his feet. Now she could rest her elbows on the wall and still watch the show.

She felt Gordie behind her, sensed him kneel, heard the quiet rasp of his zipper. Her breasts pressed against the hard stone wall.

She knew she was wet. And Gordie must have realized it as well, because he murmured as he stroked her. He curled two fingers inside her and pressed lightly. She gripped the heavy lenses, her breath broken and labored.

Gordie whispered beside her ear, "Lean forward."

She spread her knees a couple of inches and did as he asked. From the angle below, their heads would barely be visible. She felt her husband's cock enter her slowly. Her moan was a silent exhalation on the night air.

Her whole body shook with uncontrollable tremors. Between her thighs, Gordie moved purposefully. His breathing was harsh as well.

She looked through the binoculars again, trying to hold the lenses still. The Russian was still pumping away. It was almost dark now. Even with the strong magnification, only the outline of the couple below remained.

But when Katya lifted her hands to the sky and climaxed, there was no doubt what had happened.

Debra gently laid the glasses on the wall, afraid of dropping them. Her hands clenched the stone as Gordie's thrusts grew wilder. Hunger gathered in her womb and collected in a pinpoint of fiery heat in her clitoris. Her silent husband slid his arms around her and palmed her breasts beneath her top.

He squeezed her sensitive nipples. Hard. She went rigid in his grasp and choked out a muffled cry as her body imploded in an orgasm so intense, she buried her head in her arms and wept.

With two final thrusts, he ended it, his hoarse shout not as quiet as it should have been.

It was a damned uncomfortable position.

But she was too undone to move. She felt like they had been indulging in foreplay for hours. Every moment with the Russian couple had been laden with sexual overtones. And she and Gordie hadn't been imagining things.

In the house when Katya had touched Debra's breast, the other woman's sly smile had promised all sorts of sexual excess. Debra had been simultaneously thrilled and terrified. She hadn't even told Gordie yet, but at one point, Yuri had brushed her breast as well.

He'd made it seem like an accident. And the naughty caress hadn't derailed the light conversation. But he had known what he was doing.

He was nothing at all like the men Debra normally found attractive. And yet his compact, lean frame was oddly appealing. What he hid beneath his clothes was still a mystery, but his wife clearly had no complaints.

Gordie eased from Debra's body at last and helped her to her feet. The darkness was complete. It was a moonless night with only millions of twinkling stars to populate the sky. She felt the sticky warmth of come between her legs and wished they could swim right now in the inky darkness of the Aegean, the warm water caressing their bodies as they floated in secret among the rippling waves.

Gordie took her in his arms. "I still want you," he muttered. "I can't seem to get enough."

She shimmied out of her skirt and tossed it aside. The woven top was next. His hand was warm on her breast. She closed her eyes and absorbed the feel of his caress on her curves.

"Were we wrong to leave?" she whispered. "Did they want us?"

Gordie laughed softly as he abandoned her for a moment to finish undressing. "Yes. No doubt about that. But they won't stop wanting us simply because we were . . ."

"Chicken?"

He made a squawking noise as he aligned their bodies. The feel of him, all warm and male against her, fueled the simmering hunger that had never died. She had her hands on his ass, and she tried to imagine Katya doing the same. Jealousy flitted by for a half second, but it was chased away by lust. Gordie had a wonderful body. Katya would be well-entertained. And what about Yuri?

As her husband carried her inside and lowered her gently to the mattress, Debra imagined being nude in front of the Russian. Bearing the scrutiny of his steady gaze. Feeling the unfamiliar touch of his hands on her bare skin . . . between her legs . . . on her sex.

As Gordie settled between her thighs, she visualized the Russian spreading her wide, mounting her, entering her. Would she like it? Would it be odd? Would she climax?

Gordie fucked her with hard, firm strokes. The feather

mattress was as soft as the flagstone patio was hard. His weight pressed her down.

She conjured up the image of Yuri, his intense dark eyes gazing into hers, not allowing her to block him out. She imagined the broken flow of musical Russian words as he lapsed into his native tongue while he fucked her.

She gave up being shy and touched him like she wanted to. She caressed his face, his lips. She explored the tensile strength of his narrow chest, the wiry feel of the hair at his groin.

In her mind, she begged him to stop for a moment. He withdrew reluctantly. She crawled down in the bed and took him in her mouth. New Russian words followed. She felt him shake and moan.

Wildly, he flipped her to her belly, dragged up her hips and entered her. He was surprisingly strong, and she felt like a rag doll being pummeled repeatedly.

Gordie might have been omniscient, so perfect was his timing. His lips brushed her cheek as he slowed his movements. "If you want him, you can have him."

She cried out as her climax ripped through her. Later she would wonder if she had spoken the wrong name, but in the heat of the moment, it was all she could do to ride the last waves of her own pleasure as Gordie collapsed on top of her in his own release.

He moved quickly to gather her close, his arms trembling, his voice unsteady. "God, Debra, you make me insane sometimes."

"Me or the Russians?" She felt secure enough to tease him.

He played with her hair. "I can't blame him for wanting you. You're so damned sexy."

"Don't forget our dear Katya. I think she would have climbed into your lap if you'd given her the slightest encouragement."

He drew her legs over his, a position they both enjoyed. He clearly wasn't ready to go again, and she was glad. She felt completely spent at the moment.

"Are we really contemplating this?"

"Would it be so terrible?"

"I don't know. We've never . . ."

"You wanted an adventure."

"I was thinking about ancient ruins and boat rides."

"There are rides, and there are rides."

She summoned the energy to punch his arms. "I never pictured us doing this together."

"You mean sex with strangers?"

She nodded against his shoulders. "Yeah."

He pulled her close and kissed her easily. "We've always enjoyed doing new things together. This will be just one more."

But as they drifted off to sleep, Debra wondered if it might be one new thing too many.

Chapter Seven

Wesley was enjoying his solitary day. He was still in his boxers, unshaven, his hair a mess. It was supremely relaxing. And he needed this. In a few weeks he had to teach a second-term summer school class, and then in no time, fall semester would be upon them.

He loved his job, but academia had never entirely moved beyond some of the stuffy stereotypes, and there was a lot of crap that went along with his responsibilities. Evaluations, both from students and from his peers. Committee approval of course outlines. Textbook selection. Professional development. Conferences. Summers used to be downtime, but not anymore.

He put in three good hours and decided he needed to get off the couch before he turned into a vegetable. He ordered Chinese takeout from a menu they'd found in a kitchen drawer. Then he wandered into the bedroom. He'd become surprisingly addicted to the telescope, even though the altered view was not what he and Cherisse had expected.

Still, he could focus on that one strip of ocean and see all sorts of interesting stuff—oil tankers, pleasure craft, fishing boats. When he got tired of studying the sea, the tall building opposite their condo merited a passing glance. Many of the lower floors apparently were professional suites. But above about the seventh floor, the windows appeared to be condos or apartments, much like the one he was now occupying.

He moved the barrel of the telescope slowly, entertaining himself with a little harmless voyeurism. There was a lady in one office watering African violets. In another, a man in a suit talked heatedly on the telephone. A young woman struggled with a copy machine. A kid in a dental chair freaked out.

Bit by bit he panned upward. On the higher floors, he found mostly closed drapes. Until he got to one set of windows. Clearly a residence. With the bedroom's stunning occupant in full view. He was so startled, he jerked and bumped the telescope.

For long, frustrating minutes he was unable to locate the same window. Finally, it snapped into focus. *Hot damn.* A beautiful woman, completely nude, lay on a king-size bed, masturbating.

He couldn't look away.

Seconds later, when the doorbell rang, he cursed raggedly and strode to the front of the condo to pay for his lunch. Leaving it abandoned on the kitchen counter, he raced back to the bedroom and bent over the eyepiece.

She was still there. And she was still busy.

Her long red hair was spread across an array of pillows. Her knees were bent, her feet flat against the mattress. With one hand, she fondled her small breasts. With the other, she played with her pussy.

He watched, mesmerized, as she stroked her clit with a languid motion. It was hard to make out her features, but he thought her eyes were closed. She was probably fantasizing. He wanted to be the man in her dreams. Wanted it desperately. In fact, the hunger took him by surprise.

But the sheer eroticism of what he was watching grabbed him by the nuts and made him shake.

Occasionally, Cherisse would masturbate for him. But always reluctantly. And always in the dark. She said it made her too self-conscious.

The woman on the bed moved her hand more quickly. He could see urgency in every line of her body. Her hips lifted off the mattress, and she climaxed.

Wesley's dick was so hard, he was in pain. Who was she? Why was she all alone in that luxurious apartment?

The woman stood up and actually came to the window. She placed her hands on the windowsill and looked out. Now he could see her face. She was older than he had first thought. Maybe midthirties. Her flame-colored hair was so long, it actually covered one breast.

She seemed supremely unconcerned about her nudity. Probably she felt safe enough to disregard any casual witnesses. He was looking straight at her, and she had no clue. He should have felt guilty. Probably enough to walk away. But he didn't.

Moments later, she turned from the window and left the

room. Frantically, Wesley moved the telescope, scanning to see if any other portions of her home were in view. He found the kitchen. But it was empty. Most likely because the mistress of the house was in the shower.

He couldn't stand it anymore. He flopped onto the mattress and pulled his dick from his boxers. It was hard as a pike, despite the early-morning fuck. He closed his fingers around his shaft and pumped slowly.

With his eyes squeezed shut, he imagined the redhead here beside him. She wouldn't need to pleasure herself. He'd eat her until she came, and then he would fuck her senseless. On that last thought, he exploded.

Breathing heavily, he ripped off his underwear and used it to clean himself up. Naked, he went back to the telescope. His mystery woman had made it to the kitchen. She was standing at the counter, eating a banana.

The symbolism might have amused him if he hadn't been so damn horny. Still.

He watched as she finished the fruit and tossed the peel in a trash can under the sink. Then to his dismay, she picked up a set of keys from the counter and left the room.

Shit. She was leaving.

He didn't pause to think about the utter absurdity of what he was about to do. There was no way he could catch her. But such logic failed to deter him.

He stuck his legs into a pair of shorts, dragged a T-shirt over his head, and shoved his feet in docksiders. In less than three minutes he was out the door. It would be pointless to waste time with the car. The building was only two blocks away.

He jogged rapidly, ignoring the heat. When he burst through the revolving door of the lobby, he scanned the open atrium hurriedly. Two banks of elevators sat opposite each other. People streamed out, headed for work or play. But there was no sign of his mystery woman.

He caught sight of himself in a mirror and had to stifle a laugh. God, he was an idiot. He looked like he'd been on a three-day drunk.

Feeling sheepish and disappointed all at the same time, he stepped back out onto the street. And there, across four lanes of traffic, she was, patiently reading a book as she waited on a bench at the bus stop.

His heart froze and a knot lodged beneath his breastbone. He couldn't approach her. Not in his unwashed, unkempt condition. Hell.

Down the street, the lumbering bus turned a corner, headed in their direction. Unconsciously, Wesley memorized the number and the destination. But that would be useless information since she might get off at any one of a dozen stops. And from there, who knew where she might ultimately end up?

The bus drew closer. Wesley was about to lose the sensual, sexy woman of his fantasies. He acted on instinct, strolling casually across the street when the light changed. No sense in attracting unwanted attention.

The bus wheezed to a stop. The woman got on via the front door. Wesley entered at the back. Lucky for him it was one of the newer buses with the electronic swipe pad at both entrances. Only passengers using currency were required to pass through at the driver's elbow.

Wesley took an unoccupied seat and stared straight ahead, keeping his quarry in view. Now all he could think about was the moment his dear wife asked him if he wanted to have a free pass for a fling with a stranger.

He swallowed and wiped sweat from his forehead. He was pretty sure he knew the answer.

The bus made slow time with its multiple stops. Traffic lights changed. Passengers got on and off. The redhead continued to read her book. Finally, the bus pulled into the parking lot of a large upscale mall. The woman stood. And so did Wesley.

It took him only ten minutes to find out that she worked at a popular chain bookstore in the mall. In the process, he was able to get close enough to see the title of the paperback she carried. It was on the bestseller lists. A surprisingly successful story by a brand-new author. Dark, gritty mystery with intelligent writing and dry wit along the way. He'd devoured it in a couple of evenings.

He pretended to browse in the nonfiction section while the redhead went through a door in the back, apparently deposited her personal effects, then came back out and took her position behind the customer-service desk.

That was all he needed to know.

Though it bothered him to leave when he was so close to her, rational thought finally prevailed. He had two choices at the moment, go back out to the bus stop and wait for an appropriate bus heading in the opposite direction, or make a call.

Time was of the essence. He dialed the cab company.

Back at the condo, he paused to wolf down the abandoned Chinese food without even microwaving it. Then he stripped off, showered, found clean clothes, and got dressed. Cherisse ragged him about his wardrobe, but he was a conservative kind of guy. He felt comfortable in khaki slacks and a pale blue button-down shirt.

He examined his hair in the mirror. His barbershop cut was cooperating for once. Even the cowlick at his crown was mostly gone. The blue eyes staring back at him were overbright. He felt like a teenager getting ready to sneak into his first X-rated movie.

He checked his watch. Only an hour and a half had passed since he'd walked out of the bookstore. And surely even a part-time job would have shifts of at least four hours. Things were moving along according to plan.

He chose to ignore the fact that there actually was no plan. He was winging it, which wasn't his style at all. He was a planner. Cherisse accused him of being a stick in the mud at times, but he liked his routines, his simple life. What he was about to do was entirely out of character. But he could blame his wife. It was all her idea.

With his own car, he made it back to the mall in twenty-two minutes. On the way, he sketched out a tentative conversation. He was making up the redhead's part as he went along. Chances were, she wouldn't be as agreeable as he was imagining. But defeat wasn't an option.

Unless she was married. *Holy shit.* He stared blankly through the windshield. He was making one big-ass assumption. Just because a woman masturbated in the middle of the day didn't mean she wasn't married.

With a knot in his stomach, he walked inside. The first

thing he did was head for the customer-service desk and scope out her left hand. Not directly of course. He was subtle . . . unobtrusive.

Evidently not as much as he thought.

The woman with the cheerful smile and the fabulous hair leaned over the counter to where he crouched, ostensibly tying his shoe. "May I help you?"

He stood up too quickly and got a head rush. "Um, no. I mean, I'm still looking. But thanks."

She smiled quizzically and turned to help another customer.

Wesley moved away, feeling like an ass. His face was red, and his pulse was racketing away. But now he knew she wasn't wearing a ring.

He walked back to the café area and ordered an iced coffee and a danish. He consumed them slowly, struggling to come up with a plan that would convince the woman with the silky, vibrant red hair to go to bed with him.

Everything about her was attractive. The fact that she was probably five or six years older than he was didn't bother him in the least. She carried herself with confidence. And her relaxed smile projected sex appeal, whether she realized it or not.

His cell phone rang, making him jump. It was Cherisse telling him she had enjoyed a nice lunch and was off to do more shopping. He almost said something. She was his best friend. They shared everything. But he was embarrassed. There was a good chance his little attempt would crash and burn.

He would much rather share the details later, if things went well, than have to admit he had bombed out.

By the time he returned his mug to the counter and tossed his trash, he was in control. He made a pass through the fiction section, picked up a copy of the same mystery the redhead had been reading earlier, and approached the service desk. On the way, he tucked his wedding ring in his pocket.

The redhead was doing something on the computer, but she looked up immediately. "Well, hello again."

He smiled past his nerves. "I was wondering if you knew anything about this book. I like trying new authors, but sometimes you wind up getting disappointed."

Her face lit up. "I'm actually reading that book right now," she said. "So far, I love it. I'll have to admit there are some gruesome parts, but the plot is tight, and last night I read far too late."

She'd given him the perfect opening. "Did your boyfriend complain?"

Her smile dimmed and her eyes narrowed, but she gave him the answer he was looking for. "I don't have a boyfriend. At least not since I found him shagging my apartment mate two weeks ago."

Wesley winced. "Clearly, he's an idiot. Did you get rid of him?"

She sighed deeply, pausing to click out of some program on her computer screen. "I got rid of them both. Life's too short."

He smiled at her. "You sound like a smart, grounded woman."

"I don't know about that." She shrugged, leaning a hip against the counter. She was wearing a slim-cut pair of black slacks and an ivory silk tank. "If I was all that smart, I'd find a real job with insurance instead of all this part-time stuff."

"So this isn't your real job?"

"Nah . . . it helps pay the bills. Actually, I get a few modeling jobs. Now don't laugh," she said quickly before he could respond. "I know you think I'm over the hill. But I'm a hair model, so they're willing to airbrush a small wrinkle here or there as long as I keep my long locks in shape."

He held up his hands. "I wasn't going to say a thing. I think you're gorgeous. For any age. And I repeat my earlier assessment. Your boyfriend must be brain dead."

Her big smile returned. "You're good for my ego, Mr. . . . ?" She trailed off in a question.

He held out his hand, taking her softer one and squeezing it. "Wesley. You can call me Wesley. And I know your name . . . Melinda." It was spelled out on the name tag pinned neatly to her small breast.

Their palms remained linked for perhaps a second too long. She broke the connection and muttered something inaudible. Her cheeks were flushed.

He stepped closer. "Would you like to have a drink with me? Coffee . . . a cola? I know you're working now, and I don't want to get you in trouble for chatting. But I'd like to get to know you." *I want to discuss the fact that you're so horny you've been masturbating because your latest boyfriend was an ass.*

It had been years since he had tried to pick up a woman. His technique was definitely rusty. But amazingly, her eyes softened and her mouth curved in a flattered, almost bashful smile.

She wet her lips. "That sounds lovely. I have a short shift today. I'll be done in forty-five minutes. Can you wait?"

Could he wait? Hell, yes.

He managed to browse through the entire store with the exception of the children's section by the time Melinda clocked out. They met at the front by the hardcover bestsellers. Not the only things hard at the moment.

His palms were damp. When she looked up at him, her gaze was equal parts confusion and pleasure.

Her hair was a miracle of light and texture. He wondered if she sometimes bound it up in a ponytail or another less prosaic hairstyle. If he had to vote, he'd always want it just like this. Flowing, alive. So soft and alluring a man could lose himself in its thick waves.

He took her elbow in a light grip and steered her down the mall. They ended up at the food court. He'd had a restaurant in mind, but the only one in the mall was closed between lunch and dinner.

He was paying attention to the time. He didn't want Cherisse to come home and find him gone. And besides, she might even call for a ride.

He bought two Cokes and an order of cheese nachos to which Melinda confessed a guilty addiction.

Then they talked.

She was charming and funny. She reminded him in many ways of Cherisse. Smart. Sociable. Endlessly entertaining. He couldn't really imagine a scenario in which he might end up making love to her, but this flirtation was fun, nevertheless. Maybe that was all he needed. Just this little face-to-face meeting to beef up his fantasies . . . his memories of what she had been doing this morning.

They danced around the reason he was sitting with her in a mall fast-food restaurant. She must have wondered. Her face was open and her words unguarded. She put herself out there . . . while he, on the other hand, was dissembling. And being a jackass in the process. Finally he decided to come clean and see what happened.

He leaned his elbows on the table and put his head in his hands. "Here's the thing, Melinda. . . ."

She sipped her Coke, her face serene. "I'm all ears, Wesley."

He sat back and sighed. "I'm in Miami vacationing with my wife."

Disappointment filled her eyes. "Oh." She scowled. "Where's your wedding ring?"

Sheepishly, he pulled it from his pocket and slipped it on his finger. "I was afraid you wouldn't come with me if you thought I was married."

She frowned and set down her cup. "I don't understand. You went to a lot of trouble for thirty minutes in a crowded mall. Don't guys on the make usually lie about being single? If you're trying to snag an easy lay, you're pretty bad at this."

He felt his ears and neck heat. Now, instead of gazing across the table with simple pleasure, she regarded him like dirty gum stuck to her shoe.

She stood up and he grasped her wrist. "Please, Melinda. Let me explain."

After a standoff that seemed to go on forever, she returned to her seat and crossed her arms over her chest. "Let's hear it."

"I never planned to lie about being married. But I wanted to talk to you, and I thought it would help in the beginning if you thought I was single."

She cocked her head, her expression torn between skepticism and reluctant interest. "I can't decide if you're a creep or just seriously deluded."

He chuckled without amusement. "I guess that remains to be seen." He tugged the straw from his glass and twisted it between his fingers, not looking at her face while he spoke. "My wife and I have an excellent marriage. We're celebrating our seventh anniversary. She and a couple of her friends got it in their heads that we husbands should get a free pass for a onetime fling to avoid that whole seven-year-itch thing."

Her face was indignant. "And what about the women?"

"Them, too," he said hastily. "We agreed to that up front."

"And has your wife found her free-pass guy?"

He opened his mouth and shut it, stunned to realize he had forgotten to be jealous. "I have no idea."

Melinda shivered. "I don't know why they have to crank the AC up so high."

Her nipples were poking against her thin tank, and it occurred to him for the first time that she wasn't wearing a bra. He tried not to stare. Instead, he met her gaze with a wry smile. "So the thing is, Melinda, since your jerk of a boyfriend is history, and since you seem to be momentarily unattached, would you do me the honor of being my free pass? Please."

She tapped a fingernail on the table and stared a hole in him. "How old are you, Wesley?"

He felt suddenly like he was thirteen again and trying to talk to Mary Beth Franklin in his math class. "I'm thirty-two . . . almost thirty-three," he added, and then winced as he realized what a putz he sounded.

Her lips twitched. "How old do you think I am?"

He squirmed. That was a minefield he'd rather not traverse. "Um . . . midthirties?"

She grinned. "I'm forty-four."

His jaw dropped. And his unfeigned amazement must have gone a long way toward making up for his earlier behavior, because she was smiling at him again, a genuine, gorgeous smile. He straightened his spine. "Impossible." He said it gallantly, still hoping to swing things his way.

She shook her head. "Down, boy. You're cute and great for my ego, but I don't think this is a good idea."

"If you don't believe me," he said without thinking, "you can call my wife."

Melinda burst out laughing, and he felt every last scrap of his masculine dignity vanish into thin air. God, did he have to act like the world's biggest moron in front of this lovely woman?

She tried to bring her amusement under control, but her lips still quivered. "I don't think that will be necessary, dear Wesley. But I'm still baffled. Surely you didn't walk in to buy a book and suddenly decide to proposition me. That doesn't make sense."

She must have seen something in his face, because her expression went from puzzled to suspicious.

He decided it was crunch time. Time to bare his soul and hope for the best. "I saw you this morning," he said simply.

She frowned. "I don't understand. Saw me where? On the bus?"

He shook his head. "I was on the bus, yes. But that's not what I meant. I saw you in your apartment."

Now she was looking at him like she might need to call the men in white coats. She spoke gently, as though reasoning with a child. "You're not making sense, Wesley. What do you mean?"

He took a sip from his mutilated straw and sucked nothing but air. All the moisture in his mouth had mysteriously dried up. "My wife and I are renting a condo in the high-rise across from your building. The owners have a telescope. That's how I saw you."

Her face cleared and relief followed. "Well, shoot. Finally something that makes sense. So on the basis of that you decided you wanted me to have sex with you?"

"I *saw* you," he said quietly. "You were stunning."

In the few seconds it took for his meaning to penetrate, her face went white and two spots of red, high on her cheekbones, bore testament to her mortification. She tried to speak and couldn't.

He took one of her hands and held it in both of his. "It was an accident at first," he said, his voice soft and as reassuring as he could make it. "I stumbled across your window, and then I saw——"

"Stop." She put her free hand over his mouth, her voice choked. "Don't say another word." Color flooded back into her face, turning it crimson. Her teeth worried her bottom lip. "I had no idea . . ."

He stroked her palm. "You were beautiful in your pleasure. Don't be embarrassed about something so natural, so incredibly arousing."

She jerked her hand away. "It was private," she muttered, but her voice lacked conviction.

For the first time, he understood. He smiled slowly. "No, it wasn't, Melinda. If it had been, the drapes would have been closed."

Chapter Eight

This time it was Thomas who crawled into bed in the wee hours. He was probably trying to be quiet, at least in his mind . . . but his mighty sigh and the draft of cool air as he settled beneath the covers woke Melanie.

She rolled over sleepily. "What time is it?"

Hs kissed her softly, running his fingers through her hair. "Almost two. Go back to sleep.

"How did inventory go?"

"It's all done," he mumbled, already on his way to oblivion.

She'd been dreaming about Richard. She was restless now, aroused. Ready to start something. But her poor husband was barely moving.

Well, heck, she could do all the work. She reached beneath the covers and found his penis. His balls were warm and loose in her palm. Gently, she stroked and rubbed until she felt him respond.

He was still asleep when his erection swelled firm and strong in her grasp. Carefully, she straddled his waist and lowered herself onto his cock. Being filled so beautifully made her want to purr.

Her mind was still on the dream of Richard, which made her feel guilty. She tried to focus on Thomas's body. But it was dark. And he was asleep. She rode him steadily, letting her hunger build slowly. Sometimes in this position she touched herself. Tonight she closed her eyes and imagined Richard's big hand at her sex, brushing her clit.

Her breath caught. Pleasure stabbed sharply . . . remained, spread in a warm wave.

Thomas woke suddenly. "What the . . . ?" His hands came up to grip her hips. "Jesus, baby, let me know next time. I don't like missing the opening act." His voice was thick with sleep.

He rolled suddenly, putting her beneath him. It didn't take him long to catch up. He bit the side of her neck. The tiny sting shoved her to the top, but it was his whispered words of love that sent her over.

The next morning, when the alarm went off, Thomas slapped the button and burrowed closer to his warm wife. It wouldn't hurt either of them to sleep for another half hour.

But sadly, Melanie was already rousing. And he knew from experience that she wouldn't go back to sleep. She was a morning person to the max. And he usually was, too, but God, he was tired.

They lay in silence for a while, listening to the steady rain hitting the window. It was going to be a wet summer apparently, which was probably a good thing, given the recent droughts. But the heavy skies and grayish light made it difficult to work up any enthusiasm for getting out of their comfortable bed.

He played with Melanie's nipple. "Everything go okay at the gym last night?"

They were curled so closely together, he couldn't miss the way her whole body stiffened. He moved to the other nipple. "Melanie?"

Her face was turned away from him, her words muffled. "Same as usual. Two new members, though."

"Good." But two new members weren't making his wife act strangely. He put his hand between her legs. "Anything else?"

She moved restlessly in the bed. "The out-of-town guy came back."

"Oh?"

"We chatted for a bit." Without out any prodding from him, she opened her thighs.

He ran his thumb over her clit. "About what?"

Long silence.

"He thinks I'm attractive."

"Well, duh. Thank you, Captain Obvious." He slid a finger into her pussy. She was wet and warm.

"I told him I was married."

He chuckled. "That's not necessarily a deal breaker for some men. And look at you, Mel. You're hot."

Her eyes were closed, a tiny smile on her lips. "Keep

talking," she muttered, her words soft and slurred. "I love flattery."

Her hair was ruffled and mussed, her skin all smooth and silky. His boner ached, but there was more to this conversation—he was sure of it.

He played around at the entrance to her sex, driving her, and him, crazy. "What else did you talk about?"

She bit her lower lip, her back arching. "I might have mentioned the free-pass idea."

This time Thomas froze. And then a roar of lust hit him hard, drying his throat and making his hands tremble. "I see." The man must have thought he'd died and gone to heaven. "What did he say?"

Melanie turned her face toward him, her expression a mix of sheepishness and pride. "I think he wanted to do it right then."

He buried his face in her belly. *Good Lord.* "And did you?" he mumbled, his speech hindered by the fact that he was licking her navel.

"Of course not," she said breathlessly. "I wanted to talk to you first."

"To ask permission?" He was curious.

She shook her head adamantly. "No. I wanted to ask you if you thought I would regret it later."

He was breathing harshly, wrapped up in a vision of his wife screwing a stranger. "How the hell should I know?" He was losing control. He got on his haunches between her legs, and cupping her ass in his hands, he lifted her legs onto his thighs. Then he shoved hard.

Melanie cried out and climaxed, her inner muscles milking his dick almost painfully. He withdrew and slid forward again.

She opened her eyes, still clearly caught up in the moment. He waited for her to say something, but all she did was look at him. That was all. Just looked at him.

And in her hazy, sleepy, satiated expression, he saw what she was unable to hide—excitement, pleasure, anticipation, knowledge. She had gotten the message loud and clear. Her free pass would not be hard to come by.

He could have told her that. But apparently, finding it out on her own had thrilled her. Silly woman. *He* knew that any straight man from fifteen to ninety would find her hard to resist. But it was nice that she had finally realized it as well.

He was in no hurry to come. His arousal was warm and languid in this lazy morning fuck, not riding him as hard as it usually did.

He stroked her steadily, but slowly, as if they had all day to stay in bed. "So have you decided?" He gave her a hard, quick thrust, wondering if he could get her to come again.

She wrapped her legs around his waist and squeezed. "Should I do it?" Hesitation appeared for a moment. Uncertainty.

He rotated his hips, massaging the place where their bodies connected. "Do you want to?"

Color flooded her face. She looked up at him, half naughty child, half seductive woman. "I think I do, Thomas. I think I do."

That was all it took. He felt the base of his spine tighten, and he shouted as he rammed her repeatedly until he felt completely spent and he collapsed in her embrace.

Richard's cock had been hard, as near as he could tell, for twelve hours. And probably while he was asleep as well, given what he remembered of his sheet-thrashing dreams.

It wasn't a continuous erection. There were a few periods of time here and there when he had managed to concentrate on work and make rational decisions. But then a quiet moment would occur, and without any bidding from him, his libido rushed to the forefront and began weaving fictional scenarios that involved him and the luscious Melanie in every conceivable Kama Sutra position.

He nearly went to the gym at lunch, just to see her, but restrained himself. That behavior was uncomfortably adolescent when he thought about it objectively, not that he was really being objective. Everything about Melanie made his brain cede control to the head in his pants.

He ate dinner that night, wishing he could have asked her to join him. But she was married. Happily. If this happened—and he was smart enough to realize it was still a big if—if this happened, it would be about sex. No hearts and flowers. No pretty words. Just two people scratching an itch.

He sighed and shoveled a bite of baked potato into his mouth. Should he simply go with the flow and show up like he did last night? Melanie hadn't made up her mind yet . . . or at least not when he last saw her, when she had kissed him and given him a bad case of blue balls that still made him ache.

When he'd eaten all he could and paid the check, he left. After an hour of watching old sitcom reruns in his bland motel room, he changed into his workout gear and ran the same pattern as last night. Clean clothes for later. Lock up. Oh, and yes . . . a handful of condoms. He *was* an ex–Boy Scout, after all.

The gym was more crowded tonight, and he was a half hour earlier. Melanie wasn't on the floor. He pushed himself hard . . . stretches, treadmill, weights, and then a few miles around the track. To make sure he had his body under control. In case that became an issue.

He'd jerked off twice last night. Once in the cold shower he'd taken when he got home. Although he had cleaned up at the gym, the second shower had been necessary. Then in bed, completely wired and unable to sleep, he'd taken himself in hand and done it again.

So you would think the chances of his having a twelve-hour erection were pretty slim. Ha. Tell that to his prick. It was hard enough disguising his boner in dress clothes. Try doing it at a gym. Only sheer physical exertion kept him from embarrassing himself.

At eight fifteen, he headed for the showers. He was clean, dry, and antsy in twenty minutes. At eight thirty-five, he couldn't wait any longer. He sought her out.

It occurred to him that she might be hiding. That she might be embarrassed. That she might have decided to avoid him for the week.

The dull feeling in the pit of his stomach warned him he was getting way too involved in a fictional scenario—the one he'd been replaying over and over in his head to entertain himself. The one where Melanie gave herself to him without reservation.

He cursed under his breath, dried his damp palms on his pants, and inhaled deeply. Time was running out. Melanie might already have decided to remain on the straight and narrow. He sensed that this free-pass thing wasn't her usual style. It appealed to her, but it was clear that she had deep reservations.

He could understand that. He had a few mixed feelings of his own. Sex with a willing, available, sexy woman was a no-brainer. But the fact that he was drawn to her was dangerous. He had no desire to have his heart stomped on. The L word had never been a problem in the past.

But he was lonely and in need of something or someone to fill the empty corners in his life. If he allowed it, Melanie could be the sunshine.

But she wasn't his. Period. If he had her at all, it would be once and only once. A memory to carry with him over all the dreary miles he traveled.

The door to the outer area was ajar. He put his gym bag in a chair and walked across the room to Melanie's office. Two light taps from him, and then her firm, clear voice bade him enter. Her appearance took him aback.

She was wearing a simple black linen dress with a flared skirt and no sleeves. He'd already grown accustomed to her fit, capable, businesslike appearance. Suddenly, the ground shifted beneath his feet. This more feminine version of Melanie caught him off guard. Vulnerability glimmered in her eyes as she turned to face him.

She smiled. "Hello, Richard."

He felt struck dumb. "You're all dressed up." Her short hair was fluffed and waved, baring her neck. No jewelry. He'd already gathered that Melanie wasn't much of a girlie girl.

She laughed softly. "Thomas and I had dinner with friends. I just dropped by to make sure Ashanti didn't need any help locking up."

He closed the door all the way and leaned his back against it. "You have a few control issues, don't you, married Melanie?"

She wrinkled her nose and perched on the edge of her desk. It was a mistake from his point of view. The skirt now rested just above her slim knees and exposed the full length of her elegant legs.

Fortunately, his fascination with her limbs was not written on his face. She picked up a paperweight and tossed it lightly from one hand to the other. "You've pegged me, Richard," she said wryly. "I'm not very good at letting go. I like things my way."

He pretended to shiver. "Now I'm scared."

Her expression went blank before she caught his deliberate innuendo. Then she chuckled, her face lighting up and turning mere attractiveness into stunning beauty. "You're a riot. What exactly do you think I would do to you, Richard?"

He lifted an eyebrow. "Why don't *you* tell *me*?" He moved closer, watching her watch him. He saw nerves, uncertainty, apprehension . . . excitement?

When he was a foot away, he stopped. He lifted a hand to her shoulder and ran his palm down her upper arm to her wrist. "You look amazing." He traced the modest scooped neckline of the dress. Her skin was as soft as the raindrops falling outside.

He bowed his head, wondering if he was about to make an ass of himself. "Did you talk to your husband?"

She nodded jerkily, frozen beneath his tentative, so far respectable touch.

Her lack of verbal response worried him. "What did he say?"

He saw the muscles in her throat work as she swallowed. "I think I'm on my own with this one."

He hesitated a split second before lightly cupping her breast. His throat felt like he had swallowed sand. "And that means what?" Beneath the fabric of her dress, her curves were delicate but immensely arousing.

Her spine was so straight he could have used it as a plumb line. "I have to decide."

He leaned down and whispered, with his lips over hers, "I could help with that."

She made a sound in her throat and leaned into him. The small, telling movement took the starch out of his knees. His heart slugged away in his chest, making him breathless. "I want to make love to you, Melanie."

He hadn't meant to blurt it out like that. In his earlier plan, they would have done a replay of last night, talking, flirting. And then maybe ... a different ending. But walking into this room and seeing her looking like a young Audrey Hepburn had done him in.

She turned her head to the side, resting her cheek against his chest. "I didn't expect that tonight you would ... er ... that you'd want ..." She stumbled to a halt.

"That I'd want to have sex?"

"Yes."

He stroked her hair, careful not to mess up her pretty curls. "I do," he said quietly. "Very much."

"I can't go to your hotel. And my house is out."

"I understand." This would be no romantic coupling on a big feather bed with candles and soft music.

She pulled away suddenly, straightening her skirt with fluttering hands and not managing to look him in the eye. "There are still people here. I'll have to help clear the place . . . lock up . . . send Ashanti home."

His heart shot to his throat and plummeted to his belly. She was saying *yes*. A convoluted, bashful yes, but an affirmative nevertheless.

He released her completely and backed away, suddenly aware he could pounce on her without warning. He cleared his throat. "Then, by all means, go."

"And you'll stay in here? Out of sight?"

He didn't waste a second on feeling insulted. She was married. She lived in this community. She wouldn't want gossip from her employees.

He held up his hands, willing her to relax. "I won't make a sound. I swear. I'll read that magazine on your desk and wait patiently."

Liar. He was about to jump out of his skin.

She scooped up her keys and walked to the door. They didn't touch as she passed. She smiled vaguely in his direction. "I'll be back."

Melanie was shaking like a malaria victim. She never knew how she made it through the following fifteen minutes.

With smiles, and jokes, and Ashanti's help, and the utmost patience, she escorted the stragglers to the front and through the exit.

She and the other woman went around the facility, shutting off the banks of lights and turning up the thermostats. It seemed like a million years before Ashanti finally took her leave. Melanie locked the door behind her and dimmed the lobby lights.

When she turned back to her office, she felt like throwing up. But in a good way, not the I-ate-bad-shellfish-for-dinner way. More in the nature of Christmas morning when you were hoping to find a bicycle under the tree, but you were afraid it might be a magazine subscription and a six-pack of socks.

Richard was as good as his word. When she entered her office, she could swear he hadn't moved so much as a muscle. "Alone at last." She had tried for breezy humor, but even to her own ears her voice fell flat.

He stood up. And that odd freak of construction happened again. The shrinking room.

His eyes devoured her face, her body, from head to toe. He looked hungry ... starved, in fact. When she licked her lips, he closed his eyes as if he was in pain.

"Richard?"

He opened his eyes, his jaw tight. "Yes."

"I hope I don't disappoint you."

He blinked. "Is that possible?" Again, with the droll humor.

She wrapped her arms around her waist. "I'm serious. You've probably been with lots of women."

"Hundreds," he deadpanned, wiggling his eyebrows in a really bad Groucho Marx imitation.

The same thought struck both of them at the same moment. She saw it on his face.

He grew serious. "You have nothing to worry about, married Melanie. I'm clean. And I brought these." He reached in his pocket and drew out a half dozen still connected condoms.

She was relieved and intimidated all at the same time. Her throat was constricted, and she had goose bumps despite the fact that the room was not at all cool.

Richard dropped the condoms on her desk and came to get her. At least that was how it seemed. In truth, she might have moved in his direction first. They met in the middle of the room, his arms going around her shoulders, hers around his waist.

The height thing was a definite logistical problem. He lifted her without warning and set her on the desk. Now their lips were in range. He cupped her chin and stared at her mouth. Melanie's thighs pressed together. His eyes were dark and mysterious.

In slow motion, their mouths met and clung. His lips were firm, masculine. His hands cupped her head, and he tilted her neck to deepen the kiss.

She sucked in a little startled breath when he eased his hips between her legs. She couldn't stop shaking.

He pulled her closer somehow. "Don't be scared," he muttered, raining kisses over her nose, her cheeks, and then back to her mouth.

"I'm not scared," she said, trying not to let her teeth chatter. "I'm excited." Her arms went around his neck. He found the zipper at the back of her dress and lowered it gently. When she felt cool air on her heated skin, she remembered suddenly that she wasn't wearing a bra. There was nothing to impede his progress. Nothing but her tiny panties, and he hadn't gotten that far.

He didn't trespass any lower than her waist, not yet. He ran his big hands up and down her back in smooth, caressing strokes.

She found a smidgen of her usual confidence. "I want to unbutton your shirt."

He released her slowly and held out his arms. "Be my guest."

Her fingers fumbled, but she got the job done. She had already seen a lot of his torso in the gym, but baring it a bit at a time and then sliding his shirt off his shoulders seemed like a monumental step.

He stood there and let her look her fill. The hint of amused arrogance in his smug, masculine smile should have infuriated her. But she was too intrigued to be mad. His hands were on his hips, his stance a direct challenge. He lifted an eyebrow; his lips tilted with the hint of a smile. "Well?"

Her dress slipped from one shoulder, and she grabbed it, nearly tumbling to the floor in the process. "Well, what?"

"Are we going through with this?"

She decided she wasn't nervous anymore. She put her hands, palms flat, on his chest. "No pressure, but since we're only doing it once, I'm expecting a hit."

He chuckled and tugged her dress to her waist. "I stand fair warned." He chuckled again when she squeaked and tried to cover herself with both hands.

He looked around the room. "No offense, Melanie, but I have to say the amenities are lacking."

She traced his collarbone. "We're not doing the romantic bit, Richard. Just sex."

"And that means what?"

His breath caught as she grazed his nipples with her teeth, and suddenly she knew he wasn't as unaffected as he seemed. She moved one hand over his rib cage and felt the rapid thud of his heartbeat. "How should I know? You're the one with all the extracurricular experience."

His calm expression was beginning to show signs of strain. "I'm serious, Melanie. Did you mean for us to do this on the floor?"

She wanted to laugh and cry at the same time. All her focus had been on *whether* she and Richard would have sex. She'd never really gotten past the *if* to the nuts and bolts of the thing. And poor Richard was beginning to crack.

The bulge at the front of his trousers left no doubt as to his state of mind.

Here she was sitting on her own desk, nude from the waist up, with a half-naked stranger who wanted to screw her. And beyond that, her mind was a blank.

She licked her lips, fascinated when that little movement made his cheeks flush and his eyes glaze over. She scooted off the desk, still trying to hold the dress over her naked chest. He stepped back as if he was afraid to touch her. The situation was spiraling out of control, and she hadn't even seen his man parts yet.

So much for her seductive routine.

Desperate now, she scanned the bare office. A chair? She

looked at the spindly uncomfortable construction. Why in the hell had she ordered such crap?

Richard snagged her hand. "Come here, Melanie." The rough, needy tone in his voice slithered down her spine like a rolling jolt of electricity.

She allowed him to pull her toward him until they stood close enough to breathe the same air. He was big and warm. All that naked male flesh was hypnotizing her.

He took her face in his hands. "I'm done playing," he said hoarsely. "Either we do this, or I'm out of here. You're making me insane."

She looked up at him. "It's gotta be the desk."

Chapter Nine

Gordie was ready. Debra bailed.

The idea was too intimidating, too crazy. Sober, and not under the influence of a romantic, starry night, she was having second thoughts . . . and even third.

She and Gordie were conventional middle-class people who went to work, and to church, and paid their taxes, and this one time had saved enough money for an extravagant vacation. They were not swingers.

Even the word made her wrinkle her nose in disgust. She'd always imagined "swinging" as an outlet for unattractive middle-aged people who were bored with their spouses. Not once had she thought of it as an activity whereby she and Gordie might utilize their individual free passes.

But the opportunity had more or less dropped into their laps. And it sure as hell had sparked their sex life . . . first from the voyeurism, and now from the idea that something more might actually happen.

She stood on the patio in the translucent light of dawn and shaded her eyes as she gazed out over the sea. The quiet moment of reflection had become a morning ritual— one that she already knew she would miss when it came time to go home. Her sunglasses were somewhere back in the villa, but she was too lazy to go hunt them down.

Even though it was not yet eight o'clock, the sun was already brutal. Not a breath of air stirred. Heat shimmered in waves, baking into her bones and warming her exposed skin. The day would be hot, blistering in fact.

She glanced down the hillside, looking for the Russians. Their patio, for once, was vacant. Debra touched her lips, remembering the dream that had awakened her. Yuri had been kissing her beneath an olive tree. She had even felt the rough bark against her shoulder blades and had inhaled the crisp aromatic scent of herbs as his tongue teased her lips and his hands held her waist.

The dream had been more sweet than passionate. Perhaps her psyche was hard at work, trying to rationalize the potential sexual escapade as something romantic rather than lustful. Her lips twisted in a wry smile. There was no reason to dress it up. If she and Gordon took a walk on the wild side, it would be at the behest of rampant curiosity and sexual hunger. No other reason.

Was she up for it?

Yesterday, the day after their dinner with Yuri and Katya, she had panicked. She'd made Gordon drive her all over the island in their rental car, on the pretense of sightseeing. And the day had been wonderful in every way. Rocky hillsides of gnarled trees, ancient ruins tumbled like children's building blocks, quaint villages, and sweeping vistas at every turn in the road.

It was exactly the kind of day she had envisioned as she and Gordie planned their vacation. But the timing was suspect on her part. It had been escapism, plain and simple. She wasn't ready to face the Russians again, not when she was still grappling with the implications of what might occur between the four of them.

Gordie joined her by the wall, mug in hand. They had more or less mastered the art of making the local coffee, and he needed at least two cups to get going in the morning. He sipped the scalding brew slowly. The delicious scent wafted her way, making her wish she hadn't vowed to cut back on her caffeine.

She bumped his hip with hers. "What do you want to do today?"

He turned his head to scan her face, and then went back to his perusal of the scene that had inspired artists through the ages. "Are we going to avoid talking about what happened indefinitely?"

She debated the merits of playing dumb. But Gordie would never go for it. "You first," she said wryly. There was no doubt in her mind that Gordon had thought about their possible free pass incessantly. Katya was a beautiful, interesting woman. And she'd made no secret of her interest in Debra's husband.

He shrugged and spoke softly, his voice a bit hoarse and sleep roughened. "I don't want you to do anything that's threatening or repulsive to you."

"Yuri is neither." She said it flatly, at least trying to be honest about her response to the other man.

"But?"

She shifted her feet, her bare toes curling into the rough stone. "It seems wild and reckless and totally unlike us."

"Wasn't that the idea behind your seven-year-itch theory? The probability that something out of the ordinary might stave off any potential marital bumps in the road? Since we were so *inexperienced*?"

"But we aren't having any problems, are we?"

"Nope. But then again, it wasn't *my* idea."

"True. But apparently you're all over this scenario like white on rice." She heard the sour note in her voice and felt guilty. It wasn't Gordie's fault that she'd initiated the idea of sanctioned infidelity. Nor was it his fault that the Russians had made the reality both easy to accomplish and at the same time so deliciously wicked.

He put an arm around her shoulders. "We don't have to do anything at all if you don't want to. Yuri and Katya might be disappointed, but they'll get over it."

"But *you'll* be disappointed." It was a statement, not a question. She knew her husband very well. If only her self-knowledge was as fully developed. *Would* she regret it if she went back to Minnesota having missed the sexual opportunity of a lifelong marriage?

The timing was right. The location was perfect. The parties involved were congenial. What was holding her back? Her values? Her conscience? Her insecurities?

Her lack of sexual experience hadn't been an issue when

she met Gordon, because he was in the same boat. During their marriage, they'd learned a lot about how fun and varied intimacy could be. There wasn't much the two of them hadn't tried in terms of positions or kinky playacting.

But Yuri was foreign. And clearly far more comfortable with his sexuality than she was. What if he found her to be clumsy or naive or even downright boring in bed?

Gordon startled her when he spoke. She'd been so caught up in her own musings that she didn't realize he hadn't responded to her last flat statement.

He set his empty cup on the wall and turned to take her shoulders in his hands. He looked straight into her eyes, his expression determined. "Yes," he said slowly. "*I would* be disappointed. Because I think if we pass up this chance, I doubt either of us will have the courage to pursue a free-pass opportunity back home. We're on vacation. We've met two fascinating, highly sexed people. They are attracted to us. If ever the opportunity for experimentation existed, this is it."

He kissed her nose. "But I'm as serious as hell. I *don't* want to do it if you're not comfortable. Nervous and jittery is okay. Sick to your stomach is not."

She slid her arms around his neck, laying her head on his shoulder and finding reassurance in his familiar touch. "What about flat-out scared?"

He rubbed her back gently. "What are you scared of, love? I've watched the man devour you with his eyes. He thinks you're a goddess."

She kept her eyes closed. "You know me. I can say and do

stupid stuff when I'm anxious. And I don't want him to laugh at me. I'm a klutz, Gordie, and socially inept, at that."

He pulled back, frowning at her with mock severity. "Don't criticize the woman I love. And besides, we're not talking about having tea with the queen. This will be sex, Debra. And I happen to know you're an overachiever in that field."

"With you, maybe," she muttered. "That's because I'm not under any pressure to perform. I know we're good together. It's comfortable."

"Comfortable?" Now the scowl was more real. She had insulted his masculine pride.

"I meant that in the best possible way, Gordie."

He picked up his mug and turned to go back inside. "Let him take the lead, if you're worried. I have a hunch he'll take care of everything."

By late afternoon, the simmering tension in their pleasant vacation villa had reached Olympian proportions. Gordon stared at himself in the mirror, abashed to realize he was primping. He'd spent far longer than usual on his personal hygiene routine.

He lifted his arms one at a time and sniffed his pits. The damn Mediterranean heat made it hard for a guy to feel daisy fresh. He made a face at his reflection in the mirror. It was easy to act all confident and macho and tell Debra not to worry, but beneath his supposed self-confidence, he was a mess.

Screwing a stranger was great in a fantasy. The reality might be damn intimidating. Katya was the kind of woman who wouldn't put up with any swaggering shit from a guy.

She knew what she wanted and how to get it, and Debra's fears weren't that far from Gordie's own.

He didn't want to make a fool of himself.

It gave him a moment's pause to see how hot his wife looked when she emerged from the bedroom. Yuri had damned well better treat her well. Her eyes were huge in her flushed face, but she gave him a brave smile. She held out her arms. "How do I look?"

He crossed his arms over his chest. "Let's just say old Yuri will have a hard time keeping his hands off of you." She was wearing a new dress she had bought for their trip. It was a red cotton affair with some kind of abstract, modernistic print. The deep cut in front and back left her tanned arms and shoulders bare. Instead of her usual sleek ponytail, she had piled her blond locks on top of her head in an intricate knot. A few stray curls teased her ears and the back of her long, slim neck.

The material of the dress was far brighter than his wife's usual taste, but he liked it. A lot. The vivid orangey-red suited the Greek environment.

She smoothed the skirt. "Are you ready to go?"

Gordie took a deep breath and jingled the change in the pocket of his linen slacks. He'd been the one to call Yuri and Katya several hours ago and suggest a second dinner date. The stated pretext was a chance for him and Debra to return a societal obligation. He doubted whether the Russians were fooled.

He glanced at his watch. "You ready?"

Debra nodded, mute. The color had left her cheeks, and now she looked pale.

He went to her and took her face in his hands, gently kissing her forehead. "Just relax, Debra. Let the evening take its course."

Her lips trembled. "Where will we do it? Here? At their place? Oh, God, Gordie. There's a reason people like us don't fool around. Maybe we should have gone online and ordered a book or something. Surely there are rules . . . expectations—"

He put a finger on her lips to stop her nervous babble. "Fun, my love. Remember? This is all about fun." He handed Debra her tiny purse with the long, skinny strap. On similar occasions, she might have left it behind. He had plenty of credit cards and cash in his pockets. But tonight she insisted on bringing it and had carefully tucked three condoms inside.

Her earnest preparations amused him, but he dared not let it show. After all, he had a pocket of foil packets himself, but a man was *supposed* to take care of such details.

They stepped outside and he locked the door. Debra's hand was like ice, so he tucked it in the crook of his arm and tried to tease her into a more relaxed state of mind.

He led her off the patio and through the gate to the street. "Shall we stop at their villa and wait for them?" He and Debra had to pass there on the way down the hill, so it seemed silly to walk on by.

She shook her head violently. "No. I'm afraid they'll drag us inside and want to do it right now." She tugged his arm. "Let's take this side street. It loops around and comes out farther down the hill."

Gordon followed her, laughing. The evening should prove to be vastly entertaining, one way or another.

Earlier, when he called the Russian couple, he had suggested meeting at a famous restaurant with a great view of the sunset. He'd made a reservation, and now as soon as he and Debra gave their names, the rotund host clad in a spotless white T-shirt led them to a table for four near the window. The sun was still several fingers above the horizon, but already the mercurial sea was changing colors.

Katya and Yuri arrived moments later with much hugging and kissing and animated conversation. Although Gordon was on the receiving end of an affectionate, full-on-the-lips salute from the vivacious Russian woman, he managed to spare a glance out of the corner of his eye. And he was just in time to see Yuri's hands cup Debra's ass as the man enclosed her in a bear hug. Debra appeared flustered but not unduly upset.

Once again, the wine began to flow. Even so, Gordon wasn't a huge fan of the figs wrapped in grape leaves that were the appetizer.

Katya leaned toward him, giving him a nice view of her small but shapely breasts beneath the gaping neckline of her simple black dress. "Gordon," she breathed in a husky voice, "I not believe how stubborn you are. Is good to try new things." Her hand, the fingernails painted flame red, rested on his arm, lightly caressing him.

He adjusted himself unobtrusively beneath the tablecloth and smiled weakly. "In theory, but I prefer to eat things I can pronounce."

She pressed the nail of her index finger into his skin, marking him. "You pronounce my name very well, sweet Gordon." There was no mistaking her meaning.

In spite of himself, he went beet red. He could tell,

because his face was burning, and he and Debra had spent little time in the sun today. In desperation, he turned his attention to his two table mates. Yuri had his head close to Debra's, and he was speaking in a low, urgent voice.

Debra's expression was carefully blank, which probably meant she was shocked or upset or something . . . and trying not to show it.

Gordon lifted the plate of appetizers. "Another fig, sweetheart?"

Debra grabbed the morsel of finger food like a drowning woman snags a life raft. She stuffed her mouth and chewed slowly, her gaze cast down.

Yuri caught Gordon's eye. "Your wife's dress . . . is lovely, no?"

Gordon nodded numbly, wondering if he had lost track of the wine. Even though tonight's dinner was Gordon and Debra's treat, Yuri had insisted on buying several bottles of wine and putting them on his own tab. And Katya egged him on. The two Russians could drink a sailor under the table. And Gordon's head was already fuzzy.

The rest of the dinner was a blur. Between the booze, the sexual innuendo, and Katya's foot toying with his under the table, Gordon was tipsy, frazzled, and horny. Debra was faring no better. She'd tried to nurse the same glass of ouzo all evening, but Yuri kept topping it off when she wasn't looking.

Gordon watched Yuri sneak yet another glance at Debra's cleavage. She had evidently brushed some kind of sparkly powder between her breasts, because when she leaned forward, candlelight glinted off her luminous skin.

It was after ten when Katya stood up and spread her

arms, taking first Gordon's left hand and then Debra's right hand in hers. "We must go to Ammoudi."

It took Gordon a minute to catch up, but then he remembered. Ammoudi was the tiny fishing village at the base of the cliffs, with its own small beach. He and Debra had yet to make the trek down the steep steps.

He tried to be the voice of reason. "Won't the path be treacherous in the dark?"

Katya squeezed his hand, her dark eyes dancing with mischief. "Life is good with little danger—is not right, Yuri, my love?"

Her husband joined her in tugging the Americans to their feet. "We go now."

On the way, Yuri and Katya argued about how many steps lay ahead. Yuri was adamant. "Two hundred ninety."

Katya mocked him. "No. Numbers not so good for you. I say two ninety-eight." They squabbled with mock anger, leaving Debra and Gordon to tag along behind in the sweet, scented darkness.

Gordon took his wife's hand and slowed her progress so that he could whisper in her ear. "What did Yuri say to you when I was talking to Katya?"

Debra stumbled and giggled. "He kept comparing my boobs to some verse out of Song of Solomon about melons and pomegranates."

"Who knew the guy had a love for biblical poetry? Is that all?"

"Oh no," she said, laughing softly. "He told me my skin reminded him of the pale gold honey his beloved grandmother used to feed him back in the mother country."

"He wants to fuck you, my darling."

Debra leaned into him, nuzzling his shoulder. "So it would seem. And what about oh so sexy Katya? Surely she wasn't discussing current events with you."

He snorted and turned it into a cough. "Um, no. I think she's pretty much on the same page as Yuri."

Before they could compare notes any further, the other couple reached the top of the long, steep set of stairs, and turned around, waiting for Debra and Gordon to catch up. Yuri stepped forward and took Debra's hand. "Katya and I—we know the way. We help you."

And before Gordon could protest, the Russian had taken his wife away from him.

Katya rubbed a hand over his chest. "Come with me. I take care of you."

The steps would have been a risky venture in the daylight, stone-cold sober. Debra came to her senses enough in the first five minutes to realize she was taking her life in her hands, especially wearing tiny high heels that did wonders for the look of her long legs and nothing at all for stability. But Yuri was insistent. Each time she balked, he tightened his arm around her waist and urged her downward, bit by bit.

Her knees were trembling by the time they finally reached the bottom. As her adrenaline rush slowly drained away, she leaned against Yuri and tried to steady her breathing. The night seemed thicker down here. The ocean was an inky dark patch just beyond the dock and the modest beach.

By the time they reached the shore, she was more than

happy to slip out of her shoes and leave them. The small volcanic pebbles were still warm. She curled her toes into the rough mix of sand and tiny rocks and looked overhead. The stars were familiar now, but the tiny sliver of moon was new.

Yuri gave her only a moment to regain her breath. He urged her along, his voice a rough chuckle in her ear. "We walk, Debra. Feel magic of sea."

Despite her protests, he led her to the water's edge and right into the gentle waves. When she shrieked, he threw back his head and roared with laughter. Before she could protest further, he scooped up her skirt and caught it in his hands to keep it from getting wet. Now her legs were bare from her ankles all the way to the tops of her thighs.

Rattled, and feeling distinctively out of her element, she tried to turn around and look back toward the cliffs. Where in the hell was her husband? But Yuri was having none of it. He drew her a few steps deeper into the water, and then stood behind her, steadying her with one arm around her waist. His left hand still grasped her bunched-up skirt. Debra wasn't sure, but she thought he might be pressing his erection to her butt.

She felt him kiss the side of her neck. "I think you are very beautiful woman, Debra."

She shivered. The breeze wasn't exactly cool, but against her wet skin, it left a chill.

Yuri dropped his attempt to protect her dress and wrapped both arms now around her rib cage, hugging her tightly. Gradually, perhaps waiting to see if she would protest, he lifted his hands to her breasts.

Her breath caught in her throat. His touch was gentle,

but she felt it in every pore of her skin, every cell of her body. He whispered Russian words in her ear, low, urgent words that translated easily in any language.

Without warning he stepped around in front of her and deliberately scooped handfuls of water to wet the front of her dress. Her nipples responded to the change in temperature and budded tightly. He pinched one, watching her face to gauge her reaction.

She gasped instinctively and staggered backward a half step, but he caught her immediately and aligned their bodies chest to chest. Now his firm cock probed her belly. His face was scarcely visible, but the intensity of his gaze drifted over her like a caress.

He kissed her firmly, pressing his tongue between her numb lips. "I want make love to you." The fluency of his English was slipping in proportion to his need.

She needed to know where her husband was. She craved the anchor of Gordie's presence in this sea of uncertainty. "Well, I . . ."

Yuri scraped his teeth along the shell of her ear, his hands kneading her breasts and plucking at her nipples until an insistent thrum of hunger pulsed between her legs.

She tried to turn around. "Where are—"

He pulled her back to face him. "Do not worry. Katya will not let your Gordon come to harm. I want you, pretty girl."

His hand roved boldly beneath her skirt, finding her panties and slipping beneath the elastic band with startling ease. She squeezed her thighs together, feeling the shifting ocean floor beneath her feet. She spared a fleeting thought to wonder what creatures might be swimming in the opaque depths, but Yuri found her mouth again and plundered it with his tongue.

She gasped for breath, feeling the situation sliding beyond her control. Surely he didn't mean to have sex with her standing up in the bloody ocean.

She shoved a hand against his chest. "I need to speak to my husband," she said breathlessly, and then yelped when Yuri took her hand and placed it boldly over the bulge in his pants.

He rubbed her palm over his erection, groaning harshly as he did so. "Feel what you do to me, little flower."

She jerked away, her fledgling arousal dampened by the sheer absurdity of the moment. "I'm cold," she prevaricated, wondering what it would take to get this crazy Russian back on dry ground.

She pulled out of his embrace, and this time he allowed it, muttering sullenly below his breath.

Thankfully, she spotted Gordon and Katya about fifty yards away. The slim, petite woman was practically climbing Gordon's body, so much so that Debra saw him lose his footing and stumble.

Defiantly, Debra grabbed up her sodden skirts and ran as much as she was able. She made it to Gordon's side and clasped his hand in hers, elbowing Katya out of the way in the process.

The two Americans faced the two Russians, the former breathless and united in their need to restore order to the evening, the latter leaning together with their arms around each other's waists.

Katya spoke first. "We think you want sex with us. Is true—yes?"

Gordon straightened his spine. "Yes. Maybe. But not like this. In a bed. In private. At your villa. Is that so much to ask?"

Yuri bent his head and whispered in his wife's ear. Katya lifted her hands to the sky, a gesture that Debra and Gordon were beginning to recognize as one of deep emotion. "Fine," she muttered, her accent heavier than usual. "We do boring way . . . if you insist."

Chapter Ten

Cherisse decided not to call Wesley for a ride. He might be deep in the midst of his work, and she didn't want to disturb him. And besides, she wasn't the kind of woman who could carry on a casual conversation with her husband while at the same time standing beside the other man she wanted to seduce.

So she caught a cab and made it back to their condo by five o'clock. She thought it was a bit odd that Wesley hadn't called to check on her, but on the other hand, any unexpected spousal phone call during certain moments of this afternoon might have been extremely awkward.

She was still stunned that she had actually possessed the guts to initiate the beginnings of her free-pass interlude. Not that she had been completely at ease with the process. After propositioning the handsome lifeguard and receiving his tacit acceptance, she had been unsure of how to proceed. She wasn't about to go with some strange guy back to his apartment. She wasn't an idiot. But how exactly would she and Danny get from walking on the beach tomorrow morning to screwing afterward?

A hotel room close by might be a reasonable option if she and Wesley hadn't already spent so much money on this vacation. But other than that, she was fresh out of realistic ideas.

After the erotic ice-cream interlude, she'd been hot and tired and flustered, so she'd bidden Danny goodbye with a promise to meet him out on the beach at seven thirty tomorrow morning. They had exchanged another steamy kiss, and then he had walked her back to the front of the hotel, where a line of cabs waited.

Now, as she rode up the elevator in her own building, she practiced what she would say to Wesley.

It was a shock to find he wasn't home.

She dumped her tote bag on the bed and stripped off her swimsuit and cover-up. Deliberately, she posed in front of the mirror in the bathroom and studied her body. Her nudity seemed erotic suddenly, her breasts heavy with arousal. The trickle of moisture between her thighs had been almost continuous since this morning when she had baked on a chaise longue and wished for someone to touch her. Please her. Give her relief.

She lifted a foot onto the countertop so she could see her pussy. The sight of it both pleased and frightened her. Men were often accused of being ruled by their dicks. She pulled back her labia and exposed her clitoris. Was this fertile, aching, moist delta between her thighs suddenly so much more powerful than her reason?

She thought back to the moment when Melanie had proposed the outlandish free-pass idea. How had that premise gone so quickly from being shocking to terribly tempting?

She slipped a finger between the folds of her sex and probed carefully. Her thighs clenched involuntarily. She closed her eyes and remembered Danny's clean-cut good looks and cocky smile. Would he like what he saw?

She stroked her clit, letting the sensation spread slowly through her abdomen, down her legs, into her gut. Then she remembered the handy removable shower head and decided she could wait another sixty seconds.

As she turned on the water and adjusted the temperature, she heard the front door open. Ignoring her quivering need for release, she slipped into her silky, thigh-length robe and turned off the tap before moving quickly to the kitchen.

Wesley turned and smiled when she found him getting a bottle of water out of the fridge. "Hey, sweetheart. I was just getting ready to call you and see if you needed a ride home. How was the beach?"

She hovered in the doorway, her heart beating fast. She needed to get fucked. And she wanted to tell him every amazing thing that had transpired today, though she was bashful, and mindful of Wesley's earlier reservations about the free-pass plan.

As nervous as she was about confessing, it was clear that Wesley wasn't acting normally either. After downing half the bottle of water in one gulp, he now fussed with the dish towel hanging on the oven door, straightening it with military precision. After his brief greeting, he somehow had managed to avoid her gaze.

She wrapped her arms around her waist. "Did you work all day?"

He flushed. "Half of it," he mumbled.

Her own urgent need for disclosure and satisfaction took a back burner. Wesley looked about to burst. She leaned against the doorframe, amused in spite of her unappeased hunger. "Do you have something to tell me?" His fidgety behavior was unusual.

Finally, he looked up, his expression a combination of excitement and guilt. "I met someone."

Her first reaction was mixed. Surprise. A tiny blip of pique. Curiosity. And then relief. As long as Wesley was going to make use of his free pass, he couldn't stop her from doing the same with Danny.

She cleared her throat. "Where? I thought you planned to stay home all day."

He shoved his hands in his pockets. "I did. At least for a while. But then I saw her. . . ."

Now she was confused. "Saw her where?"

He cocked his head toward the bedroom. "Through the telescope."

Her eyebrows shot up. "Good Lord, Wesley. You spied on someone?" That didn't sound good. "How? Where?" The kink factor surprised her.

He met her gaze with a hint of defiance, as though waiting for censure. He took a deep breath. "I was using the telescope, looking at the water, at the new building. Nothing out of the ordinary . . . lots of offices, shops, stuff like that."

"And?"

His eyes glittered with excitement, and she realized for the first time that he had a boner. He tried to look casual and failed miserably. "I stumbled across the window of a woman who was masturbating. And I watched."

"Wesley!" She was shocked in spite of herself. Not that he had accidentally spied on an intimate moment, but that he had stuck around for the whole performance.

He eyed her bravely. "And then I followed her."

She had gone from surprise to shock to bewilderment. The husband she knew would never do what Wesley was describing. He had hunted this woman down. Maybe even talked to her. Told her about the free pass. Invited her to be his onetime lover.

Cherisse was surprised and dumbfounded and completely taken aback. Perhaps she didn't know her husband as well as she thought.

She toyed with the sash of her robe. "Is she beautiful?" It was a difficult question to ask, Danny the lifeguard notwithstanding.

Wesley finally crossed to where Cherisse stood. He stroked her cheek with the back of his hand and tipped up her chin to look deep into her eyes. "It's okay, my love. This is nothing more than a fantasy being played out in real time. But I won't pursue it if it makes you uncomfortable. I swear."

Her body reacted instinctively to his touch. This was the male who held the power to trigger her orgasm. This was the man who could probe her aching sex with his wonderful hard penis and fulfill the sharp ache that held her trapped in limbo. She leaned against him, reassured by his familiar smell, by the warmth of his strong arms as he pulled her close and hugged her. "Keep going," she mumbled. "Tell me all of it." She listened without interruption as he skated over the highlights of his afternoon. His pursuit. The mall bookstore. The conversation.

When he disclosed the woman's age, she felt marginally less threatened. "So what did she say when you asked her? Was she amenable?"

He stepped back, unable to squelch the excitement in his eyes, though he clearly tried to temper it for her benefit. "We're meeting for coffee tomorrow morning. In public. To talk."

"Oh. That sounds nice." It was an inane statement, but what *was* the appropriate response when your spouse waxed poetic about a strange woman's hair and then confessed he planned to screw her at the first opportunity? In spite of her own activities, she was indisputably jealous. Which did nothing to lessen her obsessive need to get laid at the first available opportunity, despite the fact that she was in desperate need of a shower.

She wasn't reasoning too clearly at all. All her thoughts and emotions were tied up in one huge, mental, erotic Gordian knot. She blurted out her secret with something less than finesse. "I met someone, too."

Wesley hadn't expected that. She could tell. His face went blank for a moment as he waged an internal struggle. He sighed, unable to hide his disgruntlement. "I thought you might, since you were alone today. It seemed like a good opportunity."

"He's a lifeguard."

"Young?"

She nodded.

He frowned. "Please don't take this the wrong way, Cherisse. But I'm concerned about your safety. I'm not saying don't do it." He stopped and ran his hands through his hair. Clearly, he was trying to be diplomatic. "I know you probably think I'm going to be jealous, and I will be. . . . I can practically guarantee it. But my biggest worry is that someone might try to hurt you. Women are at a disadvantage physically, and if you go to his—"

She put her hand over his mouth. "Stop. I love it that you're thinking about me and worrying. But I'm not stupid. I've already thought of all that. Believe me. That's why I've considered bringing him here."

Wesley felt a wave of relief followed by something less easy to define. "Here?" With her husband in the house? He wasn't sure he could handle that.

She chuckled at what must have been a look of complete consternation on his face. "I assumed you might make yourself scarce. And now that I know about your coffee date, it seems to me that we might orchestrate this all at the same time. Unless of course, you want to bring your hair lady here, too. After all, we do have a second bedroom."

He shook his head. "That's a bit kinky, don't you think? And besides, I'd be totally distracted knowing you were in the next room with the lifeguard."

Cherisse grinned. "I see your point. So where will you and your—what's her name?"

"Melinda."

"Ah. So where will you and Melinda go?"

"Well, assuming she agrees, I imagine we'll be up at her place."

She shook her head, her eyes a bit wild. "Are we insane? Will we really go through with this?"

He realized that he wasn't about to let her back out now. Not when it was her idea. Not when they had already involved two other people. He took both of her hands in his. They were cold. He rubbed them slowly. "You thought this was a good idea, sweetheart. A fun, crazy, let's-be-wild-and-naughty plan. And you were right."

"I was?" She didn't look convinced. For the first time he realized what she was wearing. Not much. He had a sudden urge to screw his wife, but he didn't want her to think it was because of Melinda.

He tugged her arms around his waist, pulling her tightly into his embrace so she could feel his erection. "I missed you today," he muttered. And he realized it was true. The whole time with Melinda, he'd wanted to share the feeling with Cherisse—that sensation of being nineteen and horny and out of control when it came to the female sex. He'd wanted her to see him score with another woman. Odd . . .

She bit his nipple gently. "You're full of shit. You had your fantasy day. Admit it. You never once thought of me."

He pulled back enough to look her straight in the eye. "That's not true. I was excited, yes. But I wanted you to be there to watch what was happening."

She snorted. "Right . . ."

He rubbed her back and squeezed her ass, lifting the hem

of the soft robe and finding even softer bare skin. "Okay, I know it sounds weird when I say it like that, but honest to God, I thought you would get a kick out of seeing me act like a fool. And then in the end, I thought you would probably have enjoyed meeting Melinda."

Cherisse must have believed him, because she remained pliant in his arms. His boner was throbbing; his head was full of sexual images. He slid a finger down between her butt cheeks and caressed her boldly, tickling her anus.

His sweet wife squirmed, pressing her lower abdomen against his balls and shaft. A lightning bolt of pure lust sizzled from his dick down the backs of his legs and clear up his spine. He inhaled sharply. At the moment, making it as far as the bedroom seemed an unlikely proposition. His legs trembled.

He backed her over to the counter and lifted her to sit on the edge of the slick granite surface.

Suddenly, Cherisse realized where things were heading. She shoved his chest. "Oh, not yet, Wesley. I was just about to get in the shower. I've been at the beach and out in the heat. I'm all icky."

"You're fine," he muttered. "Really." He wasn't about to be dissuaded from his mission.

When he spread her thighs and put his mouth to her lush, wet pussy, she appeared to lose the inclination to argue. As he ran his tongue over her clit in short, firm strokes, her only response was a low, guttural moan.

He had one hand at the small of her back, holding her in place. As she climaxed, he probed her passage with his tongue, wringing a cry of pleasure from her parted lips as she rode a second swell of orgasm into shivering silence, her body limp and slumped against his chest.

He scooped her up in his arms and carried her to the sofa. The living room was closer than the bedroom, and he needed to be inside her.

He ripped off her tiny robe and lowered her to the couch. She watched him undress.

Seconds later, he wedged himself between her legs and thrust hard, burying his aching dick as deep as it would go. His scalp tightened, and he groaned. God, he wanted to fuck her for the rest of the day. Forget dinner. Forget cleaning up. Forget whatever things sane, normal people did to while away a long evening.

He wanted to screw his wife.

She wrapped her legs around his waist and muttered something in his ear.

"What?" He was sweating, his lungs aching for air. "What did you say?" Why the hell was she talking? It was too late for that.

She licked the side of his neck. "I let him kiss me. Twice."

A red haze obscured his vision. Primitive emotions scrambled his brain and tormented his dick. His woman. Her lips. On another man's cock. Maybe not today. But soon. Maybe tomorrow. On this sofa. Perhaps in the bed he shared with his wife.

He shuddered as his arousal soared. God, he wanted to lock her away. But even as the thought flitted through his consciousness, he saw a vision of some fresh-faced kid screwing Cherisse.

He shook his head, but the image wouldn't disappear. He looked down at his wife. Her face was flushed. She had her eyes closed, and her breasts jiggled slightly each time Wesley thrust.

He rotated his hips deliberately. Cherisse arched her back. He knew his wife. One climax seldom satisfied. She would come again. With a little help from him. Which he was more than happy to provide.

Gritting his teeth against the need to come, he slowed his strokes and toyed with her nipples. She squirmed and gasped, but her eyes didn't open.

He knew in that instant that she was fantasizing about her lifeguard. It infuriated him and at the same time made him sick with lust.

He slid one hand into her hair and tugged. "Look at me, Cherisse." He barely recognized his own voice. "Open your eyes, damn it."

She cooperated slowly. The pupils were dilated, the irises a thin line of golden brown. She licked her lips. "What did you say?"

He ground his cock deep. "You're thinking about him." It was an accusation, not a statement.

She caught the nuance. A flush of color started at her tits and ran up her throat to her cheeks. She turned her head to the side.

He caught her chin and forced her to look at him. "I'm crammed in your pussy, but you're thinking of him. Admit it." His erection lost a fraction of its strength as he realized he was scared. Scared Cherisse was going to like fucking her lifeguard more than she enjoyed screwing her own husband.

Damn. Was he as insecure as that? The arm on which he was supporting himself trembled.

A knot formed in his belly. Cherisse's eyes were hazy with arousal, her lips swollen and full. Her nipples resembled tiny burgundy pebbles.

His throat was dry, his voice hoarse. "Answer me," he demanded, his tone more agitated than he liked.

She licked her lips a second time, and his dick pulsed in response. The muscles in her throat worked as she swallowed. "I was . . . yes. Is that so bad?"

He slid out and back in, tormenting them both. "Tell me," he muttered. "Tell me what happened. How did you pick him? I want to know it all."

She lifted her hands to his chest, stroking him, petting him as if he needed to be appeased, which he did. But it was hell on his ego to admit it, even obliquely. As she spoke, a tiny feline smile lifted her lips.

He doubted if she even realized it.

She looked straight into his eyes. "He was young. He had a great body. And looking at him made me wet. So I kinda thought that was a good sign. Don't you think?"

He stayed inside her, barely moving, his whole body taut. "I suppose."

The smile increased incrementally as though she was remembering her behavior and congratulating herself. "When I ate lunch, he was my waiter. We talked and laughed. He has a great personality. He works several jobs so he can do auditions when they come up."

Wesley told himself he wasn't threatened. So the guy was a hot, young stud actor? So what? "Tell me, Cherisse. How did you get to him?" The muscles in his arms were scream-ing from the effort of holding himself up. But he had to hear it all.

She rubbed her thumbs over his flat nipples, making his belly muscles flinch. "I flirted. And then I made it very clear that I was propositioning him. He agreed to find me when he got off work in a couple of hours. We met then. We ate ice cream. . . ."

"Ice cream?" He was having a hard time keeping track of the conversation, given the fact that his nuts were in a vise of borderline agony.

"Foreplay. Lots of licking. First the cones. Then hands."

He pumped automatically, his body straining to break the hold he had on it. "Hands?"

She ran her index finger across his bottom lip and then gen-tly forced the tip of her finger between his teeth. "He sucked on my fingers, Wesley. One at a time. Until they were all clean."

"Shit." He withdrew and lunged in again, three sharp thrusts in quick succession. He groaned. "And then what happened?"

This time her smug grin made him crazy. She was clearly proud of herself. "He deliberately smeared ice cream on his hand, and I returned the favor."

He started moving, slow, purposeful, deep slides of his penis. Rubbing her, building an inescapable friction. She smelled of sweat and sunscreen. Heat poured off his body. Their rough breathing mingled. "More . . . tell me more." His voice was barely audible.

She closed her eyes again, and this time he let her. His own lashes came down as he strained to listen.

Cherisse let go of a tremulous sigh. "I took one of his fingers deep in my mouth and sucked on it. It felt odd . . . like there was a direct connection from my mouth to my vagina. Each time I pulled, it was as if he was penetrating me. The ice cream was gone in seconds, but I continued to drag at his skin, scraping him with my teeth."

"Sweet God in heaven." His neck muscles were taut enough to snap.

She murmured, low in her throat, and he felt her inner muscles clench on his dick and caress it.

He struggled for breath. "Go on."

"I don't even know what he was feeling. All I could concentrate on was my own arousal. And the fact that I was deliberately opening myself up sexually. I gave each of his long, hard fingers the same treatment, and then when I got to his thumb . . ."

"Don't stop." The command was harsh.

She wrapped her legs tightly around his waist and fisted her hands in his hair, pulling until he winced. Her words were little more than a whisper now, almost as if she were chanting some mysterious spell to cast over the man she wanted. Or was it *men*?

She played with his ear. "I bit it. The fleshy part. Hard enough to make him wince. And I brushed my hand across his lap, testing his erection."

"He wanted you." What man wouldn't? She was a sensual woman, just learning the full extent of her power.

"He let me touch him for a moment, but it was a public place. So it didn't go far. Except for the kissing. We kissed. A lot. It felt strange. Alien. His mouth and his taste weren't you."

Another slow plunge and withdrawal. "But you liked it. You wanted his dick inside your hot, little pussy. You craved it the way an addict craves a fix, didn't you, Cherisse? You wanted to spread your legs and let him fuck you right then and there."

"I did." Her words slurred. "I even thought about how all the people would stop and watch us. I imagined being on top so they could admire my breasts. I could actually feel the hot sun on the crown of my head while he lifted his hips and forced himself inside me."

Wesley was beyond words. His only response was a feral sound that combined lust and anger and a searing regret that he had ever agreed to let another man touch his wife.

Cherisse's voice caught in her throat as she neared the inevitable pinnacle. "I could hear the ocean and feel the breeze on my naked body. And between my legs, he moved steadily, firmly . . . almost machinelike in his strokes. I wanted to cry out, to shout my release for all those people watching to hear. And then I—"

His mighty thrust and his roar of rage and hunger put an abrupt halt to her recitation. He pressed her down into the sofa. "You're mine, Cherisse. Mine, mine, mine." He punctuated his claim with one final invasion of her body that sent then both over the edge.

He heard her wailing cry at the same moment a fiery white light scorched the backs of his eyelids, and his whole body went rigid in a climax that racked him for what seemed like aeons.

When it was over, silence reigned inside the condo, except for the muted hum of the refrigerator. Wesley could feel

Cherisse struggling to breathe, so he moved to one side with a muttered apology. The sofa was generously sized, but too narrow for two adults to lie side by side.

He wiped a hand across his brow and shuddered. "I'm not sure we should call it a 'free' pass. Sounds to me like we're both going to pay a price."

Chapter Eleven

Richard knew he was as decent and law-abiding as the next guy. He paid his taxes. He was kind to animals and children. He supported his favorite charities.

None of that made him deserving of what was about to happen. Spontaneous sex with a hot, willing woman . . . no expectations . . . no strings attached . . . no awkward morning after.

How in the hell had this opportunity fallen into his lap? Was it merely a case of being in the right place at the right time? What if he had never shown up in Minnesota? Who would Melanie have picked to be her free-pass man? He found himself getting jealous of a nonexistent male and then realized that he was losing his grip on reality.

But when Melanie took him by the hand, all those thoughts that had flitted through his mind in a nanosecond were gone in a flash.

He found his voice. "The desk? Really? I'm not sure it can support both our weight."

Melanie squeezed his fingers, mischief on her face. "I wasn't proposing the missionary position, Richard. I didn't peg you for such a conventional kind of guy."

She stepped away from him and quickly cleared the middle of the smooth cherrywood expanse, then tossed him a challenging glance over her shoulder. "I assume you know what to do from here." Alarm flitted across her face. "And don't forget the condom."

He frowned. "You can trust me, Melanie. I'll take care of you, I swear."

She bent at the waist and laid the top half of her body across the desk. Then she reached behind with one hand and flipped her skirt up over her waist.

Holy shit. His knees quivered embarrassingly. But at least she couldn't see his lack of savoir faire. He approached her slowly, wanting to impress her with his finesse, his bold sexuality. A woman such as Melanie deserved to have a lover who had his act together. A man who would entertain her until she fell panting into a stupor. A sexual partner who could match her point for point.

But since he felt like a pimply teenager daring to approach the homecoming queen, it was hard to play the part of the suave playboy.

Truthfully, he rarely needed to expend much effort in pleasing women, which might have made him just the tiniest bit spoiled. But at this particular moment in time, he wished he had a bit more in his repertoire when it came to entertaining a married woman like Melanie.

He was about to be her free-pass guy. Didn't that carry some inherent obligations on his part?

He put his hands on her ass. Her barely there panties were black lace—not a thong, but a narrow strip of sexy fabric that rode the curves of her butt.

He slid a finger beneath the elastic. Melanie made a muffled sound. Her face was buried in her folded arms. Was that how she wanted it? No forewarning of what he might do? No instructions or leading on her part? Did she plan to simply submit and let the strange man do his worst as he ravaged her body?

The image of passive innocence versus carnal aggression nearly knocked him flat on his ass at the wave of raw lust it inspired. He rarely bothered to play games with the women he screwed. Their availability and eager willingness to please made any frills unnecessary.

Now, about to fuck this delightful woman, he found that he was, himself, quite eager to please.

Slowly, ever so slowly, he slipped her undies down her legs and off her feet. Along the way he paused to appreciate the sleek muscles in her calves and thighs. He wondered absently if other, more intimate muscles were as toned and, if so, whether he would survive finding out.

Melanie remained silent and passive. She shivered once, hard, as he dispensed with her underwear, but other than that, she was mute and still.

Was he being tested?

Did her quiet absence of participation mean she wanted him to elicit her participation?

His dick ached. He wanted to align their bodies and

drive into her mindlessly. If he wasn't careful, it might take only two or three quick thrusts and he'd be done. Not exactly, he'd wager, what a woman with a free pass would expect or desire.

He spread her legs a few more inches and looked his fill. Her dark pink sex was lovely. Moisture swelled there, and he touched her lightly, just to see if the slick, wet skin was as soft as it appeared.

When his fingertip made contact with her pussy, she yelped and came six inches off the desk. He grinned, knowing she couldn't see. Apparently, Melanie was as wired as he was. He petted her rump. "Relax, honey. I plan on making both of us feel real good . . . but first . . ."

He couldn't simply make this a doggie-style quickie. He might get there eventually, but he had a few variations in mind first. He lifted Melanie and urged her onto her back. Her face tightened for a moment so the position with her legs hanging off must have been awkward.

He caressed her knees. "Put your heels up on the desk. It will be more comfortable."

She obeyed, and now her pussy was in full view. He wanted to lick his lips and dive right in. But such an event required pacing, skill, nuance.

Her dress was bunched at her waist, though she still tried to keep it over her breasts. He left it for now. Somehow, with her clothing disarrayed but still partially in place, she looked even more erotic than if she had been entirely naked.

Her teeth dug into her bottom lip, and her eyes were huge. She watched him warily. But still she didn't make a sound.

He stood as close to the desk as possible so that her sex made contact with the front of his slacks. His erection flexed and arched toward the goal.

He urged her legs around his waist. "Hold me," he muttered, and his heart leaped in his chest when she obeyed instantly and without question. With one quick flick of his zipper, he could be inside her.

He sucked in some much-needed air and tried to ignore his hurting crotch. Gradually, he tugged on the bodice of her dress until Melanie let go.

Her face flamed as he studied her small, nicely shaped tits. She breathed rapidly, her gaze darting everywhere but at him.

"Why so shy?" he asked in a soft murmur. "Your breasts are lovely."

The color in her face deepened. But in her eyes he saw mortification overlaid with pleasure. Her hands fluttered loosely by her hips before landing on his forearms. She toyed with the dark hair. "You don't have to say that. I know I don't have much on top."

He bent without ceremony and sucked one hard-tipped breast into his mouth. He raked the nipple with his teeth, giving her just enough pressure to stay on the good side of pain.

Her fingernails dug into his arms and her hips lifted, even though her legs were still around his waist. He surged forward, heedless of the fact that he was still dressed. God, he wanted to fuck her.

He switched breasts, drunk on her scent and the feel of her skin beneath his palms. The more he suckled her, the more vocal she became.

But he didn't let her climax, though he paused to appreciate the fact that this woman clearly *could* climax simply from having him stimulate her breasts. Amazing. Lord knew what it would be like when their bodies were finally joined.

She whimpered in distress when he straightened and went back to looking and not touching. Her eyelids flew wide and she glared at him. "Are you sure you know how to do this hanky-panky stuff? It's taking an awfully long time."

He chuckled. "Patience, married Melanie. If I only get one shot at this, I want to make it last."

She pouted well. "Maybe I should have set a time limit. Like maybe this millennium."

He scooped her up and onto her feet, pulling her dress over her head before she could protest. Now she was bare-ass naked. He still wore his trousers and socks and shoes. For the moment, it was necessary. It was his only protection against finishing their encounter too soon.

Holding only one of her hands, he stepped back and surveyed her, top to bottom. She was one big pink blush. He cocked his head. "This gym has lots of mirrors."

Panic swept over her face. "Don't get any crazy ideas. Anyone walking by outside could see us through the plate-glass windows."

He tugged her hand, drawing her toward the hallway. "Not if we're in the exercise studio." It was the large room where group classes met. It did have windows, but none of them were on outside walls.

He wasn't sure what he had in mind, but the whole mirror thing might serve him well.

In fact, it was shocking. He stood with Melanie in front of him and stared at their reflections. From this perspective, the disparity in their heights seemed magnified. She looked small and delicate. He looked like a hungry lion about to pounce.

Melanie had trouble facing the mirror. She turned into his bare chest, burrowing her face and making it necessary for him to close her in his arms. That was what a man was supposed to do in such situations—right?

He stroked her hair. "What's wrong?" Her narrow shoulders trembled, either from nerves or from the chill in the air, or both.

She looked up at him. "It's embarrassing."

"How so?" He thought it was pretty damn spectacular, especially since he could now see her small, curvy ass in the mirror.

"You're still dressed."

He pried her arms away from his waist. "That can be remedied." He didn't wait for her help. He was afraid any assistance from her would test the limits of his control. He kicked off his shoes and socks. Then he deliberately lowered his zipper without haste, enjoying the way her gaze focused on his hands.

He shoved his pants and boxers to his feet and stepped out of them. His cock felt like the Grinch's heart. Almost as if it had grown two sizes that day.

Melanie was practically wringing her hands. But she couldn't keep her gaze on his face. She was too busy drinking in the floor show. He wasn't above preening a bit. His thick shaft bobbed eagerly, pointing to the sky and waiting for a piece of the action. The head oozed a droplet of moisture. He put his hands on his hips. "Do I pass muster? You can't always be choosy with a free-pass guy, but I don't want to disappoint you."

She licked her lips and finally smiled at him. "I'm not disappointed. And I won't be."

He turned her to face the mirror. "Look at us." For a moment they stood hip to hip.

The reflection in the mirror was not only erotic, it was deeply arousing. He urged her in front of him, her back to his chest. Now he kept an eye on the mirror as he lifted his hands and cupped her breasts.

Instinctively, she backed up into him, making him groan and curse. Her ass massaging his dick was sheer torture. He skated both of his hands down her belly to her fluff of dark hair. Her pussy was clean-shaven except for a whimsical heart-shaped patch at the top of her slit. The smooth skin around and below mesmerized him.

He watched her face in the mirror as he separated her folds and fingered her.

She groaned. "God, Richard."

He was already trying to figure out where he could lay her down and mount her when she took him completely by surprise. She slipped out of his grasp, turned around, and went down onto her knees.

When she took him in her mouth, he cursed. Between his extended period of celibacy and the fact that he wanted this woman with an agonizing urgency, she had him at flash point in mere seconds. He tried to pull back.

She wouldn't let him. She had the skill and the intuitive

knowledge to bring him gasping to the edge of a bridge he wasn't ready to cross.

But apparently she had decided she wanted control after all. Her hands on his butt kept him in place as she pulled at his shaft and clung to him while he ejaculated deep in her throat.

It was agonizingly pleasurable. His climax seemed to last forever, ripping from his nuts and making his whole body quake with seismic tremors.

When she released him, he sank to his knees as well and caught her close in his arms.

It was an awkward position. But he didn't care. He felt like worshipping at her feet.

But he had to suck it up and act like a man. Wasn't he her free-pass guy? Didn't he have duties to perform?

Blearily, he surveyed the room. In the far corner, he spotted a wire bin of those large exercise balls, and a naughty idea came to him.

When he thought he could stand, he released her and went to get a couple of mats. They weren't all that soft, but they sure as hell beat the hardwood floor.

Melanie had stood up in his brief absence, and now she helped him place the mats side by side. He could tell she was trying not to look in the mirror, but she kept sneaking glances nevertheless.

He left her for a moment to roll on a condom, and then he held out a hand. "I think we have some unfinished business, my dear."

She approached him warily, as well she might. He had plans. Oh, God, he had plans.

He stared at her, not smiling. "I want you to crouch over the ball." The purpose of the large, rubbery sphere was to help the exercise buff develop inner-core strength as well as flexibility and balance. Richard had another benchmark in mind.

Melanie hesitated only a second before complying. Now her pretty ass was posed quite beautifully. But she wasn't facing the mirror.

He nudged her around until she was staring straight ahead. "You're gonna watch, my little seductress. No closing those beautiful eyes of yours."

A range of emotions crossed her face, but the only one he cared about was hunger. He needed to know she was as greedy and as ready for this as he was. He got on his knees behind her and rubbed his cock in her butt crack. Melanie moaned and moved restlessly.

He tugged on her hair, short as it was, until she lifted her face. "Keep watching," he demanded.

Melanie was beyond being shocked by anything that was happening. It was as if an alien being had taken over her body. It didn't seem to matter if she was looking at a reflection of Richard or at Richard in the flesh. He made an impact.

The power in his large, well-honed body, the sexuality manifested in his rearing cock—all of it combined to seduce her senses. She'd gone down on him at a whim, anxious to prove she was no conservative, long-married bore. She wanted him to see her as more than available. She wanted to make him hunger for her.

The gym was an absurd place for this assignation. But

what other choice did she have? And in a way, the sheer fact that it wasn't a traditional or acceptable spot for having sex made it that much more reckless and stimulating.

He'd shocked her by insisting they leave her office. At least in there she'd had a feeling of privacy. In this big, open room, with one huge mirrored wall, she felt painfully exposed. The building was locked. No club member was going to wander through. Still, she felt entirely without protection, emotional or otherwise.

Richard nudged her again, and she inhaled sharply. For the briefest moment, an image of her husband's dear, familiar face flashed across her mental screen. How would he react when she told him the details of this tryst?

Richard moved a final time, and thoughts of her husband faded, replaced by more immediate concerns. She braced her hands, palms down, on the floor. It was pretty obvious what was about to happen. And she was ready. Maybe. Her libido was ready. Her determination was there. But some little voice deep inside her kept asking difficult questions, like the one she had asked Thomas: *Do you think I'll regret this?*

She ignored the voice *and* the memory.

She felt the head of his cock probe between her thighs and find the opening to her pussy. She was almost embarrassingly wet. He paused, whether to make sure she was ready or to ratchet up the anticipation, she wasn't sure. Either way, she responded with an instinctive backward movement of her hips, the same maneuver women had been using since caveman days.

She heard him chuckle, felt him caress her lower back. "Anxious, Melanie?"

She tensed, suddenly afraid that he was making a mockery of this ... of her. She looked at him over her shoulder. "For a man who has supposedly been celibate for a number of weeks, you're taking your damn sweet time. But, hey, I can wait if you can."

She tried to get up, but his strong, long-fingered hands clamped down on her ass, holding her in place. "Don't even think about moving," he muttered.

She saw his face in the mirror and knew, all evidence to the contrary, that Richard wanted their bodies joined every bit as much as she did. Maybe more. Their reasons for arriving at this moment might be vastly different, but the outcome would be the same.

He entered her slowly, holding her gaze in the mirror. She realized suddenly that she always closed her eyes at this point with her husband. But tonight, even without Richard's insistence, she suspected that she would have watched. She wasn't able to tear her eyes away from what was happening in the huge mirror.

Seeing it and feeling it all at the same time was doubly erotic. But the physical won, hands down.

Richard was a large man, and his penis was proportionate to his general size. Had she not been as ready, it would have been a tight fit. As it was, the pleasurable stretching sensation was incredible.

She felt him breathing raggedly, saw in the mirror the intense, tight-jawed look of determination on his face. The inevitable urge to conquer.

What worked out ever so nicely for both of them was her complete and utter willingness to submit.

He filled her and retreated in lazy, slow strokes that brought her to the edge time and again and then backed her down. The ball beneath her was not stable, and the rocking motion as he fucked her was oddly erotic.

But she wasn't getting the direct stimulation to her clit, and she wanted it, needed it to come. His weight kept the lower portion of her body trapped. Short of tumbling both of them to the mat, she had no recourse but to let him screw her at this deliberately subtle pace.

Frustration built along with hot, lustful pleasure. The ball rolled against her breasts, keeping them stimulated. She felt his hair-roughened thighs against the backs of her legs. It seemed as if he was all around her.

He stopped and tugged painfully on her hair. "You're not watching." His voice was a harsh rasp of sound. In truth, she had been so lost to what was happening inside her, she had forgotten about the mirror entirely.

She lifted her head. Now she could see the sheen of sweat on his forehead and his chest. No trace of the affable businessman remained. His tight grin was feral, the flash of lust in his eyes enough to sends shivers of genuine feminine alarm coursing though her body.

But even as those flickers of unease tempered her arousal, the thrill of the unknown remained. She was in uncharted territory.

He picked up the pace, fucking her so hard and fast she had trouble keeping her balance on the damn ball. Every stroke of his hard cock threatened to send her headfirst into the mat.

Even in his sexual delirium, he must have realized it,

because he tore himself unexpectedly from her body with a muffled growl of frustration and moved her onto her back. The mat was better than the wood floor, but it was still unforgiving. When he mounted her a second time with a hard thrust, she felt the impact on her shoulder blades, spine, and ass.

But any potential bruising was no more than a passing thought when Richard decided the time was right for the big finish. He took her repeatedly, muttering a string of broken, seemingly agonized imprecations. Her body absorbed his power, his hunger, his absolute determination to fuck her until they both collapsed.

She felt as limp as a rag doll and yet powerfully energized. When he reached between them to stroke her clit, a deep moan tore out of her throat. Her pelvis flooded with hot, crisp pleasure. One more stroke and then she shattered, mindless, helpless, in his embrace.

Richard never knew how he managed to stave off his climax when Melanie came apart beneath him. But he wanted to watch her. He wanted to study her face. She was luminescent in her ecstasy, and he felt humble pride that he had brought her to such a peak.

His own need for release was a sharp pain—a raw, insistent urge that took his breath and made him weak. But still he watched her.

She was a vibrant, beautiful woman. Strong. Passionate. Not in the least intimidated by him or frightened by his sexual hunger. She had matched him step for step in this erotic dance, and he was touched by her generosity and her willingness to be wicked and wanton.

Her eyelids had fluttered shut when she climaxed. Her chest now heaved in the aftermath with uneven breaths, and her lips were swollen and puffy from his demanding kisses. All in all, she looked like a well-fucked woman.

"Melanie." He whispered her name. Their bodies were still joined, his erect cock filling her.

She moved languorously, and finally opened her eyes. The tiny, pleased smile on her face spoke volumes.

He brushed the hair from her damp forehead. "How am I doing so far?" His words sounded hoarse, as though he could barely speak.

Her chest rose and fell in a sigh. "You keep stopping," she said plaintively. "I had my heart set on fireworks and harp music."

He flexed his hips, making both of them gasp. "From where I'm standing, I'd say you just had your fair share of fireworks, greedy miss."

She put her hands on his tensed forearms. "A girl can never have too many incendiary devices." As she teased him verbally, she taunted him physically with a firm inner squeeze on his dick.

"Ah." He was losing control. Knew it. Felt it. No matter how badly he wanted to stretch this out, he had come to the end of his rope.

He moved in and out, making her whimper. He was counting on her innate sensuality to wring out another orgasm. He flexed his hips, going deep, all the way to the mouth of her womb.

Her eyes glazed over and her chest heaved in a gasping cry. He did it again. Then he entered her from a slightly different angle and saw from her face when his erection hit that one all-important spot.

He tried to see her through—he really did. But the fireworks she'd requested exploded behind his own eyelids, and he felt as if a giant tsunami had yanked him to the top of a crest and thrown him into a violently tumbling wave.

The fire in his cock exploded in sharp bursts of completion. He hated the condom, wanted to feel every inch of her pussy as it milked him dry. But even as the flicker of regret jabbed him, his brain went blank and his body seized up in a fierce, lung-draining, heart-pounding, brain-blanking orgasm that went on and on and on until he fell on top of her, limp and barely able to move.

Neither the slender, naked woman, nor the large, naked man saw Thomas's reflection as he stood just outside the doorway.

Chapter Twelve

The climb back up to Oia at the top of the hill was equally as treacherous as the descent, but this time Debra held her husband's hand. And they took their time. Perhaps frequent sexual gymnastics kept the Russians in great physical shape, but whatever the reason, they beat Debra and Gordie to the summit.

The walk back up the road to the villas still lay ahead, though thankfully, it was far less steep. Yuri halted the group at an outside café. "We drink now," he said, summoning a waiter.

Debra sighed, but decided she might as well indulge. Perhaps another dose of alcohol-induced courage might stand her in good stead.

Yuri seemed to think it was a contest. He knocked back a glass of ouzo and followed it with a shot of Russian vodka. His taunting look at Gordon didn't have the desired effect.

Gordie was drinking, but Debra stifled a giggle when he leaned toward her and muttered under his breath.

She pretended to be overcome with passion and kissed his neck. "What was that?" she mumbled softly.

He made a show of turning to survey the crowd in the street. "I said, doesn't he know that a man's sexual performance can be adversely affected by too much booze?"

Debra snickered under her breath. "Well, Katya keeps filling your glass, so she must not be too worried about getting you in the sack."

By the time they started back, Debra was in a haze of well-being. She could handle this. It was just sex, not rocket science. All she had to do was let old Yuri have his way with her.

There were a few awkward moments back at the Russians' villa. Apparently Yuri and Katya hadn't worked out all the details in advance. After a fierce debate in rapid-fire Russian, the two hosts smiled in unison. "Is time?" They had the innocent look of excited children.

Debra felt Gordie squeeze her hand. His palm was as damp as hers. "Is time," he said hoarsely.

Debra wanted desperately to hold on to her husband, but Katya bore him away to a room at the back of the villa. Debra's throat went dry and her knees knocked as she turned back to face Yuri.

His dark eyes were hooded, his mouth set, austere. He no longer bore much resemblance to their expansive, jovial host. Instead, he had the look of a man intent on only one thing. Sex. With her.

He stalked her as she backed away in unconscious feminine apprehension. Yuri caught up in three quick strides. He cupped her face with his hands. "I want your mouth." It was an odd phrasing, but apt. His lips moved over hers roughly.

She tried to keep up, but he was slightly drunk, highly sexed, and fiercely determined. His tongue tangled with hers, probing roughly, stealing her breath. She tasted the alcohol he had consumed, felt its effects in the tremor of his fingers.

He was not that much taller than she was, but he had a tensile, wiry strength. One hand steadied her chin, while his firm arm behind her back urged her closer, forcing her to acknowledge his arousal.

She broke the kiss for a moment and gasped for air. "Can we slow this down, Yuri?"

Now both of his arms went around her waist. She and the randy Russian were locked thigh to thigh, chest to chest. He moved his hips suggestively. "Hard and fast. I take you that way. You like."

He was also arrogant and way too sure of himself. It pissed her off. "Listen, buster. I've already said I'll have sex with you. What's your big, damn hurry?"

He bit her bottom lip. "Get first one out of way. So we fuck many times."

That shut her up. And made the ache in her sex blossom into a full-fledged bout of plain old horniness. Yuri must have taken her stunned silence for acquiescence, because he dragged her toward the bedroom, muttering indecipherable words that sounded both desperate and determined.

The room was small, barely big enough to accommodate the full-size bed. The covers and pillows, inexplicably, had been stripped away and were tumbled in a pile on the rough wooden chair in the corner. Only the bottom sheet remained, and it was unbleached white cotton, no doubt fresh with the scent of sunshine and hot Greek breezes.

Yuri lowered her zipper and traced her spine with warm fingers. Her dress was still damp at the hem and bodice. It clung to her skin until he slowly peeled it away, revealing her breasts and finally her panties. He held her elbow as she stepped out of the pile of crimson cotton.

Yuri's gaze was cast down, making no pretense of looking at her face. He studied her almost-nude form for so long that she began to get restless. She didn't know what to do with her hands, so her arms hung by her sides as she concentrated on breathing normally.

Gordon had suggested letting Yuri take the lead. He'd said nothing about what to do if the Russian appeared to be struck dumb by his first glimpse of a naked Debra. She was on her own with this one.

Nerves made her tremble. Reluctant arousal caused her to press her thighs together to conceal the moist readiness of her sex. She felt light-headed with desire and confusion and too much wine, a lethal combination. She cleared her throat. "Ah, Yuri . . ."

He held up an imperative hand. "You no talk. I look now."

Still, his steady, focused gaze swept slowly over her body, pausing to inspect the mole on her left thigh, the pale, baby fine curls covering her pussy, the indent of her navel, the swell of her breasts, and finally—finally . . . her flushed face. She'd thought standing still beneath his visual reconnaissance was tough. It was infinitely easier than meeting his gaze squarely and acknowledging what was about to happen.

He touched her breast with a gentle fingertip. "Woman's body is like Russian church—gives awe."

She managed a small, incredulous chuckle. "Let's not get sacrilegious here, Yuri. I'd just as soon leave God out of this."

His fingernail scraped her nipple, making her shiver. "Sex is religious act."

"Um, no. It's not." If he was going to talk too much about churchy stuff, she was definitely going to lose her booze-assisted buzz. She spotted a candle on the bedside table. "Can we light that?" The bare bulb overhead wasn't very flattering.

Yuri turned away from her with reluctance. He took a box of matches from the windowsill, removed one, and struck it. As he bent to light the small waxy stub that looked home-made, she studied him intently.

His dark, wavy hair was thick and full. But something she'd gathered from his demeanor these last few days made her think he might be quite a bit older than she was. And he sure as hell had been around the block a few times in comparison to her sheltered life.

He straightened and blew out the match. A tang of acrid smoke teased her nose. When he reached for the switch and turned off the light, the room was plunged suddenly into intimate, cozy gloom.

Her heart beat in her throat as she realized there was no

way out. The die was cast. The gauntlet had been flung down. Ditto for any other cliché that pertained to her current situation.

The dancing flame made shadowy pictures on the white-washed ceiling. Yuri held out his hand. "On bed, my Debra. I will join you."

My Debra? Not hardly. This was a onetime offer. Still, he was a dramatic Russian. Perhaps he had a standard script for these things.

She scrambled onto the mattress with as much grace as she could muster. Lying flat on her back seemed odd, so she snagged one of the pillows and propped herself up against the headboard, lifting one knee and trying to look seductive. Thank God, there was no mirror over the tiny dresser to reflect her efforts.

Yuri paid her no mind as he stripped. Surprisingly, he'd gone commando beneath his slacks. Perhaps it was a European thing. Or maybe just a sexy Russian thing. Either way, he was naked and ready in mere seconds.

When he pulled his shirt over his head, she got her first glimpse of his chest. It was smooth and dark brown, meaning he either shaved or waxed . . . *and* spent a lot of time in the sun.

His penis was erect and handsome but not overlarge. It was uncircumcised, and as it bobbed at his groin, she could swear it almost had a personality of its own.

Yuri took his shaft in his hands and stroked it almost absently . . . like he wasn't paying attention to what he was doing. But while he stroked, he looked at Debra, as if she were a flesh-and-blood centerfold, and he was using her to jerk off to.

That odd thought lasted only a moment. Yuri bared his slightly crooked white teeth in a tense smile. "We fuck now. First time quick. Then I go slower for you."

His self-stimulation, perhaps aided by his perusal of her naked body, made his cock swell to satisfactory proportions. The head glistened in the glow from the candle, and the skin there was deep red like a plum.

He rolled on a condom and put one knee on the soft mattress. Debra lost her balance and tumbled toward him. He seized the opportunity and moved over her quickly, entering her with one fierce movement that buried his cock in her shocked pussy.

Could a pussy actually feel shock? Seemed like the answer was yes. Everything in her body stilled at his invasion. He was not heavy, but the sheer speed of his initial thrust and mount stunned her into speechlessness. Not that she wanted to talk, but sheesh . . . give a girl some warning.

She concentrated on the feel of him filling her pussy and pumping away at a staccato tempo. After the initial jolt of surprise, she had to admire his technique. It was like being screwed by a jackhammer.

Because of her nervous apprehension, it took her longer to get with the program. She was just starting to feel the first ripples of warm, sensual current fill her thighs and center in her sex when suddenly, with a hoarse shout, Yuri came, his face buried in her shoulder and his chest heaving as the last spasms of release shook him.

She lay there beneath him, stunned, disappointed, and wondering why Melanie's free-pass idea had ever seemed like a winner.

When Yuri appeared to be comatose, she stared up at the ceiling and studied the moving patterns of light and darkness. Should she slip away and go home? Gordie wouldn't like the idea of her walking alone at night, but then again, she didn't much care for the prospect of waiting around for Katya to finish with him.

Add to that her unsatisfied desire, and she was not a happy camper. This was supposed to be wild and fun and naughty. Instead, she was lying in a strange couple's bed, horny, disillusioned, and regretful.

Yuri growled something against her neck and started nibbling her collarbone. *Whoa. Apparently the man power-napped.*

He shifted to one side and leaned on his arm. That gave him access to her breasts . . . again. He plucked delicately at one nipple. "I come fast. My apology."

She closed her eyes and stifled a groan. *Damn, that felt good.* She licked her lips. "No problem. Plenty of time to take care of . . ." She trailed off, not sure how to phrase her request without sounding greedy.

His eyes narrowed. "I give you climax."

She was starting to get accustomed to his odd way with words, at least English ones. But did that last statement require an answer? Possibly not.

He left her for a nanosecond to dispense with the condom and returned to settle his face between her thighs. She was easy. Two strokes of his tongue, and she jerked and bucked and moaned in a stellar, vastly satisfying orgasm. It was spectacular.

He wiped his lips on her thigh. "We do again."

Somewhere around six she lost count. She was reduced to

begging. "Please, Yuri. Enough. I swear. You've made it up to me. We're cool. It's all good."

He ignored her and licked his way from her knee to her inner thigh. "We go for ten."

She grabbed his hair and one ear in the process. Hard tugging ensued. "Yuri. Seriously. I have to breathe." She still trembled from the last one. The man might be addicted to screwing, but he was a genius when it came to inducing the female orgasm.

She clamped her legs together, possibly smothering him, as she slammed into the next climax full-tilt, gasping and writhing as shattered.

"Please," she whispered, when she could speak. "Please, can we take a break?"

He fed her then. Grapes, figs, goat cheese. And, no surprise, more wine. He refused to let her leave the room and, instead, fetched the snack himself. Which meant that Debra had no opportunity to spy on Gordie and the Russian woman who was probably doing all manner of things to Debra's unsuspecting husband even at this very moment.

She desperately wanted to know how things were faring between Katya and him. Was Gordie as quick off the mark tonight as Yuri? Or had the alcohol he'd consumed enabled him to screw his partner long and slow, building the tension until they both snapped?

Thinking about it brought her need back to a low boil. Yuri forced another morsel of cheese between her lips. "Is protein," he murmured. "Good for stamina."

He was more creative with the grapes. He made her lie on her back so he could decorate her with the fruit. One grape resided in her navel. Three more were nested in the curls at her pussy.

Then he ate the fruit. It shouldn't have been that big a deal. The navel grape rolled into his mouth without protest. The three lower ones tickled a bit when he nuzzled her intimately and scooped them up.

But he wanted more than four. Before she could protest, he had centered two between her labia. No deeper. Nothing too kinky.

He played with his food, rubbing first one grape and then the other over her clitoris and back down. Inevitably, the skin of one split, and soon sticky, sweet juice mingled with her own damp essence.

She squirmed as heat built at her center. God, the man sure knew his produce. Every so often, his fingers took up where the grapes left off. The gradual crescendo of hunger surprised her. She twisted beneath his touch and gasped out a plea. "Yuri. Help me."

He swallowed the last grape and spread her thighs with firm hands. Again his talented tongue stroked her into a sharp, quick crest that left her breathless.

When she could breathe, she lifted a hand to his chest. "Don't you ever get tired?"

He chuckled, his face lighting up with genuine humor, for once this evening not tainted by lust. He played with her hair. It had long since fallen into disarray, and he combed through it with a tender smile. "You have good sex with Gordon?"

She nodded slowly. "The best. I love him very much. He's my soul mate."

The soft illumination cast his classic features into harsh shadows. He cocked his head, studying her dishevelment. "Does loving husband fuck you many ways?"

Her heartbeat stuttered to a stop. Alarm bells rang in her head. She summoned a weak smile. "Well, sure. We're like rabbits. Never a dull moment."

He grasped her ankle and lifted it to his shoulder. "In East we study many things. Learn how to give ultimate pleasure."

She wiggled her leg. "My pleasure's just fine, I swear. You did great tonight. And if you'll let me get dressed, I'll head home and let you get some sleep."

Yuri did something to the back of her knee that shot fire up her thigh and right into her pussy. Holy crap.

She trembled, then braced against the possibility of what might happen next. It was an awkward position, but when she tried to bend her knee, he kept it extended.

He reached into the drawer of the rough nightstand and found another candle, one that had never been burned. It was plain paraffin, perhaps an inch thick.

Debra began to get a bad feeling. She bucked in earnest, trying to get her leg back on the bed. But Yuri's strength defeated her.

He petted her pussy. "How you Americans say it? Chill out? I make you happy in your kitty."

She snorted. "That's pussy, crazy Russian man. And I'm already happy."

"Is more." He licked his thumb. Since in her current position she cold do absolutely nothing to stop him, she was forced to watch in a state of aroused suspense as he took his thickest digit and probed her anus.

Zings of illicit pleasure fanned out from the pressure he exerted. She clenched everything south of her navel instinctively. Yuri moved his thumb in a circle, making her gasp.

And then he picked up the candle. She knew such things were done. But not to her. And not by a relative stranger. "Yuri," she stuttered. "I've never . . ."

He pushed at her opening with the candle. "Until now." His quiet words accompanied the intrusion of a foreign object into her tense body. It felt huge. He took his time, nothing but tenderness in his approach. He gave her a moment to adjust and then eased the candle deeper.

Suddenly, she couldn't breathe. Her lungs quivered along with her heart, all organs jumping and wobbling behind her ribs, and her knees felt weak even though she wasn't standing. Her eyes squeezed shut.

He paused for a breath-starved moment. She couldn't tell how much of the length he had inserted. Three inches? Four?

He rubbed her cheeks. "Be brave, innocent little American woman. You like Yuri's game."

And then he began to play with her clit . . . lovely, intuitive caresses. The candle was still in place. There was no way she could come. Not like this. She was too disturbed . . . too tight . . . too afraid.

He leaned closer, forcing her leg even higher. The muscles in her thigh ached. He must have been holding the candle, because it didn't slide out.

Her body reached, aching for the release she craved, but part of her held back, terrified of what would happen if she climaxed in her current situation.

Yuri read her face and knew every thought in her head. He moved the candle slightly. "Let yourself go, little one. I am here to take care of you."

Her toes flexed, her heel digging into his shoulder. She didn't want to give in, but the more he stroked and pushed and stroked and pushed . . .

It was too much. Her brain didn't know where to concentrate. She arched her back and cried out as an intense, draining orgasm seized her entire body in a fiery grip and shook her until her world went black.

When she came to, Yuri was still lazily playing with her ass, this time sans candle. It distressed her that she felt empty now. He went down on her again, but she had nothing left to give. The rasp of his tongue was pleasant, but nothing more.

Finally, he released her foot. She curled on her side and drew both legs up against her chest. Yuri sat cross-legged on the bed, his cock erect and powerful. Their eyes met, his unreadable, hers probably full of the exhaustion she was feeling.

As he had done while standing, he once again stroked himself, as though he had all the time in the world. She knew he would want one last fuck. At least.

She wasn't sure she could handle it. She felt totally wiped out, both mentally and physically.

He was a smart man. He retrieved the second pillow from the chair and tucked it beneath her. "Get on stomach. I give you rub."

Did that mean a "massage"? She hoped so.

His hands on her back were firm and wonderful. He

knew something about anatomy for sure, because now instead of hitting the spots that triggered the libido, his steady pressure on her spine and shoulders lulled her to sleep. Just for a moment, she would let herself rest.

She was almost completely gone when she felt him lift her hips and tug one of the pillows lower. Her face was buried in her arms, and she didn't have the strength to question or protest. What more could he do?

The answer to the question came unexpectedly and shockingly. Still stupefied by sleep, she was helpless as he entered her pussy from behind while at the same time probing her ass with the candle.

The twin assaults sent waves of pleasure and tiny sparkles of pain throughout her nearly comatose body. It was like being awakened with a bucket of icy water after stumbling out of a warm bed. The contrast between her earlier contentment and this determined taking was unimaginable.

She struggled to lift up on her elbows, needing to brace herself. He wasn't a large man. In this position, she probably could have bucked him off. But despite her stunned state, she realized almost immediately that this was going to be even better than last time.

He stretched her more forcefully from this angle, and her body already recognized the violation of her ass and remembered the ensuing pleasure.

She pressed her face to the pillow and found his rhythm, rocking back into his steady dual penetration. Her clitoris had been abandoned, but oddly, her body seemed to have bypassed that circuitry and was rapidly finding another, equally satisfying path to the summit.

Her wrists ached, her ass ached, and her head ached from too much wine and the sexual excess of the night.

But none of that mattered.

Yuri pinched her ass cheeks with his free hand. He bent forward, forcing the candle deeper. She gasped and groaned and her limbs quivered. She felt his tongue trace a damp path down her spine.

He reached beneath her and found a nipple to twist and pinch until she shrieked and bucked and felt herself shatter in a million pieces that might never find their way back together.

He waited for her to catch her breath . . . barely a moment. Then he cursed in Russian, jerked out the candle, and pistoned his hips until she felt him give in at last to a gargantuan climax.

But he wasn't through. He whipped her onto her back, put her feet on his shoulders and entered with his still erect penis. The new position let him go painfully deep, so deep she felt as if he had permanently marked her.

She imagined him screwing Katya like this. And then she saw Gordie as well. Now in her head both men fucked the petite Russian woman. Yuri lifted her and supported her as Gordon stood against the wall. Gordie opened her with his thumbs and seated her on his bobbing erection.

The Russian stood behind her, fondling her ass and using the same candle to penetrate her.

The fantasy was so real, so raw, so deeply arousing that one last tremulous orgasm found its way to the top and rippled through her in a gentle wave.

She felt tears sting the backs of her eyes. She wanted

Gordie. She needed to cuddle with him and pull herself back together. This night was one she would never forget, but for now she needed the old and familiar.

As Yuri made one last thrust and reached one final blissful shore, Debra's hand clenched a fistful of sheet and wondered what she had done.

Chapter Thirteen

Cherisse didn't wear a swimsuit to the beach. She dressed for sex instead, donning an expensive bra-and-panty set in a shade of peach that flattered her coloring. The bra added to her already ample cleavage, and she wore a thin white cotton blouse that fastened up the front so she could leave several buttons open.

Her legs were average and curvy rather than long and lean, but she wore a pair of abbreviated navy shorts that hugged her ass nicely and made her feel stylish.

Shoes were a problem. She had a brand-new pair of trendy sandals, but for beach walking, it was clear that flip-flops were the best choice.

She'd wanted Wesley to sleep in, but he had insisted on driving her down to the beach. On the way, the tension in the car was palpable, each of them thinking about the day ahead. Because of the hour, Wesley found a parking spot on the street and got out for a minute. She rounded the car and went up on her tiptoes to give him a kiss. "Thank you for bringing me."

His chin was still covered with stubble, and he had dark circles under his eyes. She wondered if he had tossed and turned like she had.

He played with a piece of her hair, his hip propped against the car door. "So we're both down with the plan?"

She nodded, amused at his visible nerves...though she would never tease him about it. "Yes, sir." She saluted smartly. "I'll walk on the beach with Danny. Then I'll suggest break-fast someplace with a sit-down meal. Afterward, I'll invite him back to the condo. By then you should already be meet-ing up with Melinda."

"And when either of is—" He stopped abruptly, obvi-ously realizing that what he was about to say sounded crass. He gnawed his lip. "Uh . . ."

She smoothed his sleep-tousled hair. "I understand. We text each other. Me to let you know when the coast is clear to come home, and you to let me know when you're leaving the woman's apartment or whatever."

He rubbed a hand over his chin. "Do you still want to do this?" His gaze was troubled.

She looked around her at the quiet streets that would soon be filled with all manner of people—straight and gay, attached and single, locals and tourists. All of them looking for something in South Beach.

Was she any less of an adventurer?

Finally, she looked at her husband. Nothing about his

demeanor this morning matched the excitement he had exhibited yesterday afternoon. She sighed. "Do you?"

He rolled his eyes. "At the risk of sounding juvenile, I asked you first."

Well, damn, that was no help. She sucked in a breath and took the plunge. "Yes," she said firmly. "I do."

The slight frown between his eyebrows disappeared, and his face cleared. "Well, in that case . . ." He grabbed her close and kissed her roughly.

She retuned the kiss eagerly. He tasted of toothpaste and coffee. She felt the erection he didn't bother to hide and pressed against him boldly. "In that case, what?" Her heart was beating fast, and she was tempted to get back in the car and tell him to drive like hell.

He cupped her ass and rubbed it slowly. "In that case, my adorable, sexy wife . . . go get your man."

The beach at this hour was lovely. The light breeze ruffled the water and actually seemed cool at first. But when Danny didn't show, her blood pressure shot up and she started to sweat.

Only a few lone people dotted the sand, and it was likely that not one of them had any interest in her or her plans. But she was still embarrassed and humiliated and angry with herself. Why in the hell would a hot, young stud lifeguard want to fool around with a ten-pounds-too-heavy woman who was no longer in her twenties? A woman who had forgotten everything she had ever known about picking up a guy.

She hovered near the lifeguard stand, which was their

appointed meeting place. Ten paces in one direction. Ten paces back. She was going to have to go home and admit that her free-pass guy had stood her up. That would do wonders for her self-esteem.

Muttering beneath her breath and working herself into a state of frustrated, angry panic, she jumped a foot off the sand when a hand tapped her shoulder.

"Hey, Cherisse." There he stood in all his hard-bodied, golden blond glory. "Sorry I'm late. My alarm didn't go off."

Deep breaths, Cherisse. Deep breaths. She wanted to blast him . . . wanted to tell him that a woman's self-confidence was a fragile, delicate thing. But she didn't. She swallowed all her frazzled, manic nerves and gave him the best smile she could muster at the moment.

She tucked her hair behind her ear, wondering why she'd let vanity tempt her to leave it loose in this humidity. "Hi, Danny," she said simply. "I'm glad to see you."

He slung an arm around her shoulders as they fell into step with a natural rhythm and headed down the beach. "I wasn't sure you'd come."

The tone of his voice was casual. Perhaps he wouldn't have cared either way. He probably had enough opportunities for sex that one hookup more or less, here or there, didn't matter.

She sighed inwardly and pledged to quit overanalyzing this. It was a go-with-the-flow kind of moment.

They chatted comfortably as they walked. Danny had been in the area for a while, and he was a natural raconteur, keeping her entertained with anecdotes about famous people, local scandals, and bits and pieces of his own life.

Finally she worked up her courage and got to the point. She kept walking, not looking at him as she spoke. "I guess you figured out that I want to have sex with you."

He nodded slowly. "But I'm not sure why. You're wearing a ring."

She flushed, feeling guilty for no good reason. "We decided to spice up our marriage by each having a onetime fling. Sort of a free pass."

He made some kind of sound that wasn't quite a laugh. "Sounds dangerous."

"Why?"

"The lure of the forbidden can be a powerful thing. Makes people crazy sometimes."

"But that's just it," she said earnestly, wanting him to understand. "It's not forbidden. Not on this one occasion. We've both agreed."

"What if your husband decides he likes his free-pass woman more than you?"

It was a valid question, but Danny didn't know Wesley. Her husband was a loving and honorable man. "I'm not worried about that," she said calmly. "Our relationship is strong enough to risk something like this."

The subject was closed as far as she was concerned. But that didn't mean she couldn't pump Danny for more info. Her natural curiosity kept prompting her to ask him questions. If part of it was a desire to know something about the man with whom she was planning to get naked, then so what? There was nothing wrong with needing the semblance of a connection.

In truth, they had little in common other than a liking

for a few of the same television shows and an inclination to vote the Democratic ticket.

They walked for an hour, and the conversation and companionship were surprisingly easy once Cherisse got over her initial meltdown. Danny had a sly wit, but he wasn't unkind. Had they met in other circumstances, she would have been happy to count him as a friend.

When her stomach began growling audibly, he laughed at her and suggested breakfast ASAP.

She scanned the buildings nearby. "Do you have any suggestions?"

He stared at her with a challenging grin. "Are you a picky eater?"

She shrugged. "Not really. I'd just as soon avoid anything with raw fish or runny eggs, but other than that, what did you have in mind?"

He grabbed her wrist and tugged her in the direction of the street. "Come on. You'll love it."

"It" turned out to be a Cuban restaurant called La Familia Mia. The modest, narrow location was nothing to look at. It was tucked away on a narrow side street, and the large plate-glass front window was painted with neon scenes of Havana.

Cherisse would probably never have picked it on her own, but Danny's enthusiasm convinced her. Over coffee laced with fresh cinnamon, he teased her gently. "If I'm supposed to be your free-pass guy, shouldn't we get down to business pretty soon?"

Cherisse raised an eyebrow. "I didn't know we were on a timetable."

He shrugged, still grinning. "Maybe I'm eager."

Those three little words shifted the morning into a different gear. She felt her cheeks get hot, and she glanced away, unable to hold his gaze. A lump in her throat made it hard to speak.

He touched her hand. "Cherisse?"

She swallowed hard. "Am I your charity case?"

He frowned. "What in the hell does that mean?"

She shrugged, mad at herself for being so needy. "I'm married, and not so young. I just wondered if you were doing me a favor."

He sat back in his chair and rolled his eyes. "Jeez, women are so damned convoluted. I was *flattered*, Cherisse. Flattered that you wanted to have sex with me. I thought it would be fun with you. So I said yes. That's all. And I've been looking forward to it ever since."

"You swear?" She traced her finger in the small circle of sugar one of them had spilled on the Formica tabletop.

This time he took her hand in his. She was surprised to see that her fingers appeared small and delicate wrapped in his big palm. He held her chin and tipped it up, forcing her to look at him.

She wrinkled her nose. "Sorry. I've never done this before."

His thumb stroked the side of her face. "Are you sure it's the thing to do? There's no dishonor in walking away, though I must say I'd be damned disappointed."

She quivered when he wiped sugary residue from her top lip. He'd been feeding her fried plantains. She looked into his eyes bravely and felt the bottom drop out of her stomach.

This was not just some stereotypical guy with big biceps and a taut ass. He was a man with feelings and dreams and hang-ups like anyone else.

She wasn't sure she appreciated the insight. It was much easier when she was treating him like her own private boy toy.

She pulled back and his hands fell away. His eyes had narrowed and a slight frown appeared above the bridge of his nose.

She cocked her head and studied his face. "What's your favorite color?

"Green." He didn't miss a beat.

"Where do you spend Christmas?"

"At my grandma's in Iowa."

"Do you have siblings?"

"Two sisters." He paused and rolled his eyes. "Both older—they're pains in the ass."

She smiled faintly. He sounded like the boy next door, which was neither here nor there when it came to his availability as a sex partner.

She bowed her head momentarily and then looked into his beautiful bottle green eyes. "Yes," she said simply. "I'm sure."

Danny was the one to flush this time. He moved restlessly in his seat and lifted a hand to catch the waitress's attention. The whole time he was paying the check and finishing his drink and keeping up his end of the conversation, Cherisse noticed that he seemed tense. Was he thinking about what was going to happen next?

Finally, they were out on the street. It was almost ten, and shops all around them were beginning to open. Danny looked down at her. "What now, Cherisse?" He asked it simply, acknowledging the fact that this was her show.

She took his hand in hers and linked their fingers. "Now," she said, her heart in her throat, "now we go back to my place."

Public transportation was not the most romantic of venues for the beginning of a tryst. Cherisse had relied on Wesley to drop her off, and Danny didn't have a car. She could have called a taxi, but she didn't want him to think she was above using the bus.

So with Danny's input, they decided where they needed to stand to catch the appropriate route, and then they waited. Cherisse hated waiting. Anytime. But standing next to a stranger who might possibly, probably be seeing her naked very shortly, it was agonizing.

Finally, after about three years, the bus arrived. The passengers were an eclectic crowd. Some were plugged in to music. Others were wrestling with children. And one group— the older ones who might be headed off to jobs in the service industry—stared straight ahead, their stoic faces blank and expressionless.

Cherisse was willing to bet that not one of them was about to have extramarital sex with a stranger.

Simple things began to take on gargantuan significance— stepping off the bus, riding up in the elevator, finding the door to her condo and opening it.

She accomplished all that without freaking out, but when they stood in the foyer of her vacation rental, her muscles locked up, her brain went blank, and she went numb.

Danny stood behind her and rubbed her shoulders. "You've never done this before, have you?"

She frowned. "No. Of course not. I told you this is a one-time deal."

He moved to face her and shoved his hands into her hair, anchoring her head for a kiss that took her by surprise. His hunger was shocking. All morning he had seemed calm and laid-back . . . without a care in the world.

Had he wanted her all this time?

He ravaged her mouth, learning the taste of her, nipping her bottom lip with sharp teeth. He had a hand at her back, keeping her hips pressed to his. His erection nestled into her belly.

Her body wrested control from her mind at last, and she relaxed enough to feel the first genuine tingles of arousal. It made her feel good. Knowing he wanted to have sex with her was an affirmation of her sexuality. Wesley wanted her, of course, but to have this young, attractive man so clearly in need of her was a huge boost to her ego.

Soon even those selfish considerations faded away. She ceased to think about the free-pass aspect of what she was doing. Sexual hunger took over, driving her body to respond in instinctive, ancient ways.

Her breasts swelled and ached. The pit of her stomach quivered as coils of fire twisted and writhed in her belly and settled in her sex. She was shaking, trembling, ravenous for what Danny could give her. Sexual oblivion. Erotic excess. Primitive satisfaction.

He broke the kiss and scooped her up in his arms. "Which way?" he asked, his voice hoarse. Her flip-flops tumbled to the floor and neither of them noticed or cared.

She pointed a finger, unable to formulate words. As he strode toward the bedroom she shared with Wesley, she ran her fingers over Danny's smooth-shaven chin. It was disarming to realize that despite the fact he'd overslept, he had taken the time to prepare for her.

The bedroom door was pulled to but not closed. Danny kicked it aside, hard enough to make it bounce off the wall and hit him in the shoulder. He barely flinched.

Male behavior was unpredictable. She thought he would drop her on the bed. Instead, he set her on her feet and began undressing her.

Suddenly it seemed as if all his urgency had drained away. Her shirt fluttered to the floor. He helped her step out of her shorts and then he stopped.

She was glad she had chosen the ultrafeminine lingerie. He skated his hands lightly over her body from her neck to her waist. His gaze dwelt the longest on her full breasts. He traced the curve of first one and then the other, pausing to ruffle the lacy edge of the bra.

He bent his head and licked those same curves. He scooped the twin globes into his palms and plumped them, squeezing until she gasped. Just when she thought he would remove the bra, he stopped.

She shifted her feet, wishing she felt more confident. "I'm chunky, I know. I guess you're used to screwing skinny women."

Now his hands started at her waist and moved to her hips. He kissed her softly. "You're beautiful, Cherisse. Drop-dead gorgeous, in fact."

He played with her panties, tracing the elastic at her legs, tugging lightly at the waistband. When he palmed her crotch, she gasped and blushed. The damp nylon was a dead giveaway.

He rubbed his middle finger in the crease, pressing the fabric into her pussy. She moaned and closed her eyes. She was so close to coming, she could taste it. He continued the gentle but erotic caress, toying with the folds of her sex through the thin barrier of her underwear.

He was breathing harshly, though everything else about his behavior was infinitely tender. His thumb grazed her clitoris, and she trembled violently.

Now he dropped to his knees and pressed his mouth to the front of her panties. His hot breath made her shiver. She wanted to rip away the barrier between them and drag his head closer still.

When he stopped, she whimpered in protest. He stood up and tugged his teal T-shirt over his head. A light, golden fuzz of hair dusted his pecs and arrowed down to his groin. When he stepped out of his jeans and briefs, she held her breath. He was beautiful.

His muscles were sleek and well-defined, but he was lean and not bulked up. His penis was long and slender and curved slightly at the end. It was already fully erect. And it quivered with eagerness.

Without thinking or questioning her response, not waiting to second-guess her actions, she reached out her hand and took him in her palm. She could easily wrap both fists around his length. And she did.

His face contorted as if in pain when she began stroking him gently. Suddenly, he went rigid, and jets of white semen spurted from the head of his cock and ran down over her clenched fingers.

Instinctively, she kept up her dual massage until the last pulses of come oozed and pooled on her knuckles.

A sharp slash of red marked his cheekbones. "God, I'm sorry, Cherisse." The look in his eyes was sheer mortification.

She kissed his chest and gave one last squeeze to his penis before she released him. "Don't be silly. You're good for my ego."

She led him into the bathroom, and they both cleaned up. Their eyes met in the mirror. The commonplace rituals of soap and water were oddly intimate.

He followed her back to the bedroom and joined her under the covers. The air-conditioning was on high, and she was chilled. She still wore her pretty underwear.

He pulled her close, each of them on their sides. Now they lay chest to chest, and she realized that his cock was almost back at full salute.

It felt good pressing against her, rubbing her mound. If she lifted her leg, she could join her body to Danny's with little trouble at all. But she wanted to stretch out the pleasure . . . not let it end too soon.

He kissed her softly, tenderly . . . taking her bottom lip into his mouth and sucking on it gently.

That firm tug pulsed inexplicably between her legs as well. She was greedy suddenly, wanting orgasms by the score. Needing to screw over and over in wild, extravagant sex that went on for hours.

She brushed her fingers through his hair, traced his nose, his eyelids, his chin. "It still counts as one time if we never stop," she whispered.

He groaned, his hips moving restlessly in search of a connection with her. "I'm game if you are."

Her neck felt hot. Her limbs were tingling. "I'm warm enough," she muttered. "Get rid of the covers." She wanted to see him, to visually record the image of him in her bed for later fantasies.

He shoved aside the comforter and sheet and paused to rake a lustful gaze from her toes all the way up to her passion-flushed face. He leaned on one elbow and focused again on her breasts. He was clearly fascinated by their fullness and responsiveness.

Her firm nipples alone were enough to tell him how much she needed him and how deeply aroused she was. She wanted him to bite them, but she was too shy to ask. He seemed extremely turned on just by looking at her, and in no hurry to get rid of the sexy undies.

He placed his palm on her stomach. "Tell me what you want, Cherisse. Tell me how to please you."

She squirmed, needing the hand to move lower. "I'm easy to please," she joked. "Anything you want." Then she stopped, her innate caution getting in the way. "Well, within reason."

He threw back his head and laughed, and the moment lightened the tension between them, helping Cherisee to relax. She smiled at him lazily, bending her knee and rubbing her leg against his. "I'm generally a bit more naked in situations like this," she murmured.

He lifted an eyebrow and gave her a tight grin—one that said his arousal had not abated despite their teasing. "You look like a centerfold," he said. "I'm enjoying the ambience."

She shook her head on the pillow and huffed. "What is it with men and breasts? Besides, wouldn't you rather see them au naturel?"

He ignored her question and plucked a condom package from the bedside table. After rolling the condom on in short order, he moved over her and settled between her legs, spreading her thighs and sending a jolt through her abdomen. Now he stared down at her, his gaze hot and determined. "I'll get to the unveiling for round two," he promised gruffly. "But first I want to fuck you just like you are, all pink and soft and ripe like a peach."

He cupped her breast again and ran his thumb over the lace. "God, your tits are amazing."

He had yet to remove her panties, but that didn't seem to stop him. He put a hand between her legs and moved the narrow strip of nylon to one side. Then he held his long cock and centered it for a slow, steady push.

Cherisse sucked in a startled breath. Perhaps his cock was slender, but the length more than made up for it. She felt like he was going deep enough to fill her belly. It was an unusual sensation, deliciously so. He probed gently, realizing he was as far as he could go.

His teeth were locked in a pained grimace. "Arch your back," he begged.

She planted her feet flat on the bed, knees bent, and lifted into him. That gained them at least another inch. Now she felt pressure everywhere, like he was possessing places in her body she'd never opened to anyone. A tremor in her abdomen spread to her legs, her chest, her arms.

She knew she was about to come unglued, and he had barely begun. "Do it," she urged. "Do it now."

He was immensely cooperative . . . flatteringly focused . . . athletically adept. When he began fucking her in earnest, it was like a wildfire sweeping over the dry Florida grasslands. She wanted to savor the slow build to release, but instead, she was jerked up into a maelstrom of raw sexual urgency.

He entered her again and again, occasionally with slow, pure grace, but mostly with ragged, out-of-control lunges that made them both crazy.

Her thighs ached. Her pussy ached. Her spine ached from meeting him thrust for thrust.

He rested his forehead on hers, his damp chest heaving, and heat radiating off him like a sun too near the earth. It was odd not to exchange words of love, but she reminded herself hazily that this was all about sex.

His back bowed, his hips flexed, and his eyes squeezed shut as he chanted, "Shit, shit. Shit."

He hammered into her, taking her body like sexual plunder, ripping her out of her complacent fantasy and shooting her into a climax that lasted forever . . . or at least until her husband decided he wanted to come home.

Chapter Fourteen

Thomas staggered back from the doorway. *Sweet Jesus.* He couldn't believe what he was seeing. His Melanie, on her hands and knees, being screwed by an enormous mountain of a guy. And she was loving it. A lot.

The image was burned into Thomas's brain. Carnal. Evocative. More arousing than the most flagrant porno flick. He risked another look and trembled as lust and anger made a deadly cocktail in his gut.

He should have flown into a murderous rage. Most men would have. But instead, he was so horny, he thought he might die. The sexual arousal trumped the distress . . . barely. His dick had solidified into a steel rod. He massaged himself slowly through his slacks, wanting desperately to jerk off, but not wanting to miss any of the titillating floor show, pardon the pun.

He had never dreamed when he stopped by the gym that

he would stumble across something like this. He didn't like for Melanie to walk to her car alone after hours, so he'd dropped by to make sure she was okay. He had his own keys and knew the alarm code, so he'd entered the gym not long after nine o'clock.

As he'd expected, Melanie's car had still been in the parking lot . . . along with one other. A dark sedan with out-of-town plates. Even then he hadn't understood what was happening. He'd walked into the outer office and stopped dead when he heard the noises inside.

Sex noises. Panting, heavy breathing, Melanie's little cries of pleasure.

He'd been caught in a net of conflicting emotions. And the most surprising one had been jealousy. For all his big speeches and magnanimous posturing, he was sick with it. He wanted to burst through the door and rip the guy's genitals from his body. How dared he touch Melanie? How dared he taste her mouth, feel her breasts . . . inhale her essence? The whole scenario turned him psycho.

He'd hidden just outside Mel's office, risking one quick peek through the crack where the door met the frame. His tiny slice of the erotic picture was enough to tell him what was going on.

He slumped against the wall, not worried about being caught. The two inside wouldn't have noticed if he had cleared his throat or shouted their names, so intent were they on each other.

It had caught him off guard when the big man decided to move the game to another venue. Thomas was forced to scramble beneath Melanie's desk until they were gone. After a decent interval, he'd followed them to the large exercise classroom, led by the sound of their voices.

This bit of voyeurism was far more difficult. He was easily able to peek through the door and see the entire scene played out in the mirror. Every last sensual detail. Melanie's lithe, slender body. Her lover's streamlined bulk. The moment another man slid his dick into Melanie's pussy and fucked her hard.

Thomas ground his teeth together against the urge to groan in amazement. *He'd agreed to this? Was he a moron?* It was entirely his fault that Melanie was at this very moment getting pounded by a strange cock. Thomas might as well have pimped for her.

All he would have had to do when Mel brought up the idea was to talk her out of it. She respected his opinions. If he'd convinced her it was a bad idea, she would have dropped it.

But no . . . he'd been all smiles and congeniality, assuring her that she should go for it and that he would think about it as well. Now Melanie was exercising her option (why in the hell was he suddenly full of puns?), and Thomas was hiding in the shadows like a stalker, watching while another fellow played sex games with his wife.

The couple in the room changed positions. In the mirror, Thomas watched the pale pink ball roll slowly out of his field of vision. Unfortunately, the duo on the mat didn't disappear. Melanie was on her back now, and the guy was mounting her enthusiastically.

Thomas saw his wife's legs go around the man's back . . .

heard his wife moan . . . saw both of them strain and shudder in each other's arms.

Thomas slid down the wall and plopped butt down on the floor. Frantically, he lowered his zipper, released his prick, and gripped it. It hurt to touch himself. That was how wound up he was.

He squeezed the shaft, running his thumb from the base up over the head. The mix of pain and pleasure left him breathless. He came close to whimpering like a little girl. He cupped his balls in his free hand and rubbed them slowly. *Holy hell.* He felt like razor blades were raking the inside of his dick.

He tried to pump vigorously, but the stimulation was too much. He was forced to go slowly. The sounds from inside the room were a muffled counterpoint to his frantic, jagged breaths, his grunts of discomfort.

He wanted to come . . . desperately. But fear of discovery hampered his efforts. And the more he thought of being found out, the harder his cock became.

He sobbed out her name under his breath. *Melanie . . . dear God, Melanie.* But no one was coming to his aid, least of all his wife. He grabbed his cock in both hands and worked it violently. He was no longer able to separate the agony from the pleasure. It was all one big knot of sharp, pounding sensation.

He closed his eyes, imagined the scene in the mirror, remembered the moment when his wife's lips had closed over that man's cock, and suddenly, in one sharp, devastating burst, he groaned and cursed and exploded in a massive orgasm that was more pain that pleasure.

He was trembling and shaky, his hands sticky with his

own come, when he heard voices again. Shit. They were finished. He caught the two sides of his zipper together and stumbled to his feet. He was forced to shuffle awkwardly around the corner and crouch beside the vending machine until the coast was clear.

From here he could neither see nor hear the denouement, but perhaps that was his punishment for being such a clueless dickhead.

Melanie found her voice. "I can't breathe. You weigh a ton."

Richard wheezed something that sounded like a cross between a laugh and a protest, but he rolled to one side. He kept one big arm across her stomach, perhaps to anchor her to the mat in case he decided they weren't finished. He was a man with strong opinions.

Melanie floated in a sexual haze. She *felt* finished. In fact, she felt like the survivor of a war game. But simmering just below the surface was the knowledge that she could be persuaded, with very little effort, to spread her legs again... making her every bit as easy as that slut on the high school volleyball team who'd tried to sleep her way through all the jocks.

Melanie closed her eyes and drifted. Richard's heavy arm was not an unpleasant weight. Without it she had the strange notion that her body might levitate toward the ceiling, light and sated and happy.

He groaned and rolled to his side, resting his head on his hand. "Well?"

His eyelids were at half mast, and he looked rumpled and sleepy and satisfied. But the gleam in his eyes was predatory, nevertheless.

She arched her neck and lifted her arms straight over-head. Her muscles had just gotten a very unorthodox work-out. "I'd give you a nine point five."

He frowned. "What was the problem?"

She rolled her eyes. Men, always so competitive. "That's a fabulous score."

"I can do better," he muttered. He closed his eyes. "A salesman always strives for perfection."

She tugged the hair on his chest. "Can't you be satisfied with what I gave you?"

He lifted on eyelid. "Apparently not. Clearly, I'm not ever going to be satisfied when it comes to you."

That was nice . . . syrupy, but nice.

She glanced at the clock on the wall. "Oh, shit." She scrambled to her feet, looking frantically for her dress. The woman in the mirror was an embarrassment.

He reared up on both elbows this time. "What's wrong, darlin'?"

"Thomas will be expecting me home. He'll think I've been mugged."

"So call him."

She wriggled her hips into the dress, slid her arms through the holes, and did a contortion dance to get it zipped. "I can't. He'll be able to tell from my conversation that I've had sex."

"Seriously?" Richard was still reclining, big and nude and endlessly tempting.

She smoothed her skirt. "He says my voice gets all low and smoky after we do it." She paused to glare at him. "Get up, for heaven's sake. Grab your stuff. We both need to get out of here."

She scooted him to the door, her hands all over his bare ass. "Hurry."

Thomas followed them surreptitiously. At least Melanie now had some clothes on.

He lingered in a side hallway while the man she called Richard went back into her office with her so they could gather up the rest of her things and his.

Thomas hovered in the shadows, waiting for them to exit the outer office. He was forced to endure the sight of Melanie, in her sexy black high heels, going up on tiptoe to kiss the guy good night.

She wasn't tall enough. The guy lifted her off her feet with ease and covered her lips with his, kissing her long and hard, his massive arms wrapped around her waist. When he released her, she slid down his body, making him groan. Thomas assumed the guy had another boner.

The man cupped Melanie's face. "Are you going to leave me like this?"

"I told you it was a one-shot deal." Thomas swore he heard regret in her voice.

The man took her hand and placed it over his crotch. "We could consider this all one incident."

Melanie's small hand moved slowly, massaging the guy's enormous erection. "I can't," she said simply. "It wouldn't be fair to Thomas."

Both lovers walked to the front doors, the man's arm around her shoulders, her body close to his.

Thomas had moved behind them, wraithlike, so he could hear their goodbyes.

Melanie stroked the man's arm. "Thank you, Richard. You were amazing."

He shrugged, his expression wry. "That's cold comfort, married Melanie. I feel like I've won the lottery and then found out my ticket was a fake."

She winced. "Don't say that. You're going to find a woman so perfect for you, you'll wonder why you ever thought you were happy going it alone. I promise."

He gave her one last kiss. "If you stumble across another free pass, give me a call."

Melanie followed him out and locked the doors. Through the glass, Thomas saw them exchange one last brief kiss, go to their separate cars, and drive away. Clearly, Melanie was too distracted to notice her husband's car parked in the shadows.

Thomas waited until they had cleared the parking lot, then went out as well. The route home was the same one they always used, so it wasn't hard to tail his wife.

He drove on autopilot, his brain fried by what he had seen and done. This wasn't his life. This was a damn soap opera.

Fifteen minutes later, he saw her drive up to their house, use the remote to open the garage door, and pull inside. When the door met the ground, Thomas parked behind it.

He sat in his vehicle waiting for the upstairs bedroom light to flip on. She was probably wondering about her husband's whereabouts.

Eventually, he let himself in quietly and went up the steps. The carpet muffled any sounds he might have made. When he walked into their bedroom, Melanie was standing in front of the dresser. She was still wearing the black dress she'd had on at dinner.

She whirled around, her hand over her heart, clutching a pair of pink cotton panties to her chest. "Gosh, Thomas. You scared me to death. Where have you been?"

He wanted to say "out" in a snotty, dramatic voice, but he resisted.

Instead, he made some noncommittal answer and crossed the room. He took her shoulders in his hands and gripped them. It required every acting skill he possessed not to let her see how upset and freaked out he was.

He forced a smile. "I've been horny all evening since you went back to the gym. Did you spike my wine at dinner with some mysterious aphrodisiac?"

His teasing words seemed to confuse her. Her gaze was troubled. When he cupped her breast through the black dress, she stiffened.

He ignored her body language and kissed the side of her neck, opting for the plain, unvarnished truth. "I want you," he groaned. "Now."

She pushed back, her face first pale, then rosy. "Let me shower first."

He held her at arm's length. "Is that so you can wash away the smell of another man on your skin and between your legs?" He said it quietly, as though it was a normal question.

Melanie trembled in his grasp. "How did you know?" Her eyes were huge. She was agitated and guilty-looking, and sexy as hell.

"I went to the gym a little after closing to make sure you got home okay. When I unlocked the door and went in, I found you—"

Now she was dead white, apprehension written in her expression. Her sharp interruption held panic. "How much of it did you . . ."

He released her and folded his arms across his chest. "Pretty much all of it."

She gulped. "I didn't know it was going to happen tonight, I swear. I would have told you before. And I was planning to tell you at home . . . later. . . ."

He grinned tightly, though to tell the truth, his gut was churning and as unsettled as a storm at sea. "Calm down, Mel. I'm not mad."

Her chin wobbled. "You're not?"

He unfastened his belt and started unbuttoning his shirt. "Nope. We talked about it . . . agreed to it. . . . You did it . . . end of story."

She followed him around the bedroom like a puppy as he tossed bits and pieces of his wardrobe here and there. She didn't seem to notice that he was now wearing only his boxers and that his erection made a bold tent in the fabric. He hadn't added anything else after his last, conversation-stopping statement. He was waiting to see what Melanie would do or say next.

He stopped suddenly, and she bumped into his back. She stumbled. He turned and caught her, dragging her to his chest and holding her tight. "Mel?"

She circled her arms around his neck and clung. "I adore you, Thomas. You know that, right?"

It pained him that she thought he needed reassurance, even though she was right. He kissed her softly. "I know. Don't worry about me. I can deal with the awful pictures in my head."

She punched him in the arm, her nervous giggle laced with relief. "Don't joke about it. You're making me self-conscious."

"Well, we wouldn't want that." He lowered her zipper and tried not to remember who else had carried out a similar action that evening. "Step out of this."

Melanie struggled slightly but obeyed. "I'm serious, Thomas. I need a shower."

He tumbled her to the bed and moved over her, sliding a knee between her legs. He kissed her roughly. "I need *you* . . . now."

He actually tore her panties. The look on her face was priceless. Her mouth moved but nothing came out. He pinned her to the mattress with his hips. "Cat got your tongue, Melanie?"

She swallowed hard. "I don't understand you," she whispered.

He shrugged. "I'm apparently not a highly evolved male. Not only does it make me damn hot to think of fucking you after he's had you, but I also have this strong need to stake my claim." He cupped her breast and squeezed it. "Can you deal with that?"

He shed his boxers and ripped away the remnants of her expensive undies. Melanie watched him, big-eyed. He got on his knees between her spread legs and stroked her thighs. This was the intimate view to which her free-pass guy had been privy. The man must have thought he was the luckiest bastard on earth.

Thomas tried to imagine seeing Melanie's supple, toned body for the first time, tasting her sex, touching her soft skin. His erection swelled to painful proportions. He remembered the first day he'd met her. He'd fallen in lust instantly and in love during the next month. They'd married not long after.

She was watching him warily, as if she was afraid to say or do anything that night set him off. Even though he'd maintained his facade of cool, civilized manners, she knew him well. She'd probably picked up on his inner turmoil. He felt the need to apologize somehow, but he'd be damned if he would. He couldn't help the way he felt.

He was brooding, not willing to give in to his sexual hunger. He could hold out. Maybe.

She tried to sit up. "Are you okay, Thomas?" Her expression was troubled. "I'd never intentionally do anything to hurt you. And I really did think you would be the one to do this first."

He scowled. "How do you know I'm going to?"

She sat cross-legged, exposing every one of her secrets to his lustful gaze. He shivered and closed his eyes, his palms on his thighs. He sucked in great lungfuls of air, trying to find calm.

She stroked his knee. "You promised you would think about it. I don't want you to get bored with married sex. If you find someone who attracts you and is available, why wouldn't you?"

He settled down beside her, stretching out on his back and wincing at the ache in his groin. He was in a bad way. He tugged her hand. "Get on top." He wanted her in a position in which gym guy hadn't taken her.

Melanie straddled him and lowered herself onto his cock. The feeling was indescribable. As she sheathed him in her tight pussy, it was like being squeezed by a warm, wet glove. He panted, concentrating on anything that would enable him not to come instantly.

That would be hell on his ego at the moment.

Melanie was like a dog with a bone. She leaned down to play with his nipples. "Will you?" she asked huskily. "Will you use your free pass?"

He gripped her butt, holding her still for a moment. He was on a hair trigger, and he couldn't bear another long, slow slide without coming. He reached up to fondle her breasts. Their delicate beauty matched the rest of her body. When he twisted her nipples, she squirmed.

Melanie bit her bottom lip, her eyes closed, her hands resting on his collarbone. She was indescribably beautiful to him. He pinched her tits gently. "Yes," he growled. "I will. But there are conditions." He flexed his hips, making her whimper.

"Tell me," she muttered. "Where? When?"

He lost it. His wife wanted him to screw another woman, and all he wanted was to stay right here in Melanie's pussy forever. He lifted her slowly, encouraging her to ride him. He was done talking.

The scent of her skin and the perfume she wore every day

enveloped him in a haze of lust. Was it his imagination, or could he really smell the other man's touch on her body? The thought both aroused and enraged him.

He played with her ass, traced her waist, glided his palms over her rib cage. Melanie rocked back, leaning her hands on his thighs. The new position made it easy for him to toy with her clit. She loved that. He watched her face, studied the play of emotions reflected there.

Her body quivered with need, and he sensed the moment she was close to climaxing. Tonight, he was determined for both of them to reach the peak together. He stroked her slowly.

"Come for me, baby," he whispered. "Show me how much you love getting screwed."

She opened her eyes, and in her gaze, he saw that she was remembering. Shit. It made him nuts. He went wild, fucking her like a crazy man. How could he have let it happen? His nuts tightened, his swollen cock probed her as far as he could go, and with a ragged shout, he filled her with come, something that her mystery man couldn't do.

That last stupid thought was what stayed with him through the shattering moments when he and his wife clung together, riding the wave of a mutual orgasm.

Long moments later, he cuddled her close. "I was wrong," he muttered. "Turns out I'm a bit jealous after all."

She yawned and rubbed her eyes, as cuddly and cute as a kitten. "You needn't be."

He sensed that she was going to drift off to sleep quickly, and he had to ask. By tomorrow he would lose his nerve.

He massaged her scalp, loving the feel of her hair beneath

his fingertips. When he extended his touch to his slender neck, she moaned and stretched luxuriously, sighing finally and tucking her head on his shoulder.

"Melanie?"

"Hmmm?"

"I want to give you my free pass."

She frowned, her eyes closed. "That doesn't make sense. I've already had mine."

"I'm serious." He let her keep her eyes closed. It made his confession easier. "Promise me you'll take it." He stroked her back.

"Whatever." Her voice was slurred.

He played with her ear. "How long before he leaves town?"

"Who?"

"Your free-pass guy."

"What does it matter? A couple of days, maybe."

She got irritable when she was sleepy. He whispered in her ear, "I want you to screw him again."

He thought that would shock her awake, but apparently she was farther gone than he thought. He nuzzled her ear. "Did you hear me . . . Melanie?"

She snored softly.

He shook her gently. "Baby, this is important. Listen to me. I want you to use my pass."

She sighed deeply and opened one eye. "I'll give you a million dollars to let me sleep."

He kissed her cheek. "Did you hear me?"

"What?" she wailed. "What can't possibly wait till morning?"

"I want you to have sex with him again."

This time he knew she had heard him, because her mouth did a fishlike imitation and every trace of drowsiness left her eyes. "You what?"

"You heard me. I'm giving my pass to you. I want you to tell the big guy that it's his lucky week. He gets to score with my hot wife one more time."

She blinked owlishly. "But why?"

He kissed her softly, sliding his tongue between her lips and teasing hers. "Because I want to watch."

Chapter Fifteen

G ordon had never really cared for aggressive women. He'd fallen in love with Debra because of her sweet, generous nature. She was feminine and strong, but she had a softness about her that appealed to his masculine need to protect and defend.

Katya was nothing like Debra. And frankly, though he'd never dare admit it, she scared him a little. As she dragged him through the house with an iron grip around his wrist, he wondered if he'd be able to get his dick up in the face of such blatant domination.

The room to which she led him was bare except for a mattress on the floor. Perhaps it was intended as an extra bedroom, but the wooden plank shelving on one wall suggested it might also serve as a storage area from time to time.

Gordon winced inwardly at the lack of ambience. He was a guy, for God sakes. He didn't need candlelight and all that romantic shit to have good sex, but this austere cell of a space made him think of prison.

Katya obviously saw no need for gentle foreplay. She shed her dress, shoes, and undies with lightning speed and waved an imperious hand. "You take off clothes."

Damn. If he had acted more quickly, he wouldn't have suffered through her staring at him, hands on hips, eyes mocking his uncertainty. He undressed slowly, ruefully aware that his penis was limp and quivering. This was not how he usually orchestrated things.

And now the Russian woman was probably wondering if she had gotten the bad end of this deal.

She had a small, sly smile on her face—one he had begun to associate with her sharp, dramatic personality. When he finally stood before her, fully nude, he felt his face heat as she studied his package—one that was not anywhere near ready for delivery.

He lifted his chin and met her gaze, look for look. She was leaner than his wife, with smaller tits and a narrow waist. A dark cloud of curls covered her sex. Perhaps nothing in the individual aspects of her petite body shouted sexuality, but the parts when viewed as a whole made an exotic, alluring picture.

She lifted an eyebrow and a shoulder in tandem. "You no like Katya?"

The heat in his face moved to his neck and burned brighter. "Of course," he stuttered, feeling lame-ass and socially clumsy. "You're very pretty."

"Pretty? Ha!" She sneered at him. "Pretty is not what man want in bed. He need tigress."

Gordon gulped. "Ah, I don't know if—"

She cut him off with a flick of her hand. "We fuck. You see."

Well, hell. He smiled placatingly. "I'd like to kiss you, Katya. A little foreplay." He paused. "Do you know that word? Foreplay?"

Her frown was black. "I know word. Is not kissing. You tame tigress."

She'd lost him completely. *Tame tigress?* What in the devil did that mean?

She bent and reached into a leather satchel on the floor. This view of her ass and pussy gave him his first flicker of genuine arousal.

But in seconds she had straightened and was holding out her hand. "This for you. Make tiger purr."

His mouth went dry and his dick flexed. "This" was a black leather whip with a braided handle and a long, skinny tail. Holy mother of God. She wanted him to whip her?

She pressed it into his hand, and in doing so managed to align their bodies, the leather instrument in between them. Her fingernails raked down his chest from his collarbone to his nipples. She put some force behind it, leaving deep red scratches.

His hand clenched on the handle. "Katya, I—"

She gave him the kiss he had asked for, all dueling tongues and sharp teeth and clinging lips. Finally she released his mouth. "We have fun . . . you see."

She went to the rough plaster wall and faced it, her hands outstretched. For the first time, he saw the iron hooks just below the low ceiling. They looked like what a Greek farm wife might use to dry ropes of aromatic herbs and vegetables.

Katya looked at him over her shoulder. "Restraints in bag. I wait."

His knees felt funny, and his stomach bounced and twisted, but he didn't hesitate more than a second. He rummaged in the satchel and pulled out two narrow canvas strips of cloth. Katya remained silent, thank God, while he bound her wrists to the iron hooks.

She looked pagan and yet not at all helpless in her confinement. When he was done, she spoke without looking at him. "Show passion, weak American boy. Make tigress ready for fuck."

The insolence in her voice struck him on the raw. Was he no more than an object of fun to her? A seminaive, boringly conservative toy?

The spark of anger he felt enabled him to consider the task at hand with a bit of enthusiasm. Tame her? Shit. He'd show her what he was made of.

He tested the whip in the air, and immediately realized that it would not be easy to master the perfect stroke. He coiled it a second time and tried again, this time forced to smother a yelp of pain when the damn thing ended up wrapped around his knee. Finally, he bunched part of the length in his left hand and attempted a third practice run.

The leather popped with a loud crack, and he grinned as triumph filled him. But when he turned to where Katya stood in silence against the wall, his confidence waned.

What if he did it wrong? What if he really hurt her? How in the hell was he supposed to go about this? He cleared his throat. "You ready?"

She made no answer. But he saw her hands clench around the bonds he had secured.

He took a deep breath, raised his arm, and let fly with the whip. It caught her across the back of the legs. Katya made a small sound and her shoulders flexed. A thin red line appeared where he had struck her.

His chest heaved. Lust roared through him, thick and hot as a river of lava, finally bringing his penis to life. He was embarrassed that this turned him on, but he was not about to stop until Katya gave the word. The tigress would be tamed one way or another.

He gained confidence and skill, enough to keep the force of the strikes in check. Even if Katya was into severe pain, that wasn't his thing at all. He wasn't about to break her delicate, golden skin.

By far, the most enjoyable target was her ass. He returned to it repeatedly, crisscrossing the twin globes with ruby patterns. Katya was tough. Her feet remained firmly planted, and though she muttered words in Russian from time to time, she made no protest . . . no plea for mercy.

His erection had grown to painful proportions. And as much as he enjoyed his role at the moment, he craved full body contact, with his aching cock plunging into her and pummeling her into submission.

His feelings toward the Russian woman were a disturbing mix of anger, lust, intrigue, and uncertainty. At last, he stopped. He lowered his arm to his side, the length of the whip trailing on the floor.

He dropped it and went to her, resting his hands lightly

on her back. Slight pink lines traced the history of her pun-ishment. He ran his thumb over one raised welt. "Did I hurt you?"

He hated what he was feeling at the moment, unsure if she would berate him or laugh at him or thank him. Or none of the above.

She turned her head, her usually flashing eyes bright with tears. "You not hurt Katya enough. Tigress will turn on you. Rip you. Kill you."

Whoa. Stop the truck. This was way beyond playacting. He stroked her hair from her cheek and kissed her shoulder softly. "Why such violence, Katya? Why the need for punishment? Sex should be tender and fun." He untied her wrists and stepped back two paces as she whirled to face him, her hands clenched in fists at her side.

She tossed her head, her stance aggressive. "What do milk-faced American man know about Russian passion? We burn. We crave. We tear beneath skin to raw core of self. Sex is fire and heat and agony."

His stomach did that weird thing again, and his erection weakened. He tried to smile. "Sounds painful. Couldn't we just fool around?"

She grabbed his dick in one red-taloned hand and clenched her fingers. Pain made him gasp. He was afraid to move. "Um . . . easy there, girl. I need my man parts if we're going to do this."

Her other hand captured his balls, subjecting them to similar pressure. For a moment, fear—plain, cold fear—enveloped him and brought sweat to his forehead. This was not what he had signed up for.

Katya laughed, her face finally lightening to the extent that he recognized the fun-loving woman who had flirted and downed Russian vodka with him in days past. "I make joke." She released him and turned her back.

He gulped in air and massaged his dick. Was the Russian schizo? Or was he seeing glimpses of the real woman beneath the almost manically cheerful playmate.

He cupped her shoulders, ran his hands down her arms. "I think you are an amazing woman. Not sure about all the punishment shit, but no worries. I'll play whatever games you like. I'd be honored." For some unfathomable reason he felt the need to protect her from herself.

What the hell kind of weird, fucked-up relationship did she and Yuri share?

She allowed him to hold her, his arms wrapped around her from behind, his hands toying gently with her breasts. Her head fell back on his shoulder. She sighed, a long, deep sigh of pleasure. "You have nice hands. Katya like."

He plucked lightly at her brownish nipples, making her squirm, raising the tempo of her breathing. She remained docile for the moment, letting him explore her belly, her soft pussy hair, her upper thighs.

He dropped to his knees and pressed kisses everywhere he had inflicted a stripe. With his left hand he steadied himself on her hip. With his right, he parted her sex and found her clitoris.

Her whole body quivered when his fingers probed her pussy, finding it wet and swollen. He turned her around so he could lick and suck to his heart's content. She tasted like an exotic dessert.

He took his time, learning the things that made her moan and plead. Soft Russian words and phrases fell from her lips like gentle rain, bathing him in a cocoon of fantasy. Again and again she climaxed, her throaty murmurs balm to his ears. This was what he wanted.

When her knees gave out, he carried her to the mattress. There wasn't even a sheet. He frowned as he lowered her carefully. She seemed fragile to him suddenly, as though her earlier aggression had been nothing but a protective shell for her vulnerable inner self.

He moved beside her and curled an arm beneath her neck, settling his body hip to hip with hers. "Does Yuri abuse you, Katya?" he was troubled enough to ask.

Her eyes went blank, and then she laughed with genuine amusement. "Yuri adore Katya."

"Then why the whip? Why the need for punishment? Why all the tigress talk?"

She rolled to her side and sat up, her hair tumbled around her face, her eyes glittering with some unnamed emotion. "I like it—how you say it? Rough?"

He stared up at her, perplexed. "Always?" She sure as hell had seemed to enjoy his tenderness a few moments ago. But now the insolent gleam had returned to her eyes.

She propped up a knee and wrapped her thin arms around it. "In Russia is hard for women. I want feel strong. Tough. Most men like."

He heard a hint of vulnerability in the unspoken question. He remembered his stone-hard erection. "I like," he said, unwittingly following her syntax. "But hurting you doesn't seem appropriate or necessary."

Her eyes narrowed. "Then maybe I hurt you."

His balls tightened. He hadn't seen that one coming. He rolled to his side and nonchalantly moved his thigh to protect his manhood. "Does there have to be hurting?"

It was supposed to be a teasing question, but Katya didn't smile. She moved with the speed of a striking adder, shoving him to his back and going down on him with a hungry mouth.

Her teeth raked his shaft even as she sucked him so hard, he thought his eyeballs would roll back in his head. In spite of, or maybe even because of, his apprehension, his cock swelled and thickened rapidly, forcing her teeth apart and making her work to keep him between her lips.

His thighs were sprawled apart, with Katya half lying across his body. He lifted one knee to get more comfortable. His arousal built steadily, making him hungry to mount and fuck her.

Now she had one hand on the base of his shaft as she sucked him while the other hand tortured his nuts, separating them and squeezing them and raking them with sharp fingernails until he gasped and trembled.

He felt his body tighten and knew he was going to come. But he didn't want to, not yet. Not like this.

His brain scrambled for reason. He could persuade her to stop. He could suggest a conventional fuck for starters. He needed to be the nice guy in the scenario.

The more he struggled mentally, the more Katya played him like an instrument she had mastered and now wrung the utmost response from. Heat gripped him. He felt his cock surge and pulse. Oh, shit, he was so close.

Katya leaned in, her words nothing more than honeyed temptation. "Come, my lusty American. Come for Katya." And then she thrust one sharp-nailed finger up his ass.

Pain and pleasure slammed into each other, making him cry out and writhe in knife-edged agony. Then he cursed and groaned and struggled in her grip until his world exploded like a star fragmenting into the night.

Aeons later, he lay limp and shivering on the hard mattress. Katya had disappeared to God knows where. He reached out mentally to his wife. *Debra, baby . . . are you all right?* What had Yuri done to her? Was he as sexually unpredictable as his volatile wife?

The door opened with a soft whoosh of air, and Katya returned, still naked, still smiling at him as if nothing out of the ordinary had happened.

She knelt beside him and offered him a glass of water. He rose on an elbow and swallowed half of the contents in three gulps. His throat was raspy. His head felt as if his brains had been ripped out and the resultant cavity had been stuffed with cotton balls.

He finished the drink and handed the glass to her. "Are my wife and your husband finished?"

"Finished?" Her expressed was perplexed.

He sat up, raking his hands through his hair. "You know what I mean. Are they done having sex?"

She studied his face, her own expression impossible to read. Then she shrugged. "I listen at door. Hear Debra beg. Yuri good lover. She like many times."

He wished he could share Katya's confidence. He was concerned about his wife. But he couldn't exactly march in there and demand that Yuri release her. Debra had gone of her own free will into the Russian's bed.

Katya interrupted his painful musings. "I whip you now?" She said it with the hopeful expression and tone of a kid asking for a candy bar or a bicycle ride in the park.

His poor, abused body responded like a Pavlovian dog. Two parts arousal, one part well-founded apprehension. But the conditioning was already working. He seemed to want what the Russian woman had to dish out.

He closed his eyes and prayed he wasn't making the biggest mistake of his life. "Sure," he said evenly. "But be gentle."

Her throaty laugh made the hair on the back of his neck stand up in alarm. But he followed her to the wall docilely and allowed himself to be bound as she had been before.

He wasn't prepared for the first blow. Katya was no novice, and unlike him, it seemed she had no qualms about inflicting pain.

He gritted his teeth and locked his knees. In all honesty, he'd never dreamed it would hurt this much. His eyes watered, his lip bled from where his teeth bit down hard at the apex of each blow.

He pressed instinctively into the wall, the rough plaster abrading his erect cock. He willed his dick to lie down and play dead, but the more Katya punished him, the more his hunger grew. He'd never explored the odd kinship between pleasure and pain, but tonight he was getting the short course.

Every time he braced himself for another slice of the whip, his body climbed higher and higher. He found himself unconsciously rubbing his shaft against the wall, craving the ultimate stimulation that would bring relief.

He lost track of time. His ass was a meld of bright, stinging pain. His back and shoulders felt raw. His knees quivered from the strain of remaining upright.

In the end, she broke him.

"Stop," he cried out, his voice little more than a croak. "Enough."

She ceased immediately, and the room fell silent. He sensed her approach him, felt the whisper of her breath on his sweaty back.

She massaged his shoulders, making him flinch and quiver as the salt from his perspiration irritated the swollen whip marks.

She spoke softly, almost inaudibly. "We fuck now?"

His head dropped forward, his brow against the wall. "Yes," he rasped. Anything to end this torment of unfulfilled lust.

He yelped when he felt her hands at his ass. He thought she was untying him. Instead, he felt fresh alarm as she forced something into his anus. The whip handle. Sweet heaven.

He cleared his throat. "What are you doing?"

She stroked his lower back. "I fuck you. Then you fuck me. We both happy."

Happy was not a word he would have used to describe tonight's escapade.

He gasped when she probed deeper. Had she even slicked up the damn thing with any kind of lubricant? It was fairly thick, and he was in serious discomfort. Oh, hell, let's call a spade a spade. She was inflicting major pain.

Though he cringed from it mentally, his poor deprived cock was happy to get with the program. He was so hard, he wasn't sure he'd be able to ejaculate when he finally got the chance.

She reached around him and gripped his cock. Now, in an erotic tandem, she stroked and pushed, stroked and pushed. He was sure his eyes crossed, and he squeezed them shut, trying in vain to resist the torture.

So much pleasure in one place, so deep a hurt in the other. She made it impossible for him to enjoy the ride to the top. Or was she making the journey darker, scarier, more ultimately thrilling?

Her small, agile fingers explored his cock in every configuration. The skin on his dick was tight, the shaft engorged to the point of pain.

But nerve endings in his anus made him tremble and shudder as hot ribbons of agony spread through his abdomen and assimilated into the searing pleasure writhing through his cock.

He'd thought the whipping was tough to endure. That was child's play compared to this. He pressed away from her, trying to elude the dual assault. "Let me come, Katya. Please. I beg you. I can't stand this." His male pride lay in ashes.

She picked up the tempo. "Come then, stupid man. No fight. Yield. Yield to Katya. Yield to sweet release. Feel ecstasy when you leave body. Fly high."

He felt himself losing his hold on reason. His arms and legs were numb, his torso a seething, shuddering hub of feelings. Euphoria. Dread. Fierce, exultant, almost-to-the-crest feelings of invincibility and ultimate defeat.

He braced his feet. His eyes stung from the sweat rolling down his forehead. He felt like he was suffocating. He muttered a curse and then screamed. God, he actually screamed when the end came.

It was nothing he'd ever experienced and nothing he wanted to find again—a dark, seductive place where his body embraced the fiery pain, transformed it in a violent cataclysm, and slammed full-tilt into an electric current of climactic release that ripped through him like a tornado and left him weak and spent in the aftermath.

He was barely able to stand when Katya released his wrists. He stumbled after her to the bed and fell facedown on his stomach. He felt her lie beside him, but after that, there was nothing but blankness.

Later, thinking back on the incident, he was never sure how long he was out of it. He awoke to the now familiar feel of Katya's hands on his cock.

His body flinched instinctively, especially when he felt her rubbing something that felt damn good into his asshole. He stirred and murmured, but she pressed him down. "Don't move. This help. Katya make better."

He let her violate him one last time, this instance a healing one. Whatever she used soothed and cooled the residual pain.

When she was done, she moved away for a moment and then returned to snuggle beside him. She took his arm and lifted it across her waist. The two of them lay there in the dark with no sound but their breathing.

His body felt heavy, his limbs like lead. Katya wiggled closer, her breasts brushing his side, as she bit his ear lobe. "I wait. You rest. Fuck soon."

He wanted to whisper out a protest. Seriously? Did she think he was a damned machine? His respect for Yuri grew. The wiry Russian must have a libido like a fucking nuclear reactor.

Gordon pretended to sleep again. His options were clear. No way was he getting out of this room unless he screwed Katya. So he was just going to have to man up and do it. But getting his cock to cooperate might be an issue, especially since he was pretty sure he had lost all feeling below his waist.

He deliberately summoned an image of his beautiful wife locked in a carnal embrace with Yuri. He saw the Russian's hands on her ass, imagined his jet-propelled dick hammering away at her.

Beneath Gordon's belly, his cock stirred. He rolled to his back with a groan. "Eat me, Katya."

She was happy to oblige. The wet sucking sound she made, combined with the feel of her mouth moving up and down his shaft, did the trick in minutes. It might not be his best erection, but considering the circumstances, it was a miracle he'd gotten it up at all.

He rubbed a hand across his face, smothering a yawn. "How do you want it?"

The question seemed to confuse her.

He motioned with his hand. "Me on top? You? Whatever you want." He was feeling magnanimous.

Katya's eyes gleamed as she studied his erection. Her smile broadened. "I have idea."

She backed up to the wall. "Tie hands. We stand up."

In spite of his exhaustion, a fresh sizzle of anticipation ripped through him. The woman was a constant surprise.

He quickly fastened her wrists to the hooks, this time with her facing him and not the wall. Katya looked far too satisfied. It was time for a little payback.

He picked up the whip and fluttered the thin, frayed ends over her nipples. She bit out a word in Russian, and her eyes closed.

He looked behind him and found the jar of ointment she had used to soothe his ass. He unscrewed the lid, ran his middle finger though it and turned back to his captive. She stood, eyes closed, waiting.

Without any warning at all, he pushed his hand between her thighs, found her anus, and shoved his finger into her. She shrieked and bucked, forcing him to clap a hand over her mouth. "Not a sound," he muttered.

It was fiercely satisfying to probe her repeatedly and watch her response. She fought him. She tried to dance away, but her nipples were the telltale sign. Katya was enjoying his attentions.

The naughty play was priming him far too well. He left her only long enough to wipe his finger on his pants and pull a condom from his pocket. He sheathed himself and faced her.

"Time to tame the tigress," he muttered. He spread her legs, lifted her ass, and surged into her with a wicked thrust that plastered her back and butt to the wall.

Katya moaned and tightened her vaginal muscles, clenching his shaft in pure pleasure.

He fucked her slowly, so tired he could barely stand. "Is this how a man declaws the tigress?" he asked, panting at the exertion of supporting her weight and lunging upward at the same time.

She glared at him. "Katya not weak." She dug her heels painfully into his back. "Katya take."

It was a moot point as to who was taking whom. But he was damned tired of wrestling with her. He gave up trying to be gentle, or tender, or even conciliatory.

He rammed her over and over, undoubtedly bruising her ass. But he didn't care. If she wanted to get fucked, he would oblige.

She came seconds before he did, a thin cry ripping from her throat as he shot his load, shuddered for long, aching seconds, and put an end to his onetime free pass.

Chapter Sixteen

Wesley made it through an awkward hello, two cups of coffee, and a stilted conversation before he popped the question they both knew he was going to ask. "Will you have sex with me, Melinda?"

Her hair was up in a French twist this morning, and he couldn't wait to undo it all and let it cover the both of them as they fucked. He'd worked himself into a high state of tension, which was the only thing now keeping from having an embarrassing woody in public.

Melinda had been joking and laughing, and she seemed genuinely happy to be spending time with him. But his blunt question put a shadow on her face.

She leaned forward, with her elbows on the table, and she unwittingly gave him a nice view of her chest. "Are you sure, Wesley? I worry about what your wife will think even if she agrees, and besides that"—she grimaced, biting her lower lip and looking unhappy—"I'm really a lot older than you, and I'm not—"

He cut her off. "Don't even think it. You're an incredibly beautiful, confident woman. I get hard just looking at you."

She turned pink, her expression pleased and abashed. "Thank you, Wesley," she said softly. "I have to admit that this last month has been hell on my ego. This is a lovely and unexpected surprise."

He sobered suddenly. "I suppose if you think about it, I'm using you. That doesn't make me any better than your bastard of a boyfriend."

She patted his hand. "This is mutual. I'm offering to be your free pass, and you're proving to me that my sex life isn't over."

He snorted. "Don't be ridiculous. You'll have men lusting after you for another two decades. You have that look that will always draw male attention."

Her lips trembled, and he suddenly realized how much she had been hurt. He got to her feet and took her hand. "Come on, lovely lady. Let me prove to you I know what I'm talking about."

Her condo was far different from the one he and Cherisse were renting, but no less comfortable. Melinda had made it a retreat, filled it with homey touches that revealed her personality.

The living room was romantic and welcoming with deep soft sofas and chairs and a vivid Oriental rug. The air was scented with something subtle that evoked forests and wildflowers. It would have been a comfortable place if he hadn't been so jumpy.

She hovered nervously once they were inside. When she offered wine, he accepted, hoping to make her more at ease. He didn't point out that it was still morning, since she seemed prepared to indulge.

He saw her drink two glasses in a row, and he smothered a smile. She had nothing to worry about, but only the sex to come would reassure her on that point.

She kicked off her sandals, so she was wearing only a thin silk tank top similar to the one she'd had on in the bookstore, and a flowing, ankle-length gauze skirt, both in shades of green. She was tall for a woman, and she held herself with an elegant grace.

He went to her and toyed with the strap of her top, his tanned fingers dark against her skin. "Don't be shy with me, Melinda." He took her hand and pressed it to his erection. "I want you so much, I ache."

Her eyes grew wide and some of the tension left her shoulders. She licked her lips. They were a lovely color, but bare of any lipstick. She reached up to kiss him softly. "My bedroom is this way."

Before they undressed, he made an unorthodox request. "May I brush your hair?"

She wrinkled her nose. "Really?"

He nodded, his throat dry. They sat on the bed, with her perched at the edge, and him with his legs spread on either side of her hips. She gave him a wooden brush that looked far more expensive than the dime-store kind, but what did he know about feminine junk like that?

Slowly, he removed the hairpins that kept her pretty waves in place and dropped them on the floor. He fluffed and separated the heavy strands with his fingers, and then began to drag the brush from the crown of her head down through that glorious mass of color and light.

It was soft, so soft. And it bounced and shimmered with a life of its own. No wonder she was in demand for commercials that touted beauty products for hair. Hers was incredibly lovely.

He kept at it for a long time. Her head was slightly bowed, her body warm between his legs. When every strand was smooth and sleek, he tossed the brush to the floor. Then he buried his face in her neck and inhaled the scent of her shampoo.

He felt her tremble when he slid his arms around her and toyed with her small breasts through the silk of her top. Again today, she had worn no bra. The slide of silk against bare skin was warm and sensuous.

After several moments, she put her hands over his. "I don't mean to be rude, and I love what you're doing, but shouldn't we get started?" She turned to face him. "I have to be at work by twelve thirty."

The nasty dose of reality shocked him and made him uncomfortable. Of course she had a life. So did he. And this was not some romantic chick flick. This was the equivalent of a nooner.

He smiled stiffly, feeling out of sorts and ticked at himself. "You're right. I'm sorry."

Awkwardness entered the room. He and Melinda both undressed themselves, not at all what he had hoped for. When they were each nude, they stood on separate sides of the bed facing each other. He wasn't sure how she wanted him to proceed, so he pulled back the covers and climbed in, feeling not so much horny as uncomfortable.

After a second's hesitation, she joined him. Her sheets were smooth and soft and smelled like her hair. Her body wasn't touching his. Both of them lay still.

He reached for her hand. "Melinda?"

"Yes?" That one word was filled with a host of emotions, not the least of which was fear.

"Is it all right if I touch you?"

She chuckled breathlessly, lightening the mood. "I think you should, Wesley."

It got easier after that. He stroked and petted her for a long time, learning the curves and planes of her body. She seemed uncomfortable when he glided over the soft swell of her belly . . . so he abandoned that and returned to her tits. Since she was on her back, they were almost flat.

But they still looked and felt erotic to him. The drapes were partially open, and there was enough daylight in the room to see clearly. Melinda's skin was pale. She was a true redhead—that he knew for sure.

His hand moved between her legs and she gasped, tightening her thighs automatically. He continued to stroke her slowly until she finally relaxed and let him see and feel her femininity.

Her sex was amazing, full and plump and glistening. He used a finger to test her wetness, to tease her clitoris. But still she lay almost dead still beside him.

Was he doing this wrong? Did she not find his body attractive after all?

He leaned over her and kissed her gently, as if he had all

the time in the world. Her lips clung to his, but he realized that her hands were clenching the sheet, white knuckled.

He wrapped a hank of her hair around his hand. "Relax, Melinda. Let me do this for you."

Images of watching her masturbate filled his head, made his cock swell painfully. He wanted to be the one today to give her a satisfying climax.

He touched between her legs again. This time she made a little groaning sound. Her body went lax, and he knew he had won her trust.

He went slowly out of necessity. He had to learn where and how she liked to be touched. Her little sighs and restless movements clued him in. Soon she was panting, her hips shifting in the bed, her back arching.

His erection brushed her hip, not that he'd planned it, but her reaction pleased him. She reached for his penis and closed her hand around it.

He sucked in a breath and almost lost his rhythm, but he quickly went back to where he'd left off. It was hard to concentrate with his aching cock in her fist. He hoped like hell she wouldn't damage him when she came.

He circled her clit, applying a gentle pressure and then skating right over the top. Melinda whimpered, shuddered, and pressed into his hand. She released him and grabbed his neck with both hands, pulling him down.

Her eyes opened, cloudy with desire. "I want you inside me, Wesley."

He couldn't have resisted her invitation even if he had wanted to. He ripped open a condom package and handed it to her. "Do this for me."

Watching her hands roll the latex over his dick made him dizzy. He moved on top of her and settled between her legs. Her hair spread out on the pillows like a mermaid's in a tidal pool.

When he touched the head of his cock to her pussy, he let is rest there. "Your boyfriend was insane. A man would have to be seriously fucked up to let you get away."

He pushed slowly, seating his length inside her, making them both sigh raggedly. He smiled at her, feeling goofy but determined. "Would you mind getting on top?"

Her brow creased. "Okay." But her affirmative was uncertain at best.

He rolled them both until he was on his back. "I don't have female-domination issues, I swear. But, God, I love your hair. And I want to see it over me when I make you come again."

She laughed aloud, suddenly looking years younger than he knew her to be. "This is your free pass, Wesley. My job is to give you your heart's desire."

She moved her body sinuously, making him curse. "Damn, woman. Do that again."

She did. Over and over. Driving them both crazy. He lifted his hands and grabbed fistfuls of her hair, anchoring her to him. The curtain of red-gold enclosed them in a cocoon of intimacy. A ray of sunlight sneaked past the drapes and set Melinda's long, full tresses on fire.

Wesley felt a little fire of his own. It seized him unexpectedly and triggered a sharp, embarrassing orgasm. He knew she hadn't gone with him, and he felt like a clumsy teenager too quick off the mark.

She moved to his side so he could stand up and get rid of

the condom. Then she touched his leg. "Quit looking so pouty. We're not finished."

He smiled wryly. "Men don't pout."

She left the bed and crouched in front of him. Sixty seconds of a good blow job later, he was back in the batting cage. She led him to the window.

He followed obediently, ready to let her do anything if he could continue screwing her.

She placed her hands on the windowsill, much as she had done the day he'd watched her through the telescope. Leaning forward and tilting her ass in his direction, she turned to give him a naughty look over her shoulder. "I wonder if anyone is watching."

Wow. That sly, little comment made his dick hard and ready. He moved behind her and spread her legs. The height wasn't exactly right, but if he bent his knees and thrust upward . . .

The moment when he joined their bodies made both of them groan. He fucked her slowly, looking out the window, seeing the condo where at this very moment Cherisse was probably having sex with a hot, young lifeguard.

He imagined his wife pausing to look through the telescope . . . spotting Wesley . . . meeting his gaze. His arousal bumped up about a thousand notches, and he squeezed Melinda's ass. Her movie-star hair cascaded down her narrow, white-skinned back.

This position was making his knees scream in protest. He pulled out and dragged Melinda down to the soft carpet, mounting her with clumsy haste. He was shaking, craving an orgasm like a junkie needing a fix.

Melinda squirmed when he reached between them to play with her clit. He moved his hips and his hand in unison, once . . . twice. . . . Suddenly, he and his onetime lover locked eyes and both went over the precipice together. The end seemed to last forever, little ripples from her pussy squeezing him over and over until he had nothing left to give.

He felt a great, inexplicable affection for the woman beneath him, but more surprising than that was his driving need to get home and fuck his wife.

A half hour later, Wesley stood on the street that ran in front of both buildings and looked at the tiny screen on his phone anxiously. Nothing. He had worked himself into a fine frenzy of jealousy when five minutes later, his wife's text message popped up: *Come home.*

That was it. Two words. *Come home.* He walked swiftly, his head filled with pictures of Cherisse and a strange man. He vacillated between horny curiosity and a jealous need to pretend nothing had happened.

In the lobby of their building, he stood at the bank of elevators and pushed the button impatiently. Finally, the doors opened. Three other people joined him. All their stops were before his.

Finally, he stepped off on his floor. A man was standing quietly, ready to catch the down elevator. The guy was blond . . . young. . . . *Oh, shit.* Wesley reeled mentally as he made the impossible-to-miss connection. This was Cherisse's free-pass guy.

The other man's gaze met his, then slipped away with indifference as he moved past Wesley. Wesley's heart pounded, his hands fisted at his sides. The atavistic response took him totally by surprise. He paused, almost ready to step back into the enclosed space and do something to the guy—grill him, punch him.

Civilized instincts prevailed. The doors began to close. The other man had his back to the wall, looking curiously at Wesley, perhaps wondering why he was lingering. At the last second before the doors came together, Wesley could have sworn the guy's eyes widened in startled recognition.

But the elevator doors closed, breaking the odd moment and releasing Wesley from his imitation of some poor schmuck who had been frozen by a stun gun.

He hurried down the hall, used his key, and went to find his wife.

She was in the bedroom, still wearing her simple shirt and shorts. Her back was toward him because she was looking through the telescope. The bed was neatly made as it had been when he'd left that morning. There was no sign of anything out of the ordinary.

He stopped in the doorway, his throat thick with an inexplicable lump. Emotions flowed through him—love, gratitude, quiet lust. Cherisse seemed, for the briefest moment, a stranger to him.

He studied her intently. Seven years ago, give or take a few days, this stunning woman had consented to be his wife. It was a mystery to him why he was so blessed. Without false modesty, he knew he was an average guy in every way. Fairly intelligent, decently good-looking, moderately talented in the bedroom.

Picking up a strange woman had been a lark—a crazy,

unconventional, out-of-character move that would serve as a pleasant fantasy as the months passed. As arousing as it had been, as much fun as he'd had, it was just a blip on his radar.

The woman standing across the room from him was his life. The knot in his throat grew bigger, and he clenched his jaw. He wasn't a deep guy. He didn't spend a lot of time analyzing his feelings. Even when Cherisse had first proposed the free-pass idea, he hadn't paused to sort out his mixed emotions.

But this experience had taught him one crucial lesson. He loved his wife—madly, passionately, the way all those men in sappy chick flicks adored the female leads. And it startled him. He felt self-conscious, not sure how to approach Cherisse.

She sensed or heard him and turned around. Her lips curved in a small smile. "Well, hey there. I didn't know what to think when you didn't answer my text."

He blinked. "I didn't?" Apparently, he'd been so wrapped up in what had just happened with Melinda and what he was imagining had just happened with Cherisse and her mystery man, he'd flown down the street, not pausing to even send a two-word text as she had.

He shifted his feet, his hands in his pocket. "I guess I was in a hurry to get home. Sorry."

She cocked her head. "Did it go okay?" She paused, obviously flustered. "Well . . . I mean . . . did you have a good time? Wesley? Did you?"

He felt himself turning red. "Yeah." He looked down at the carpet. "It was fun. How about you?"

She blushed as well, nodding jerkily. "It was very nice."

God, they were acting like middle school kids comparing notes on the Web porn they had watched.

He finally got his feet to move and went to stand beside her. He put his hand on the barrel of the telescope, staring blindly out the window without benefit of magnification. Across the way, Melinda's windows reflected the noontime rays of the sun.

He slid an arm around Cherisse and pulled her close. "I love you, baby."

She put her head on his shoulder and sighed, a long exhalation of breath that might mean something if he'd been able to interpret her subtext. "I adore you, Wesley." Her soft whisper brought the lump back to his throat.

They stood side by side, neither of them speaking, for several long seconds. He hadn't anticipated this level of awkwardness. The free-pass idea had included an agreement to share all the wicked details afterward, but he found himself willing to let that provision slide.

Maybe later he would want to know. Later . . . when they were back home in Minnesota and curled up in bed, teasing one another into full-blown arousal with the titillating details of their Miami escapades.

But for now, he just wanted to hold her, to feel the unbroken bond between them, to know that everything was the same. He stroked her arm. "I have something for you," he said softly. He released her long enough to reach into the drawer of the bedside table and pull out a box wrapped in white satin paper.

She half turned, her expression quizzical. "Our anniversary's not for two more days."

He brushed a kiss on her cheek and pressed the small, rectangular package into her hands. "I can't wait, Cherisse. Open it." He'd carried it from home and kept it hidden all this time.

She removed the paper carefully, barely even tearing it. He waited impatiently. When she pulled off the lid, she made a little sound of surprise. "Wesley!"

She lifted out the contents and held it up. Months ago, he'd been browsing online for an anniversary gift, something unique, something that would let his wife know exactly how much she meant to him. He'd found a Web site run by an Irishman who designed jewelry. The pictures on the site had caught Wesley's eye, and he and the Irishman had e-mailed back and forth until Wesley came up with precisely what he wanted.

The necklace was an amazingly narrow but flexible twist of copper. Dangling from it was a hammered disk, maybe an inch in diameter, with two Celtic symbols and several words etched into the luminous copper.

Cherisse held it in her palm. "Oh, Wesley. It's lovely. Put it on, please." She turned her back to him and held up her hair. "Do you know what the writing means?"

He fastened the catch and caressed the nape of her neck before turning her around. "I should," he said, feeling pleased with himself. Cherisse really liked it, he could tell. "I ordered it specifically. The gist of the message is basically *love for all eternity.*"

Tears welled in her eyes. She leaned forward to kiss him, her hand still at her throat, caressing the dangling charm. "I can't believe you found something like this. I'm really touched, sweetheart. You're a wonderful, thoughtful husband."

He grinned, feeling lighthearted and happy and damn grateful for his life in general. He pulled her into his arms and hugged her. "I'll still want you when we're both using walkers, you know. You're a hot chick."

She giggled, her arms around his waist, her boobs pressed to his chest. "Will we always be this happy?"

He shrugged, feeling his cock rise predictably. Her body did that to him. Every time. "Yes," he said simply, "because we know that what we have means something."

"That's nice," she murmured.

He paused, his damn throat choking up again. "It's never been just sex with you, Cherisse, even in the beginning. That's why when we're in bed together, it keeps getting better and better. You give me something no other woman can. You give me your heart." He stopped there, dead sure she would understand what he wasn't saying.

The tryst with Melinda had been fun. The sex was great. He was glad he'd gotten past his jealousy to sign on for the free-pass idea.

But already it was a fading, pleasant memory. His future lay with the woman in his arms.

Cherisse loosened her hold ... stepped back ... took his hand in hers. "Make love to me, Wesley."

They undressed each other slowly, savoring the odd mix of peace and passion. She insisted on leaving the necklace on. When she was nude, the splash of copper around her neck gave her a graceful pagan beauty.

He didn't pause to wonder about the man who had occupied

this bed so recently. It didn't matter. No matter how that guy had fucked Cherisse, it wouldn't be like this. It wouldn't be like drowning in layers of tenderness. It wouldn't be heat and happiness mixed together. It wouldn't be love.

They played around with each other forever, teasing and tormenting, but never giving in to the rising passion. By unspoken consent, they let it build slowly, their need spiraling higher and higher

Foreplay had never been so sweet. Wesley groaned as he roughly stroked her breasts, seeing her pretty nipples turn so hard and rosy, he wanted to suck at them like tart, ripe raspberries.

Cherisse sat astride his chest, facing his feet. She grasped his ankles for balance and took him in her mouth. With her pussy in kissing distance, he didn't miss a beat. He licked her lazily, careful not to let her peak.

His penis had swelled to painful proportions. Cherisse's warm lips and mouth encased him in wet, sucking heat. He gasped. His hips pumped unconsciously, straining toward the final prize.

Wesley trembled, trying to continue eating her, but distracted by the driving need to come. When she bit down, her teeth trapping the head of his cock, he clenched her ass so hard, he left finger marks on her butt.

"God, baby, either stop or suffer the consequences." He wasn't sure what he was demanding.

She rose with nimble grace, pivoted, and slid down over his erection with one fluid movement. That initial joining stunned them both. He saw her response on her face, felt his own in the straining, throbbing ache in his dick. This wasn't going to last.

"I can't wait to get home and fuck you in our own bed," he muttered. "All night. Until we both fall asleep too sated to move."

She smiled down at him. "Happy anniversary, Wesley. I think you're going to like your present."

He froze in alarm. "Oh, hell, it's not another free pass, is it?"

She was still laughing when they both tumbled into a slow, sweet release. So it took her a bit to answer. She flopped on his chest, her breathing labored. "Don't worry, my love. From now on, you're mine, all mine."

Chapter Seventeen

Melanie went to the gym the next day as usual, but she hid in her office. She couldn't decide if she wanted Richard to come back or not. From what she'd gathered about his schedule, he had a couple more nights before he had to leave town. Would he want to see her again? Or would he be as freaked out as she was about facing her and vice versa? Maybe he'd skip his workouts to avoid running into her.

Last night's conversation with her husband was riveted in her mind. . . .

You want to what? She'd been stunned, barely able to speak.

Thomas's face had been serious, his eyes hot with some unnamed emotion. *I want you to fuck him again so I can watch. That's how I want to use my free pass.*

But why? Won't it upset you?

He stared at her, brooding, sulky. *I can't explain it, Mel. But I've got to see him fuck you again.*

And you'd rather watch me than make it with another woman?

What can I say? I get off on seeing you do it with a strange guy. Watching you both in the gym tonight . . . hell . . . it made me nuts, but at the same time, I couldn't tear my eyes away. Ask him again. Please. Tell him the price of admission is me seeing the whole damn thing. Discreetly . . . not in the same room. But close.

And if he says no?

Thomas's eyes flashed with self-deprecating male knowledge. *He won't, Mel. I promise you . . . he won't.*

So now here she was, closeted in her tiny office, afraid to go out on the floor. She monitored the day's traffic flow from her computer. Every time a member logged in, she could see it. Thomas's entrance would show up differently since he wasn't an official member, but she'd at least notice if someone had come in using a temp pass.

So far, no one had.

She skipped out for lunch at a nearby deli and checked her e-mail while she tried to come up with a plan. Even if Richard came in, he might not try to make any contact with her. He'd probably do his workout and leave.

She'd told him loud and clear that their sexual encounter was a onetime deal. He had no reason to think she might change her mind. So how would she explain a follow-up invitation?

Finally she went back to the gym. The day dragged on forever. She talked to Cherisse during the afternoon and learned that she and Wesley would be home soon. Her friend's voice had been smug and full of glee. Apparently, Cherisse and Wesley had *both* used their free passes while in Miami. Melanie knew the whole story would be forthcoming when Cherisse got home.

Debra and Gordon would by flying back in several days as well, their trip much shorter than Wesley and Cherisse's. Hopefully, their vacation had continued to be as wonderful as Debra had reported in the beginning.

Melanie paused a moment to be jealous. She really did have to get someone in place as a second-in-command so she and Thomas could get away for a break. They both deserved and needed some intimate alone time.

She skipped dinner, not in the least bit hungry. Her nerves had her belly tied up in knots. About seven she ran though a punishing workout and showered afterward, marginally less stressed, but no less worried about how she was going to pull this off.

It was almost eight when Richard came through the front doors. She ducked into her office before he spotted her, and grimaced when he never even glanced in her direction. Outwardly, he looked like a man getting ready to exercise. Nothing more.

She timed him with her watch, and was right on target when he headed into the locker room to shower. Fifteen minutes later, she hovered in her assistant's empty office, her heart in her throat, and waited to intercept him.

It was not as easy as Thomas had said it would be.

She called out to him. "Richard, can you come in here for a moment?"

He hesitated and stopped, taking a long moment to turn

around. No smile lit up his face. His body language was one big negative.

She smiled gamely in the face of his sobriety. "Please. I need to talk to you about something."

His reluctance was almost insulting. Finally, he walked toward her. The fingers of his right hand were clutched around the handles of his gym bag, his keys fisted in the other palm.

When he was several feet away, his gaze met hers. His eyes were wiped clean, blank of any expression other than a bland courtesy. "What is it, Melanie?" His voice was perfectly even, his tone matter-of-fact.

She backed up two steps. "Let's talk in my office." Something resembling a grimace flashed across his face, but he followed her. She sat behind her desk. He sprawled in one of the small chairs.

The silence lengthened. Try as she might, she couldn't see any bit of affection or familiarity or even simple male lust. Perhaps last night hadn't been as memorable for him as it had been for her.

She fussed with her pen and cleared her throat. "Here's the thing, Richard. My husband saw us last night. He slipped in while we were—" She stopped. It wasn't easy to say it aloud.

During her stumbling opening monologue, Richard had tensed visibly. He sat up a bit straighter in his chair. "Should I be watching my back when I go out to my car? Is he a good shot?"

His black humor, wry though it was, defused her anxiety a fraction. "Not at all," she said slowly. "He liked what he saw."

Richard frowned. His gym bag had been in his lap. Now he dropped it and his keys on the floor and put his hands on the arms of the chairs. "Maybe you'd better elaborate. I'm a little lost." He shook his head. "Are you sure he doesn't want to castrate me?"

"Maybe a little." She'd always thought honesty was the best policy. "But it turned him on. A lot. So he made me a proposition."

His brows narrowed. "I can't see how this concerns me, married Melanie."

She felt like her throat was closing up, and her voice was hoarse when she finally squeezed out the words. "He's giving me his free pass. I'm supposed to ask you if you're interested and/or willing to be with me again, with the caveat that you let him watch."

He got to his feet and paced the small space, agitation in his sharp, hasty movements. "To fuck you again, you mean. 'Be with you' is a weak-assed euphemism for what we did. We need to be adults here."

She winced. "Sorry. It's hard for me to say this, after my big speech about onetime deals." She paused, troubled by his bad mood. "Have I upset you somehow? You don't have to say yes. I know I'm asking a lot. Please don't be mad at me."

She stood and came around the desk to face him. "Talk to me, Richard."

He ran his hands through his hair, his eyes filled with turbulent emotion. "I loved screwing you last night—really loved it, Melanie. But I went home to my empty bed and made peace with the fact that I'd never get to touch you again. Now, damn it . . . now here you are dangling the apple from the Garden of Eden again and making me wonder if I'm going to get bitten in the ass."

"Only by me," she joked.

He wasn't amused. "I don't mess around with married women as a rule. I made an exception in your case. So pardon me if I can't be blasé about the possibility of a jealous husband setting me up for an opportunity to kick my ass. Or worse."

She risked his displeasure and moved closer to touch his arm. "Thomas is not like that. He's a very gentle man, I swear."

"Honey, no man is gentle when his woman is in question. It brings out the warrior. Trust me on this."

His voice had softened at the end, and finally, his gaze was as open and honest as it had been when they first met. He grinned halfheartedly. "Don't sacrifice me to the wolf. I'm attached to all my body parts."

He lifted her and sat her on the edge of her desk. They looked at each other for a long moment, remembering. . . .

She raised an eyebrow, wondering if it was impolite to persevere. "So will you?"

He put his hands on her shoulders, massaging them gently. "Screw you . . . or let him watch?"

She smiled at him, enjoying his dry wit and his slow Southern drawl. "Both. And honestly, Richard," she said, smirking at him, "after last night I didn't think I would have to work quite this hard to convince you."

He kissed her briefly and brushed her cheek with his thumb. "Yes to the first . . . no to the second."

She frowned. "That won't work. He only offered the free pass if he could see what was happening."

"So you said."

"Then how—"

He took her mouth again, this time in a carnal kiss, all tongues and teeth and masterful technique that left her breathless. "I'll fuck you again, sure. But I think your crazy husband should join us."

The following day Thomas thought he might be having a heart attack. And it was his own fault. What kind of man agreed to have a threesome with his wife and a stranger?

A desperate, horny man.

Somehow, Thomas had lost the upper hand. He'd been the one to set the parameters. And this Richard person had outwitted him by upping the ante. The guy was willing to have sex with Melanie (*duh*), and he was willing to let Thomas watch. But he was daring Thomas to take a far more active role.

Thomas adjusted the front of his slacks and groaned. He was still at the sporting-goods store, but in a couple of hours he would be meeting Melanie at their house along with . . . *Richard*. He growled the word in his head.

Melanie was probably clueless about what was going on, but Thomas had been a slave to testosterone for a lot of years, and he recognized the posturing. Richard had issued a challenge. He'd refused to perform with Melanie for Thomas's benefit. Instead, he'd turned it all back on Thomas, making him decide yea or nay.

The unspoken message was clear. *Put up or shut up.* Maybe

Richard thought Thomas would refuse. But then, in that case, the big guy would miss out on another opportunity to be with Melanie. The more Thomas analyzed things, the more he was confused.

Giving up his free pass to have sex with some imaginary woman was no big deal. He hadn't been keen about that idea to start with. All he had wanted to do was fulfill a long-standing fantasy by watching his wife make love to another man.

Nowhere in his imaginings had he ever craved a three-some. Okay, well, maybe in his adolescence when he saw himself with a set of blond twins. But, heck, that was pretty standard fare for a masturbatory mental flick.

The reality of sharing a woman—and not just any woman: his wife, damn it—that was going to be one hell of a scenario.

His stomach rolled until he popped an antacid. This Richard guy had a lot to answer for.

When Thomas pulled up in the driveway, two cars were already there. The one he didn't recognize was parked to one side. Thomas stopped just behind his wife's vehicle and turned off the engine.

Their house was a two-story brick one with white columns. Melanie's prized azaleas flanked the front door. It didn't look at all like a residence where naughty sex was about to take place.

He opened the front door and stopped cold when he heard Melanie laughing. *Hell and damnation.* Apparently, the party had already started without him.

Following the sound of voices, he discovered them in the

living room. They were both fully clothed and upright, so he took that as a good sign. Snorting inwardly at his twisted humor, he plastered a smile on his face and stepped into the room.

Melanie had never been so glad to see Thomas in her life. She and Richard had arrived ten minutes ago, and every cell in her body was stressed. How in the hell had her seven-year-itch, free-pass idea come to this?

She held out her hand to her husband. "Come here, sweetheart. Meet Richard."

The two men shook hands, almost identical expressions of aggression on their faces. Oh, Lord, this was going to be a challenge.

Heavy silence sat like an unwanted guest in the room. Melanie started to hyperventilate. This wasn't a freakin' dinner party. How in the hell were they supposed to get to the bedroom?

She shot Thomas a pleading look. He didn't take the hint. Richard stared at his shoes.

Frustrated, surprisingly horny, and tired of this duo of macho men and their little-boy games, she stripped off her blouse and unfastened her bra.

Bare from the waist up, she stared them down. "I'll be upstairs when you gentlemen are ready."

Richard choked back a laugh. She was one hell of a woman. His gaze met Thomas's. "Your wife is an original. You're a lucky man."

Thomas's posture relaxed a bit. "Yes," he said quietly,

"she leads me a merry dance, but I don't have any complaints." He motioned toward the stairs. "Shall we?"

Richard walked in front, feeling the other man's gaze bore into his back. He'd been sure Thomas would refuse the change in plans. Richard had been satisfied with his one evening with Melanie, and he didn't want to drag it out. Too much of a good thing and he would end up with a serious crush that would be hard to get over.

But Thomas had surprised him.

At the top of the stairs, Richard paused. Thomas didn't make him ask. He pointed to the correct door.

Inside, Melanie waited in the bed, stark naked, with the covers thrown back. Her courage and sheer guts amused and aroused Richard. She was a bright, feisty, determined woman. And sexy as hell.

Richard was not inexperienced by any means, but this was new for him. He and Thomas never looked directly at one another as they undressed. Finally nude, they stood on either side of the bed with Melanie in between. The symbolism was not lost on him.

Melanie had been flushed when they first came in. Now she was pale. Fortunately, Thomas took the lead. He put his knee on the edge of the mattress and crawled in beside his wife.

Richard swallowed his unease and made the same move on the other side. He didn't touch Melanie at first, not that he was afraid to, but because he wanted to see how this would unfold.

Thomas kissed his wife tenderly, running a hand from her breasts to her thighs. The embracing couple looked right together. Richard definitely felt like the outsider.

Melanie caught his eye over her husband's shoulder. She lifted a brow as if to say, *Feel free to join us, Richard. Jump right in.*

He rubbed his groin surreptitiously. He'd been hard almost since the moment he slid into the car and followed Melanie from the gym. Even with the awkwardness of entering another man's house and preparing to screw another man's wife, he was fully, painfully aroused.

He touched Melanie's thigh, smiling faintly as she flinched. Thomas didn't seem to notice. Richard tangled his fingers with Melanie's, squeezing tightly. He had access to her left breast, so—what the hell? He leaned over on his elbow and licked one delicate nipple.

Melanie jumped, and at the same time, Thomas realized what had happened. Two male gazes clashed.

Thomas broke the visual standoff and gazed down at his wife. "Prepare to be wowed, my love." And he winked at Richard.

After that, things zipped along nicely. Richard moved to the end of the bed and massaged Melanie's feet, leaving Thomas to kiss his wife. Melanie's reactions spurred them on. Every caress, every kiss, made her sigh and mutter and writhe in their embrace.

The two men were careful not to bump into each other. It was weird at first, but the more they turned their attention to Melanie, the less it mattered. She was sensual, sexual, and real. Richard didn't know how else to describe it. Her raw, natural responses were unfeigned, unscripted. She made him ache.

And he wondered bleakly if he would be searching for

those same qualities in every woman he met from now on. Thomas was licking his wife's neck, grazing her ear with his teeth, sucking at her earlobe. Richard seized the opportunity to move his hand between Melanie's slim, soft legs and find her clitoris.

She went rigid when he first touched her and then slumped back into the mattress with a long, low groan. Every nerve in his body quivered with the need to bury himself between those legs and re-create a few memorable moments from last night. But he couldn't. Not with her husband so close. It was a damnable situation, but he'd asked for it, and now he had to see this through.

Melanie's sharp, shocked cry signaled her orgasm. When Richard thrust two fingers in her pussy, she climaxed again. Thomas kissed her roughly, muffling her moans. He was wild, his tongue penetrating her mouth in a clear mimicry of what both men wanted.

Richard choked back a frustrated oath. In spite of himself, he sneaked a glance at Thomas's cock. It was rigid, dark red, and angry-looking. Richard was abashed to see that it was also long and thick. So much for that contest.

As he watched, Melanie reached for her husband's penis and stroked it with a confidence gained only after many years of intimacy. Thomas shuddered and rolled to his back. Melanie followed him, leaning on one arm and running her hand over her husband's chest.

It was clear that for the moment she had forgotten Richard's presence. It gave him a funny feeling in the pit of his stomach. In spite of the fact that he had seconds ago stroked her to climax, and regardless of the wild and crazy sex they had indulged in the night before, Melanie had turned naturally to her husband.

For a brief, insane moment, Richard contemplated dragging her back to him, mounting her, and shoving his dick deep into her pussy, pumping over and over until this damnable ache was soothed.

How Thomas would react was anyone's guess, but Richard wasn't betting on the other man's good nature in such a circumstance.

Now Melanie was licking her husband's small, flat nipples, raking them with her teeth and making Thomas curse and grab the sheets in his fists. She slid a thigh over Thomas's leg, pinning him down. Her hand went back to his cock, stroking it with a smooth motion.

She might as well have been touching Richard as well, so real was the sensation he felt in his penis. He shut his eyes, breathing roughly, imagining what pleasure Thomas was experiencing at this very instant.

But he couldn't stay blind to the moment. He couldn't keep his eyes closed, couldn't look away.

Melanie slowed her hand, barely caressing Thomas's cock. She fluttered her fingers from his balls to the fat head of his penis, tormenting him with butterfly touches that made the man groan audibly.

Richard massaged his own dick, wondering if either of them would notice if he jerked off.

And then Melanie did something that shifted Richard's world from anticipation to sharp regret. She kissed her husband's lips and then smiled down at him. "I love you, Thomas."

Richard witnessed the moment and felt as if he had trespassed on something sacred. What he saw in their faces was something he'd never experienced. They were entirely attuned to each other's needs, completely devoted, permanently committed.

At one time Richard would have mocked such a conventional suburban relationship. Now he felt the unmistakable sting of envy. And he knew in that second of clear insight that he had to do the right thing. He eased from the bed and began to dress. At some point, they noticed he was gone. He could tell from their faces they were embarrassed that they had been rude.

Rude? Not really. They had simply been a couple in love, connecting on the most basic level.

He finished putting on his socks and shoes and grabbed his shirt and belt. His prick hurt. He was physically miserable, but mentally back on steady ground. As he moved toward the door, he looked at the naked pair on the bed.

He smiled wryly, though it was an effort to pretend he was okay. "I think I need to leave. It's wrong for me to be here. The two of you have something very special, and as much as I enjoyed being with Melanie last night, that's as far as it's going to go."

Melanie sat up, pulling a corner of the sheet over her chest. Her face was troubled, and in her eyes he saw that she really felt something for him. Not love . . . probably not even affection. But something.

He stopped in the doorway. "It's okay, married Melanie. Don't sweat it." He reached in his pocket, pulled out a credit card–size piece of paper, and tossed it on the dresser. "I'll let myself out, and by the way . . . I won't be needing this last free pass."

Melanie turned to Thomas, stunned by what had just happened. Downstairs, she heard the gentle slam of the front door. She bit her lip. "I feel terrible. Should I go after him?"

Thomas shook his head, pulling her into his arms. "Let him go, love. This was my mistake. I never should have suggested giving him another shot, and I sure as hell shouldn't have asked to watch." He pulled her onto his chest, settling her into a comfortable position. "And when he suggested a threesome, I should have realized he was blowing smoke. He thought I would refuse, or he never would have mentioned it."

She wiggled around, whispering an apology when her knee almost damaged his very important man parts. "What a weird night."

Thomas snorted. "What a weird week, don't you mean? Next time you decide to get me some kind of off-the-wall seven-year-itch anniversary present, do me a favor, sweetheart. Shoot for a set of golf clubs."

She kissed him to shut him up and rose on her knees in order to slide down over his cock. Impressively, it hadn't wilted, even during Richard's awkward departure.

She shivered and closed her eyes at how good it felt to connect with her husband . . . finally. He filled her, made her whole. As they both began to move in a sensual dance for two, she smiled down at him. "No more crazy ideas from me, I swear. But I was thinking that when we do finally get away on a vacation, I've heard about an S and M cruise that might be fun."

He clamped one hand over her mouth and gripped her ass with his other one. "Shut up, my love. And I say that with the utmost affection and respect. Shut up and make love to me."

Chapter Eighteen

D ebra followed Yuri out onto the patio. It was hard to read her watch in the gloom, but she thought it was sometime after one a.m. They had dressed in silence. She thought the Russian might conceivably have gone another round with her if she'd allowed it. But she was done, at least for now. She wanted to see her husband.

Katya and Gordon stumbled out of the house at almost the same moment, making Debra wonder if the Russians had somehow predetermined a schedule of sorts. The two couples moved toward one another, separated, and reassembled in married units without saying a word.

Katya and Yuri shared a passionate kiss. Debra ignored them and hugged Gordie, her head buried in his shoulder, His strong arms came around her, making her feel safe and warm and loved.

She whispered in his ear. "How was it?"

He seemed a bit shell-shocked, but he answered readily, "Not what I expected."

An odd note in his voice told her there would be more of the story to come later. She shivered a bit, feeling the breeze kick up and ruffle her hair. The night was romantic, full of shadows, sweet scents, and the caress of the wind. Reality seemed far away.

Their indefatigable hosts offered more wine. Debra took a glass because it was easier than refusing, but she did nothing more than sip. Gordon did the same.

For the first time in their acquaintance, the Russian couple seemed subdued. Yuri drained his glass and tugged Katya by the hand to where Debra and Gordie perched on the wall.

Yuri touched Debra's cheek and smiled at Gordon. "You not go home yet. We have one last—um, how you say—moment?"

Debra frowned inwardly. *Moment?* What in the heck did that mean? Katya was quiet. Yuri leaned toward them, his wine-scented breath a bit hoarse either from the late hour or from fatigue.

His teeth gleamed in the darkness. "We have quilts. Is nice to fuck outdoors. Husbands and wives. You want?"

Debra's nipples tightened and she shivered. She did want Gordie . . . so very much. And she didn't want to wait until they got home. The entire island was sleeping. How risky could it be?

She squeezed Gordie's hand. "Are you game?" She stroked his chest, already imagining the feel of his cock as it pushed into her.

Gordie blinked and cleared his throat. "If that's what you want."

The Russians had disappeared inside, presumably to get the quilts. But Debra spoke in a low voice just the same. "You and I have had fun watching Yuri and Katya do the exhibitionist thing. Don't you think it might be exciting to pretend that some voyeur is watching us, too?"

"I doubt anyone could see us in the dark."

She giggled, feeling young and crazy and in love. "Exactly my point."

He shrugged. "Okay, then."

The bedding Yuri carried out was enough to make two comfy pallets. To Debra's consternation, instead of using each end of the patio, Katya and Yuri prepared the love nests side by side.

"Oh, shit." Gordie's shocked, whispered expletive echoed her sentiments exactly.

"Surely they don't expect us to—"

He cut her off with a hard kiss. "Yes, they do," he muttered. "And since you've already given them the go-ahead, we're screwed."

"Screwed? Very funny."

Katya and Yuri stripped off their clothes with not even an iota of modesty. Soon they were on the ground, kissing and fondling in earnest.

Debra looked at Gordon, barely able to make out his expression. "Well?"

His hands went to her shoulders, and he slid the straps of her dress down her arms. Then he reached around for her zipper. "We're wasting time," he said, his words raspy. "Let's do this."

Making love to Gordie was especially sweet after the unexpected, boundary-pushing session with the Russian. Debra had no qualms, no anxieties, no need to protect herself in any way. The familiar touch of her husband's hands on her body aroused her and made her feel as if she was floating. It was deliciously uncomplicated.

He was tender and slow in his caresses, but he was insistent. She wouldn't be allowed to passively reach her climax tonight. Gordie wanted it all.

She touched him at his groin, finding his erect shaft and stroking it. Out of the corner of her eye, she saw Katya perched on Yuri's cock in a position Debra and Gordon had witnessed before. She was making no effort to be quiet. Her cries in Russian echoed on the night air.

Debra moaned when Gordie sprawled between her legs and ran his tongue over her clit. She'd thought she was far too exhausted to do more than go through the motions, but fresh hunger, unexpected and sharp, flooded her belly and radiated outward to her arms and legs. She closed her eyes and arched her back.

Suddenly, Gordie moved away with a hoarse protest and Debra felt delicate hands on her legs. Katya had elbowed him out of the picture and was now enthusiastically licking Debra's sex.

Oh, hell, no. Debra struggled to close her thighs, but the woman was strong. Katya knew her way around a pussy. She hit every erogenous spot, murmuring praise and excitement.

Debra reached for Gordie, but he was crouched at her side, hands on his thighs, seemingly spellbound by the sudden turn of events.

Katya slithered upward, sprawling her small, lithe body across Debra's. Soft skin met soft skin. Breast met breast. Her mouth closed over Debra's shocked lips, her tongue darting inside.

Debra felt as if every bone in her body had turned to water. She was helpless and embarrassingly aroused, not so much from Katya's attentions as from the knowledge that Gordie was intent on watching, his cock furiously hard and weeping moisture from its tip.

Debra didn't return the other woman's kiss. That simply wasn't in her repertoire. But she submitted, because it felt nice and she was miles away from home in a sexual fantasy that had somehow become very real.

With Katya French-kissing her, and Gordie doing an imitation of a stone statue, that left Yuri free to join in the fun. He moved closer and ran his hand up Debra's leg, ending up at her already swollen clit and rubbing it with lazy strokes.

Debra felt torn in a million gut-tightening directions. It was hard to absorb the dual stimulation. Katya's lips were everywhere, kissing, biting, sucking. But it was Yuri who made her body arc and quiver and ultimately burst into flame as her climax swept through her body.

She was still shaking in the aftermath when the Russians moved aside and Gordon pushed his body into hers. He and she both cried out. The connection was bittersweet. It seemed as if years had passed since they had last screwed each other, and even the familiarity was tinged with a wicked excitement and an extra dollop of eroticism.

Gordie rode her slowly, giving her time to build to a second orgasm. He whispered words of love, of admiration, of gratitude. She turned her head and watched Yuri mount Katya in the same position. The Russian woman thrashed wildly. Her gaze met Debra's. The two of them locked eyes, each knowing that she had been with the other's mate a short time ago. But there was no challenge, only a smug recognition.

Debra felt the shock of that visual connection, ruefully aware that it added to her excitement.

Gordie moved faster now, hitting a spot deep inside her vagina that made her close her eyes and catch her breath. Overhead, the stars tumbled in crazy circles.

From somewhere far away, she heard Katya cry out. A deep, rolling wave of intense pleasure drew up in Debra's womb like a wall of water gathering steam to crash onto the sand. She dug her heels into the quilt, feeling the hard stone beneath. "Gordie!" She couldn't hold back her cry. It spilled from her lips at the exact moment that her husband rammed his cock deep and deeper still, pitching them both into the final, quivering release.

In the silence that fell afterward, she realized that Yuri and Katya must have hit the peak almost in sync with their American guests. They lay cuddled in a tangle of arms and legs, murmuring softly to each other.

Debra absorbed the feel of Gordie's weight anchoring her to the hard floor of the patio. Without it, she might have floated up to the stars and never returned. He rolled to his back and muttered something she didn't quite catch. When she leaned over him to ask what he'd said, Katya came up behind her.

She put a hand on Debra's bare rump. "Katya taste Gordon. Is okay?"

Debra was relieved that the woman was not about to have a go at Debra again. Debra looked at Gordie with a grin and tickled his nipple. "Sure. Knock yourself out."

Gordie yelped when Katya went down on him. Debra smirked at not being the one under attack, but her smugness was short-lived. Yuri lifted her, again with that deceptive strength, and moved her to the other quilt.

She struggled to get on her feet, but he held her down by the simple expedient of anchoring her hands over her head and using his lower body against hers to keep her still.

He kissed her several times, and her body responded, caught up in the memories of Yuri's enthusiastic lovemaking. He pushed his thick erection into her belly. "You let Yuri take you one more time?"

He found her clit with his shaft and massaged the sensitive nub until Debra squirmed and gasped. She chanced a sideward glance at her husband and decided he wouldn't care, considering the fact that Katya was now perched across his shoulders, allowing him, or perhaps cajoling him, to eat her pussy.

Yuri moved again with wicked skill, and Debra tried to free her hands. He chuckled low in his chest. "Tell me, Debra . . . yes or no."

She felt the heat burn deep inside her and gave in without a whimper. "Yes."

The man was a damned acrobat. He kept her wrists immobilized with one hand, retrieved a condom packet, tore it open with his teeth, and rolled the condom on. Somehow, Debra had expected this time to be a slow, lazy possession.

She was wrong. He shoved inside her with a force that made her gasp. With her hands unable to hold on to him, or anything for that matter, she was helpless. She lifted her knees and planted her feet.

He liked that. It forced him deeper into her vagina. She felt him swell and then start pumping again. She knew she would be sore tomorrow. He gave no quarter, entering her again and again and again, until he went rigid, muttered an unmistakable curse in Russian, and strained against her until he could go no longer.

His weight was not unpleasant, but she hadn't climaxed. And she wanted to. Badly.

Yuri finally rolled away and disposed of the condom. Gordie was fucking Katya now. His gaze met Debra's, his expression hard to read in the dark.

Debra watched, aroused in spite of herself. To see her husband moving on and into another woman's body gave her an odd feeling, almost like jealousy, but not quite. More a wistful regret that she wasn't able to feel and share what was happening with him this very moment.

Yuri came back to her in mere seconds. Her arms still lay limply over her head. His fingers twisted her nipples. Then he secured her wrists with one big hand as he had done before. Her momentarily dormant desire flickered and flared brighter.

"Yuri..." She whispered his name, wondering if it

bothered him at all to see his wife being screwed by another man.

As far as she could tell, Yuri had never once looked toward the other pair. His concentration and focus were solely on her. He was on his knees. Now he slid an arm under her butt and pulled her up on his thighs, so high her shoulders were the only part of her still making contact with the hard ground.

He held her captive with one strong arm while his other hand toyed and probed between her legs. He separated her labia, tugging this way and that at the tender flesh. Debra squirmed, frustrated that he wasn't hitting the spot that ached and throbbed.

He entered her barely an inch with his forefinger and pressed upward. Sensation rippled through her pussy. Her hips arched.

She moaned in protest when he abandoned her sex and used that one same hand to touch her forehead, trickle a path down her nose, glide over her chin. He traced the valley between her breasts.

She tried to jerk free, wanting to force him into a more intimate caress. But his grip tightened inexorably. Damn, the man was strong. He continued his playful assault, circling her belly button, diving in, circling it again.

Her hips moved restlessly. She felt the storm gathering, a gigantic crest of pleasure building steadily, swelling her sex, trembling through her body.

At last Yuri made it south again. He cupped his hand over her pussy and held it there. The pressure was warm, comforting, but she needed more.

She dug her heels into his hips, panting, so tired she could weep. "For God sakes, Yuri, do it. Please."

He started talking in Russian, low, impassioned strings of words that sounded like a prayer or a chant. Finally he released her arms, but she didn't have the strength to bring them down beside her body, so she left them extended above her head, the image of a willing sacrifice.

Yuri bent and blew on her clit, a warm rush of air that stimulated unbearably, but wasn't enough to push her over the edge. She trembled violently, reaching for the peak, desperate for release.

He waved a hand and Gordon appeared as if by magic. Debra's husband's hair was tousled, his eyelids hooded, his mouth a tight line. Yuri looked first at Debra, then Gordon. "We men . . . we finish own wives."

Debra thought she was past the point of caring *who* finished her, but she was wrong. As Gordie hovered above her, her eyes misted and her heart leaped in recognition. This was her mate, her other half, the key to her soul.

He moved between her legs gently, soothing her when she flinched. Her skin felt tight, painfully sensitive, hot beneath his touch.

He joined his body with hers in a mighty thrust, and above his shoulder, Debra saw a flash of pure white light arc across the sky. She closed her eyes, feeling as though the meteor had infiltrated her body, burst through her circulatory system, and smashed into her pelvis.

She jerked and moaned. The climax was stunning in its intensity. Gordie shook like a man in the grip of a fever. He pounded the mouth of her womb, taking his own release and shuddering through the multiple contractions of her vagina on his penis.

Neither of them had any knowledge or awareness of the Russian couple until it was all over. Debra shivered as Gordie pulled the sides of the quilt over their naked bodies. Their damp flesh cooled rapidly.

Debra drowsed, wondering how they would ever have the energy to get dressed and go home. She muttered her question to Gordie, and he hugged her more closely to his long, muscular frame.

"Rest a bit," he said, the words slurred. "And then we'll leave."

The first rays of sunlight were peeking over the mountaintop and spilling into their corner of the village when Gordon finally roused. He was aghast to realize that dawn had come, and he was still lying where he had fallen asleep the night before.

Every bone in his body ached. Sleeping on stone was pretty stupid, especially when he and Debra were paying for a perfectly nice bed just up the street.

He shook his wife's shoulder. "Wake up, honey. It's time for us to get out of here."

He looked around to see if the Russian couple was still asleep as well, but they were gone, along with the quilt they'd been lying on.

Gordie frowned. That was odd. He reached for the articles of clothing scattered around them, careful to protect his modesty with the quilt. No telling who might be up and around, looking out at their neighbors with curious eyes. He'd just as soon not put on a show.

After he was decently clothed, he nudged Debra again and helped her into her dress. She rolled her neck and yawned. "Did Yuri and Katya go back inside? I can't believe we slept here all night. My back feels like somebody has been beating on it."

He pulled her to her feet and folded the quilt. Sounds of morning activity were beginning to fill the air. When he stretched as well, Debra looked at him with a raised eyebrow. "Well, what do you think? Should we say anything or just disappear?"

"I don't know. My head's fuzzy from all that alcohol they kept plying us with."

"Tell me about it."

They tiptoed to the door, and Gordon eased it open. They both paused in shock. The kitchen was bare. When they explored further, they realized that all traces of the Russians' presence had disappeared.

The sexual fantasy/free pass had gone up in smoke as if it had never happened.

Debra was the one to spot the small folded piece of paper taped to an iron hook in the spare room. Gordie reached for it, his groin stirring as he was bombarded by mental images of whipping Katya and vice versa.

He unfolded the paper. Debra read over his shoulder. The handwriting was spidery and uneven.

Dear American Friends:
  We have very early flight, so we not bother you. We thank you for the sex. Yuri say to me that you are handsome, hot-blooded couple. Make good Russians.

Greece is land of ancient discovery. Many gods have sex under hot sun. Warms blood. Makes joy.

We wish you long life, happy marriage, much sex.

Love, Katya (a tigress for Gordon)

Debra tugged his earlobe. "What's this about a tigress?"

He stuffed the note in his pocket, feeling his cheeks flush. "Just one of her games." He put his arm around Debra's waist, leading her from the room. "Let's go home, my love. I'm exhausted."

As they walked up the hill, the sun burst out in full glory, painting the housetops with gold and signaling the start to another blistering day.

Gordon felt like a different man from the one who had arrived in Santorini just a few days ago. If Debra's plan with the free-pass idea had been to shake up their marriage, she had succeeded. But as much as he had enjoyed parts of this week's incredible sexual adventure, he doubted he'd ever want to repeat such a thing. He was content and happy to be with his wife and no one else as long as he lived. And that knowledge in itself was a hell of an anniversary gift.

He unlocked the door to their villa, and they stumbled inside. Showering seemed like a waste of time to him, but Debra insisted. When they were clean, they tumbled into bed like innocent children and slept the day away.

Five or six hours later they surfaced to the sound of a church bell ringing in the distance.

Gordon listened to it, and a kick-butt idea popped into his head and took root. He turned onto his side and played with his wife's breasts. She was still groggy, but she smiled with her eyes closed.

"Debra?"

"Hmmm?"

"Tomorrow's our anniversary."

She nodded her head, mute.

"Why don't we find a church here on the island and re-new our wedding vows?"

That got her attention. Her lashes flew open, and she stared at him. "Where's my husband and what have you done with him?"

He grinned sheepishly. "I'll admit I'm not the most ro-mantic guy in the world, but being here has done something to me. I want to remember this week forever."

"The sex or the whole week?"

He pinched her cheek. "When your husband is trying to make a grand gesture, it's not polite to throw past indiscre-tions in his face."

"Indiscretions?"

"What would you call it? I think we went way beyond the free-pass stage."

She sighed and stretched luxuriously, her breasts pale pink and morning soft. "I'd call it Russian roulette. And I'm just happy we survived."

Epilogue

It was raining the day Melanie and Thomas got back from their Caribbean cruise. She couldn't wait to call Cherisse and Debra and make plans to meet at their favorite coffee shop. Since Thomas and Melanie had departed for their trip on the spur of the moment to take advantage of a sudden cancellation, it had been several weeks since the friends had seen one another.

The following morning over lattes and apple Danish, the three women compared notes. Cherisse's lifeguard, Wesley's hair model . . . the crazy Russians, Melanie's handsome businessman.

There was much squealing and giggling and many red-faced confessions. And in the end, a contemplative silence laden with memories.

Girlfriends were the best when it came to sharing the good stuff, and naughty adventures in particular.

Before they left, they toasted Melanie for having the insight and the guts to come up with the free-pass idea.

She smiled modestly. "Thanks, guys. But looking back, I see how easily it could have backfired."

Debra smiled as she picked up her pocketbook and rose to her feet, eager to get home and tell Gordon all the juicy gossip. "True, but it turned out way better than any of us could have possibly imagined."

The other two stood as well, and Cherisse blushed. "It was way better than any fantasy I've ever made up in my head. And it's had residual effects. Wesley has been insatiable ever since we got home."

As they reached the door to go out to the parking lot, a young man wearing the uniform of the coffee shop held out his hand. "Would you like one of these?"

Melanie took one and flipped it over. "What are they?" she asked, studying the small card.

The kid, barely twenty, smiled and flashed a cute dimple. "It's a free pass for the dessert of your choice."

All three women burst into laughter, making the young man blush with a puzzled look.

Cherisse touched his arm lightly and apologized. "Thanks, but no, thanks. We're all three over the limit, but we appreciate the offer anyway. Why don't you give them to some other hungry women?"

And then Cherisse and Melanie and Debra walked outside, eager to start on the next seven years of marriage, happy to have outwitted the dreaded seven-year itch. . . .

About the Author

Elizabeth Scott enjoys hearing from readers. She can be reached at lizybeth13@aol.com or visit her at www.myspace .com/authorelizabethscott.